Acclaim for Lorraine Adams's H

"Mesmerizing. . . . A ripping read. . . . A tale of American justice gone awry."

—*Los Angeles Times Book Review*

"Remarkable. . . . Brilliant. . . . Compelling and haunting. . . . Adams creates an exquisite tension in a character who is at once unseen and yet hunted, both estranged from society and deeply enmeshed in a complicated social order. . . . [*Harbor* is] a work of art that lifts the veils of many of our assumptions that have formed since 9/11." —*The Boston Globe*

"[A] great, gutsy first novel. . . . Outstanding."

—*Entertainment Weekly*

"Fascinating. . . . [Adams] writes convincingly from within the hearts and minds of her characters. Though topical, the narrative flies well beneath the headlines." —*The Oregonian*

"A chilling story of identity and loss culled from real-life experiences. . . . A cautionary tale that asks readers to be open-minded. . . . [Adams] never loses sight of a story that alternates between incredible moments of joy and sadness."

—*Pittsburgh Tribune-Review*

"Insightful. . . . Adams adds welcome shading to the usual portrayal of the war on terror." —*U.S. News & World Report*

"A disturbing tale where suspicion is enough to trump innocence and the consequences of naïveté are potentially disastrous. . . . Adams humanizes the terrorist threat and convincingly shows how a confined worldview can breed generalizations that may hatch tragic consequences." —*San Francisco Chronicle*

"Brilliant. . . . A strong and disturbing book."

—Annie Proulx, *Book-of-the-Month Club News*

"Adams displays a gift for detail and character that takes us fully inside the complex systems of survival, kinship, and religious ideology which form Aziz's world." —*The New Yorker*

"Adams is a sharp observer of the current war-on-terror politics. [*Harbor*] counters the media's easy perceptions in our age of xenophobia by immersing readers in the depths of myriad characters."

—*The Dallas Morning News*

"Mesmerizing. . . . A timely and grippingly written book, *Harbor* helps give the war on terror a human face." —*People*

"Adams drags her characters through the wheels of fate and makes them sing. . . . [Her] sentences move with speed and visual economy, but also contain poetic beauties. . . . A compelling story with great characters—timely, suspenseful and profound."

—*Ruminator Review*

"A powerful look at America through immigrant eyes that is not only timely but essential in our post–9/11 society."

—*Fort Worth Star-Telegram*

"[Adams] writes with verve and is so convincing that it often seems that this is a true story instead of fiction. . . . A story about complex interaction between human beings of greatly differing cultures, written by an author of enormous talent."

—*Deseret Morning News*

LORRAINE ADAMS

HARBOR

Lorraine Adams, a Pulitzer Prize–winning writer, was educated at Princeton University and was a graduate fellow at Columbia University, where she received a master's degree in literature. She lives in New York City and is at work on her second novel.

HARBOR

LORRAINE ADAMS

VINTAGE CONTEMPORARIES
VINTAGE BOOKS
A DIVISION OF RANDOM HOUSE, INC.
NEW YORK

FIRST VINTAGE CONTEMPORARIES EDITION, SEPTEMBER 2005

Grateful acknowledgment is made to the following for permission to reprint previously published material: **Buckhorn Music Publishing Company:** Excerpt from "One Day at a Time," by Kris Kristofferson and Marijohn Wilkin. Reprinted by permission of Buckhorn Music Publishing Company. **Hal Leonard Corporation, Scarlet Moon Music, Inc. and Universal Music Publishing Group:** Excerpt from "On the Other Hand," words and music by Don Schlitz and Paul Overstreet. Copyright © 1985 Screen Gems-EMI Music Inc., Scarlet Moon Music, Universal-MCA Music Publishing and Don Schlitz Music. All rights for Don Schlitz controlled and administered by Universal-MCA Music Publishing. All rights reserved. International copyright secured. Reprinted by permission of Hal Leonard Corporation, Scarlet Moon Music, Inc. and Universal Music Publishing Group. **Penguin Books Ltd.:** Excerpt from "The Conference of the Birds" (16 lines from pages 47, 75, 123), by Farid ud-din Attar, translated with an introduction by Afkham Darbandi and Dick Davis (Penguin Classis, 1984). Copyright © 1984 Afkham Darbandi and Dick Davis. Reprinted by permission of Penguin Books, Ltd. **Warner Bros. Publications U.S. Inc.:** Excerpt from "Windmills of Your Mind," words by Alan and Marilyn Bergman, Music by Michel Legrand. Copyright © 1968 United Artists Music Co., Inc. Rights assigned to EMI U Catalog Inc. (Publishing) and Warner Bros. Publications U.S. Inc. (Print). All rights reserved. Reprinted by permission of Warner Bros. Publications U.S. Inc., Miami, Florida 33014.

The Library of Congress has cataloged the Knopf edition as follows:
Adams, Lorraine.
Harbor / Lorraine Adams.—1st ed.
p. cm.
1. Algerians—United States—Fiction. 2. Illegal aliens—Fiction. 3. Stowaways—Fiction.
4. Violence—Fiction. I. Title.
PS3601.D38H37 2004
813'.600—dc22
2004040916

Vintage ISBN: 1-4000-7688-9

Book design by Pamela Parker

www.vintagebooks.com

Printed in the United States oif America
10 9 8 7 6 5 4 3 2 1

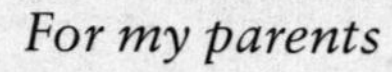
For my parents

My eye conversed while my tongue gazed;
my ear spoke and my hand listened;
and while my ear was an eye to behold everything visible,
my eye was an ear listening to song.

—Farid ud-Din Attar

HARBOR

1

Water never warms in American harbors. They had told him. Shivering, on the high deck of a groaning tanker, told more. He made out a far field of whitecaps many feet below. By the prow, the wind was pulling back the flags into flat, clear pictures. His beard whipped past his face; his overlong hair flew east. His hands and neck burned from insulation he had torn from a crate in the hold that most likely, he realized, after a few days of scratching skin to bleeding, was asbestos. He willed himself to stop but woke to blood caking his shins, under his nails, ridged in his ears. The cold tightened him into a pain that killed sleep.

Aziz could sense there might be other stowaways. On his second try, one he had befriended turned him over to ship's security, who beat him with mallets, rowed him from the anchored vessel, and deposited him in the care of the harbor police, who pistol-whipped him into unconsciousness and three weeks in a dirty hospital, where his mother cried at his pillow and his brothers brought armloads of food she had cooked, sheets she had washed, an amazing pair of cotton mittens, soft as new white feathers, for his slowly oozing hands. He never saw the informant again, but his brother told him the miscreant had died, not violently but all on his own. He had disappeared for days until his friends found him dead in an alley. It turned out the betrayer had fallen and hit his head.

Now, on his third try, his eyelids were blistered. Some kind of wet kept coming from his ears, which were stoppered, as if someone had poured india rubber into them. After fifty-two days in the hold, his eyes, so long in dark, had just this moment adjusted to the blaring morning. And so he jumped.

He hurtled down in the air for long seconds to the ocean's surface, whacking into a cold all his preparation had not prepared him for, plunging what seemed to be too far. He tucked his elbows against his rib cage, kicking, and kicked more and farther, all of him roaring up, up, get up. His head popped into the wind and he opened his eyes, locating the pier. He had not gone too far. Stroking across the surface, his arms wore ice sweaters, mercifully insulated from any feeling. On they went, arms of his, down and back, down and back, heavier, heavier, his arms so heavy he wanted to sleep. So he did. He let himself rest, into the deeper water, feeling the weight of it, hoping for its relief. There was something about the possibility of light that came to him. It was like the lamp his mother read beneath. He saw her bent head.

Someone else had jumped with him. He could feel hands at his neck. Maybe more than one. They were choking him. He fought, and at the surface he gurgled out the water in his lungs and saw he was alone. It was then fear found him. He swam in a screaming whistle of panic. There were no thoughts now, just the pumping of his heart. He had been swimming, he guessed, for three hours, or maybe three minutes. He looked a little—squinted, really—and saw he was nearly at the pier. Once there, a ladder, rubberized steel, was slipping from his hands, but then he realized it was grooved this rubber, or was it rippled steel, and his hands were too numb to think they could hang on. So he imagined that they could, and his hands then obeyed this concept, and up he went, peeking over there and down that way to make sure he was alone.

He was. He ran. His jumpsuit, stolen by his father to match the uniforms of the crew, was sopping. Again the command went to his body: You are not cold. Again the body conformed with this idea, and his thinking cartwheeled into the next necessity. There it was—near the Boston train tracks—an abandoned signal booth.

He stripped and started wringing out his clothes. The uniform was canvas, rough and punishing to his blue hands. It is nothing, he told his hands. You are here to function this way, for me, for the future. He had gotten the first of the water out when his hands began to bleed. He dropped the uniform. He would die here, asbestos sickened, ears and eyes mortally infected, the cold finishing him. He pictured his body, stiff across the tracks, as if he had died in the act of trying to gain a conductor's attention. Then he saw them.

Across the tracks flutters of newspaper pages, hundreds of them, touched down and rose up like kites. He ran toward them in his putrefied underwear with his stretched socks flapping at his ankles. There were so many that even the wind could not keep all of them from him. He gathered them in his arms, scooping and diving like a gull. When he thought he had enough, he sprinted back to the booth and carefully put them inside, securing them with a rusted loop of wire in case the wind gusted in through the door. He pulled off the socks and briefs and laid them and the uniform on the gray stones along the tracks. He closed what was left of the door. The window had been broken, but only slightly, and he began pulling the newsprint toward a slant of sun on the floor, where he lay, building a frail tent that eventually settled into layers of his own heat to warm him.

"He's drunk."

"No, he's a homeless."

He heard them. With no English, he didn't know what they said, but he saw in their faces that he was frightening. Back in the signal booth, he had decided what he would say—or, rather, be. He would say nothing and pretend he was deaf. That is how he acted, that is how he was thinking of himself, and that was how this family he had just passed should see him. There were two toddlers, both boys, and their mother and father, getting out of a car. He had tried to hurry past them, but he had discovered it was impossible; his legs would not accommodate his idea of hurrying, and instead he had to be satisfied with a shuffle.

He moved into the blocks of the city, to the skyscrapers, the corridors of shadows so cold, so mean. The sun was out near the water, but that was not where he could find anyone or anything that might warm him. He imagined he would find a church. That was what he was looking for—they allowed people inside, come what may, and he would sleep there, maybe under the altar, or maybe he would find a heavy silk robe in a back room and wrap himself in it, and a priest would happen on him. He was imagining the priest, kindly and old, a face that beamed and was mostly a face of love. How he needed such a face. As he was constructing its possibilities in his head, someone said "Brother." And so did another one, this time emphatically: "Brother." They were speaking Arabic to each other. He stopped. The two men, standing near a cart, a cart selling sweatshirts and mugs that said BOSTON, kept talking. The conversation in his head went silent for the first time since he had said goodbye to his father.

Men who spoke Arabic. He had not anticipated anything even remotely this lucky. It was such a gift, such a wonder, that for a full ten seconds he stood rooted to the street, his coldness receding. It would not be good to be who he really was—that much was easy. Deafness, no, but perhaps down on his luck, unstable, if only slightly. He would not beg, no, something more permanent had to be gotten out of this marvel of two men speaking Arabic.

"Brother," he said, and was surprised at the sound he made. It was a whisper. "Brother!" he shouted, producing only a speaking voice.

They did not hear him. But then, one of them saw him, out of one eye at an angle, and caught his breath.

The other man turned to see, and when he did, Aziz shouted again. "I am sick, help me! I have lost my home." But when he looked at them, their faces were made entirely of fear, nothing else. He began to feel their fright welling up inside him and the urge to run was enormous, bigger than he could counter, and as he started, he fell, hard, on the pavement, scraping his bare palms, his elbow, reopening the thin scabs from wringing his ship's uniform, succeeding in shielding only his cheeks and his eyes, from which tears as hot as tea were spilling.

They wanted to take him to a hospital, but he would not let them. So one of them took him to a mosque. He was Egyptian. He worked in a Radio Shack. He went into the mosque talking on his cell phone and came back with donated sweaters, pants, shoes, and a sparkling aquamarine ski jacket. Then he drove Aziz to an apartment in the suburbs, where a wife accepted him with no expression into a hallway with blush-colored broadloom stretching into rooms with white furniture.

The Egyptian took him to the bathroom, where there was a tub that was white, new, and clean. The man explained that there was hot water, right from this handle. Aziz's parents did not have hot water. Water came in an urn, carried up the hill from the well that everyone shared, and he and his brothers had spent a good deal of their time working out who would be responsible for doing this and who would get excused from it. His mother could have never done it herself, nor would they have ever let her.

The man explained that this was a shower, and he wanted to say, *Yes, I know what a shower is; my father managed a hotel for European tourists and I have seen them, I have used them,* but he had decided that appearing to be meek and stupid was by far the better course. It also seemed clear that the man did not need to question him too closely to feel an obligation to help him, in however rote a fashion, and that he had little interest in pinning down whether Aziz had jumped off a boat or was a vagrant so imbecilic he could not remember how to bathe.

When the temperature was right, which the man was extremely

concerned would be so, putting his hand in and out of the water and turning the handle by bits, he told Aziz to clean himself, to put on the mosque clothes, and that there would be a meal for him in the kitchen. And then he said, "Don't worry," and smiled an unaccountably radiant smile that Aziz was entirely unprepared for, and he dropped his head quickly because he did not want this man to see him cry again. When he looked up, the man was gone, the door had closed, and the room was filling with steam. A long high mirror over a pair of sinks was clouding. He walked to it. He looked. He saw a man he knew was himself—of course he knew that—but he was also stained and chapped, almost burned, but he had not been near a fire, he knew, he remembered he had not. He had lobster skin in places, a fearful red on his arms, and then when he looked his elbows were like the wattle of the young roosters his father kept in the back, a glistening crimson he had to keep rubbing the mirror with a towel to see.

He needed to rest on the floor. He could no longer stand. He was crying as quietly as he could, holding himself around his knees on a towel, trying not to spoil the white tile, but he gave up and pulled all the towels he saw in the bathroom down to the floor and lay there on them, watching the water rain in the tub.

He began unbuttoning his uniform, and then he tried to take off one of his socks, and there was his blistered foot, so gelatinous he gasped at the first tug, and then he was shaking. He was faint, and the vertiginous delay in his motions, the slowing of the sound of the shower, finally, finally scared him. He understood that realizing was what was making him weaker than he was. He had to pay attention; he must, above all else, after everything, not let his personhood disintegrate on this bathroom floor in this Egyptian's apartment. This was what breakdowns were, he said in his own head, enunciating silently, precisely, the sound of his inside voice reminding him of how that voice had been with him in the hold and it was with him now. All a breakdown was was coming up to this kind of a situation, and instead of taking the other sock off the person began howling, or whimpering, or indulged in the real pleasure—for there was no other way to think of it—of feeling how wretched, how lost, how utterly unthinkable and mad everything in his life had been, culminating in a screaming he could not stop and the Egyptian bursting in, while down the hall his children hung anxiously on their playpen bars and the stolid wife pretended she was unconcerned, when inside she was screaming too, something like *I am not able to go on, I cannot go on, I will not go on.*

He pulled down the uniform and stepped out of it. Then he put one of the towels into the tub, because he did not want to see his clotted bits swirling on the white, and he didn't want to slip. He put his hand into the rain of water, and it was hot, but not too hot, and the kindness of the Egyptian's tinkering flooded through him, causing more tears. He put his foot into the tub and on the now-wet towel. He had to grab the side of the tub with his hand and the pain was fierce, but he was no longer shaking and he was only a little dizzy. He forced himself, slowly, because he did not want to shock his system—or he had an idea there might be such a danger after having been cold for so very long—and as he put his shoulder and his neck and part of his back into the falling water, he realized his back was not hurt at all, not the skin, only the muscles were terribly sore. The hot water began to loosen them. He kept his hands out of the water and pushed his head back into the shower and cried, cried and cried as the clarity of the warm sweet water seemed to wash into his brain, not just through his hair. He began to say an old prayer his mother had taught him, his first one. He said it over and over, like a song, while he took the soap and endured the sting it brought. He didn't look down at what swirled away from the towel in the tub's bottom. He just washed and washed and rinsed and rinsed. And when the water started to lose some of its warmth, he turned it off and wrapped the towels from off the floor around his head, and his back, and his legs, and he sat there, humming a little, until he heard the Egyptian tap on the door.

"Are you all right?"

"Yes."

"Good. Good. No hurry."

But he did hurry. Because by then there was chicken cooking. It was a rich crackling sound of oil and the starch aroma of rice. He fumbled with the clothes, which did not fit, and finally he figured out he would have to use a too-large T-shirt as a belt to keep the pants from falling. He put on three sweaters and he kept a towel on his head, because his hair was wet and his beard still long. Now, clean, he looked like a boy. He was twenty-four years old, and he looked as if he were twelve—a twelve-year-old who was dressed up in a beard. He was more than slightly ridiculous.

He opened the bathroom door.

There were men gathered in another room; he could hear them talking in low voices. And women too, who were helping the wife in the kitchen. From one of the bedrooms there were sounds of more women and more children. He moved toward the sound of the men's voices. But then one of them came around a corner and said, "This boy, look at this boy who came from such cold!" And there was a competition of voices, and more men came toward him, and he looked in the kitchen and saw that the women were not veiled—of course they would not be—but were wearing blue jeans and skirts and sweaters and jewelry and makeup. And one of the women came toward him with a plate, piled with chicken legs and rice. She looked at him, without any fear but with something of what he had hoped the imaginary priest would have looked at him with, and asked in English and then slowly, in perfect Arabic, "Do you want something to drink?"

2

He slept. In the morning, the wife came into his room and gave him juice and chicken sandwiches. He ate them and fell back asleep. This went on for three days. On the evening of the third day, he took another shower. In the mirror he checked carefully on his worries. The blisters on his eyes had flattened and begun healing. His elbows—reddened, still, but no longer as painful to the touch. Hands—scabbed over. Hair, beard—still a wild nomad. His teeth ached—what was that about? Had they hurt before? He couldn't remember.

He could not get the water in the shower the right temperature. He turned the dial and scalded. He turned, wrong, again, over. Just as he was about to give up and find the Egyptian, the water flowed a strong warm. He crawled in using his previous method, this time improving it somewhat by placing the towel on the tub's side as well as its bottom. He could tell his ears were still blocked. His feet—well, he almost threw up when the water first touched them.

As he dressed, he was thinking about what was next. It was time for the number. Six one seven, two eight two, twenty-five forty-six. It was Rafik's. And it would be easy, he hoped, to call it from this Egyptian's apartment. The plan had been, once he called Rafik, Rafik would come get him, and then, once at Rafik's, he would call his mother and father. He wondered how many times his mother would have liked to call Rafik. He wondered how many times she did. It was expensive, fantastically so, but he knew that after three weeks—which is how long it took Rafik to make the journey three years ago—his mother would be quiet, and then angry, and then shouting, and then weeping, and then, finally, would come the last awful quiet, which is where, he estimated, she had been for at least a month.

He saw her in his parents' bedroom. His father was in a chair praying near the window. She kept her head at the foot of the bed, which is how she always took things the worst. "I am on my head," she would say. Then, sometime later, "I am on my head." His father would say, "He is fine. These are not trains that run on time." She would have a handkerchief on her forehead, one that was moistened with water and a lemon. "I am dead now," she was saying. "Cover my eyes; all is lost to me."

The Egyptian and his wife and their two children, a boy who was still a baby, really, and a girl slightly older, were seated around a table in the dining room. When he walked in they all looked up and smiled. The girl said, "Up at last! Up at last!" The wife was wearing a nurse's dress and shoes. She headed into the kitchen to get him a plate, and the Egyptian seemed pleased with himself about something that had nothing to do with Aziz. "A good day," he said. "A very good day."

The wife was back with a lamb stew, and Aziz was drunk fast, looking at it. As she put down his plate, she said, "I am going to bandage those feet after dinner."

"And I will help," said the Egyptian. "There is something very wrong with your eyes," he said, looking satisfied at having discovered this and said something about it.

The wife nodded. "I think I have something for them too."

He was shoveling down the lamb, nodding and smiling in dopey heartiness. They began talking about the wondrous thing that had happened that day, but he had missed the first part of it, and now it was all a something or other of "and the thing about it was" and "that is what I had believed, all along." The boy was throwing cereal. Some of it landed on Aziz's now-empty plate. It was Cheerios, what his father's hotel had for tourists and the French would not eat. Aziz tried to catch the boy's eye, but the boy was too young and busy. Just then, he knew he had to go.

"I have a friend, a phone number. I must call it. I cannot impose on you one day more."

"Oh," said the wife.

"Well," said the Egyptian. "That is good you have a friend."

"Are you—" the wife began.

"You were in no shape when we found you, but now—" He turned to his wife.

"You are a little better," she said slowly.

Something else was called for to be said, at least in Aziz's family something would have been, but he could tell that this family operated under other rules. It was not any of their business what had caused his dereliction, his suppurating feet, his barely understandable excuses about having lost his home. He said the phone number to them, and the man said, "Come, I will let you talk at my desk."

They entered the hushed order of his den. The computer was on, the screen making buzzing stars, and there was a shallow light over the keyboard. He could feel the pride the Egyptian felt at this den, and for a sliver, Aziz sensed the man was boasting or gloating, or going through something not nearly as virtuously kind as Aziz had assumed for him. But it was gone as soon as it came. "There is no need to dial the six one seven," he was saying. "Just the rest."

Aziz pushed the buttons, put the receiver to his ear, and listened. He felt an unexpected desolation because the receiver at his ear was almost familiar, but the sound of the open line, and the sound the numbers made when punched, and the ringing sound—they were unlike any phone sounds he had ever heard.

"Hey."

"Rafik?"

"Cousin!"

"Oh, my uncle!" The old words opened him.

"You are all right!"

"I am!"

"Where are you?"

"I am here, in Boston, I swear to God."

"No!"

"On my mother's head, I swear it."

"This is unbelievable. This is such good news!"

"My parents?"

"Oh, cousin, they called every day this week."

"Can you come get me?"

"Tell me where you are, I will be there."

Aziz looked up, and the den folded back in on him. The Egyptian was listening intently, perhaps for the first time since he had been with him. Or maybe this was the first time Aziz was able to notice. The Egyptian looked puzzled; he did not understand the way they were talking. It was their urchin patois from Arzew.

In his best school Arabic, Aziz said to the Egyptian, "My friend needs to know where to come. What should I tell him?"

The Egyptian looked worried.

"Everything is fine," Aziz said too fast, fear draping on his shoulders, his eyes getting that squinting look that he knew did not bring confidence. You look like a pickpocket, his father would joke. Stop doing that with your eyes. The roundel of his brothers and mother and sisters teasing him about it played in his head. *Stop,* he pleaded. *Stop it.*

"Let me talk to him."

"Wait, Rafik, wait."

He could hear Rafik barking to someone who was with him. He had heard he had a girlfriend, an American.

"May I speak to your friend?" the Egyptian asked, perhaps too formally.

"He . . . he . . . does not speak well," Aziz tried to explain, haltingly, sounding to himself like a raving liar, the kind who was possibly violent, never believable.

"He does not speak Arabic?"

"He does, he does. He is Algerian." There, he had said it. This was the problem, something about that.

"Algeria. You have bad troubles there."

"Yes."

"There are many from there that have come here."

"Yes." His chest was pulling downward, or maybe his last ribs? No, it was a stone the size of his head on his chest.

"Let us meet your friend at the mosque," said the Egyptian, sour and bored. "I will drive you there. I will tell him how to get there."

"Rafik, we are going to meet you."

"Who?"

"Me, and—" He could not call him the Egyptian, but he had no memory of his name, so he said, "The kindest man who has helped me. I am at his home."

This did not remove the expression from the Egyptian's face.

"But I can come there."

"Cousin, it is better this way."

"Why? I am ready to leave this minute."

"The mosque is a good place to meet."

"But where is it?"

Aziz looked imploringly at the Egyptian. "The mosque—where is it?"

"Excuse me," the Egyptian said. "I must talk to my wife first. Please wait."

His bowels were shrinking and hot. Perhaps they were going to call the police on another phone. Americans always had two phones, had he not heard that? And these were more Americans than Arabs, more Americans than Egyptians.

He should have talked to Rafik alone without the Egyptian present. But he could not tell Rafik where to come; he did not know this address, or the town. He did not even know the name of this family.

"Rafik."

"What is going on?"

"I cannot say, but listen."

"I cannot hear you."

"Listen, something is wrong. You know the tall buildings."

"Aziz, there are many tall buildings."

"But when you are walking, first off the ship, after you swim."

"Aziz, there are all different places—one place may not be the place you think it is. There is not one place with tall buildings."

"There is not?"

"No!"

The man was coming back into the room, but this time his wife was with him.

"My wife wants to speak to your friend. Because of her work at the hospital, she will understand him." A swooshing of reprieve went through Aziz. He smiled so largely that his eyes disappeared. He was goofy, eagerly handing the phone to her.

But the man's expression, it was actually worse. He looked not just worried but in a great hurry. He was, Aziz saw, angry.

"Yes," the wife was saying. "Yes." She was serious.

This would not end with police, but it must end soon. He looked at the clock. It was almost seven-thirty.

"The mosque is in Everett. . . . Oh, you are in Everett. That is very good."

She was speaking a Tunisian kind of Arabic. Rafik had spent time in Tunisia, time Rafik's family knew nothing about. Aziz knew his own mother would not want him to be going to Rafik if she knew. But it had to be Rafik. He was the only one from Arzew who had done this before, and it was always somebody like Rafik who could do something like this that first time.

She was giving Rafik the address, but she was not smiling.

"In an hour," she said. She looked at her husband, and for the first time Aziz saw she thought her husband was a fool. This, more than everything else that had changed since he called Rafik, stunned him. He must get out of the apartment. He was not sure he should accept the ride to the mosque with them. What if they did not take him to the mosque? What if they were planning to take him to the police?

She hung up and drew in a breath. He could see she would not by word belittle her husband in front of this problem he had brought home.

"Please wait," she said to Aziz. She and the husband left the den and closed the door.

A cab. He had no money.

A bus. Less money, but still money.

Run out of the room, out of the apartment building, and find this Everett. How many mosques could there be in Everett?

But he remembered Rafik saying, "There are many tall buildings." There might be dozens of mosques in Everett, and besides, he would never ever be able to walk there in an hour.

He could run out of the apartment and find a phone at a church, as he had planned.

But now he was away from Boston; he knew that. He was in a suburb. And even if he was able to call Rafik, he would be unable to tell Rafik where he was. He could not read the signs; he could not ask anyone. It had been a bad thing to leave the city. He should not have done it this way. He should have stuck to his plan about the church.

They were back.

They sat on a sofa opposite the computer. Aziz stood by the computer. He tried to remember what the best approach in a situation like this was. Was it better to level with them, to say, I know you are upset, I think it is because I am Algerian, I hope you know you have nothing to fear from me. Or did that make whatever was disturbing them more alive, because he would be putting it into words? Words made not yet real things real. It was undeniable. So, the other way. He would act as if the anger and the worry and the smart wife and the dumb husband were something he had not even noticed. Was that the better choice?

"We had considered taking you to the authorities," the Egyptian said at last.

He let a silence lengthen.

"Because the Algerians, they are very dangerous. They are crazy," he continued.

"You told my husband you were Moroccan?" the wife interrupted. She could not help herself. Aziz knew that this was the question. If he answered rightly, he would be talking to his mother that night. But what was right? To ally with the wife? To say, No, I did not tell your husband I was Moroccan. In that answer, she could be confirmed in her delighted assessment of her husband's lying ways and thus feel kinship with Aziz and see Aziz as honest, most possibly strong. Or to ally with the husband? To say, yes, I told him I was Moroccan, which the husband could view favorably, because Aziz had covered for him in front of his wife. But the Egyptian knew Aziz had not claimed to be Moroccan. What if the Egyptian were a larger person than he appeared? He might be one who did not fear being exposed in a lie. He might be a principled person, a person who would then recognize, without any doubt, that Aziz was the kind of person who would say *anything* to appease. Aziz would be the kind of person who posed. That kind of person would not be from Morocco. A Moroccan was from a country of peace. A poor country, a desperately difficult country to come from, but it was not a country where people stuck neighbors' heads on shovels beside front porches and went to their funerals crying false tears.

It had been a miracle that he had heard Arabic so soon. But it was to be his undoing. Because anyone who spoke Arabic knew what Algeria was. He had been seduced and rightfully betrayed by his own need for the comfort of being understood. He remembered how each time he had tried before, he had gotten a little closer. First, he tried to get on the boat by delivering a pizza, and they laughed him off the ship. Then, his brother rowed him to the ship anchored offshore, not right at the dock but still in the harbor, and he successfully hid, but he was deceived by the boy, now dead. This time, he had gotten all the way to Boston, only to be taken to the police by an Egyptian couple he had thought were his salvation. What would become of him? He would be deported. And where would he wind up? Home. He wanted to be there. He wanted to be there; in this moment, he wanted nothing more. But the years had taught him that at home he would be having the same kind of conversation he was having this minute, only with different people. He had skedaddled and twisted and been lucky all the times that were possible and allotted to him back home. But with this couple, in their den with its silver lamp and white sofa, there was the possibility, however remote, of a right answer.

"I will tell you honestly, I do not know what I did or did not tell your husband because I have been out of my mind, too sick to know who I was or where I was. And you have been so kind as to take pity on me. But I am not Moroccan. I am Algerian."

"You act like a Moroccan. I have known many Moroccans," the wife said, still tense but less so.

"Yes, he is just like a Moroccan," the Egyptian said soberly.

"You could have said anything, the shape you were in," she added. "Those feet! I must bandage those feet before we take you to your friend."

She got up. Aziz made a step as if to leave the den.

"Sit down," she said. "Sit down."

He edged onto the sofa.

She bent over. She squatted. Aziz felt he had one smile left. But she did not even see it. She was intent on his socks. For some of the seconds while she pulled on them, he was sure he would scream. He closed his eyes, and then he was steady.

3

Rafik gave him the rundown. It was a one-bedroom apartment. There were five of them. Two of them had girlfriends. One girlfriend came only on weekends. The other, Rafik's girlfriend, was rich. She was a receptionist at her father's company, taking a year off from college. She drove a BMW. It was a convertible. So the bedroom was Rafik's, since he had her with him every night. The kitchen had a bed but only on weekends, for the guy with the weekend girlfriend. That left the living room. Two guys slept on a pullout sofa and another on the second sofa. So Aziz got the chair. Everyone was Algerian. But only Rafik was from Arzew. The rest were from Oran or Algiers. Two of them had known Rafik in Germany. One had known him in Paris. One had known him in Tunisia. One had just met him in Boston.

They all took to Aziz. There were beers and stories told. No one could pass up a chance to hear about a stowaway. Except for Rafik, they had all come on visas and then stayed. They flew here with their own passports, checked baggage, and wallets thick with calling cards. Before Aziz, Rafik had been the only stowaway they had known. Rafik's status among them rested in part on his stowaway story—that and the fact that he had won and kept Heather, the rich American girl. Rafik was taller than the others. He was muscled and lifted weights. He had taken up cycling; his titanium racer was there in the corner of the living room, a gift from Heather's father. Aziz was so tired and drunk by dawn, he fell asleep on the floor near one of its skinny tires.

It was quiet when Aziz awoke. No one was in sight. At work, he guessed. "We'll be able to get you a job at Heather's father's company," Rafik had told Aziz, on the drive to the apartment from the mosque. "But don't tell the others, because I haven't done the same for them. They work every day for nothing. But you are like family. My mother, your mother—like babies in the same cradle! I will tell her father, and he will do it. My word is precious with him."

In his long acquaintanceship with Rafik, Aziz had learned that three-quarters of what Rafik told him was false. So he did not count on any job with Heather's father. Nor did he expect to see a BMW parked out front. When the BMW did materialize outside the apartment as they drove up, Aziz was momentarily amazed. But the truth of it would be revealed in time. Heather had been in the bedroom with the door closed when he arrived and never emerged to join them. This could very likely be a neighbor's car. With Rafik, there was always a pull in the sweater.

As he got up from the floor, he remembered his mother. All the shades were drawn, the time of day not clear. He must find the phone.

The apartment was many cheap possessions. What caught his eye were the posters of Madonna that seemed to come from Algeria. She looked French. Maybe one was a Madonna impostor—but no, she was the real Madonna. It was always a guess with her changing hair. He looked at her belly, smooth like milk. Did Rafik's girlfriend have such skin? How could any woman who was really what he knew a woman to be want a man such as Rafik? He scanned for pictures of someone who might be Heather, but there were no photos of friends or family, only Tour de France shots of cobra-helmeted racers that had been torn from a magazine and pasted on the back of the front door and spiraled through the hall into the living room; could it be a map of the tour's winding through the hills of France? He followed it along the wall. Oh, here was a photograph of Rafik! He had put himself, on his bicycle, right in the race, next to a pair of crashing bicycles, as if he had pulled ahead of them.

And the sofas. One of them was not actually a sofa, he realized, but a cot, which had been outfitted with pillows to make a sofa back. The pullout sofa was a futon that folded. His place of rest, the chair, was a baby-blue plastic lounger that was part of an outdoor furniture set, the rest of which—a side table, a chair, and a footstool—were nearby. There was not a phone that he could see.

He turned the corner to the kitchen. There was a folding card table, two television tray tables scrunched against it, a school chair with a desk attached, and two beanbag chairs, which were too big to fit in the kitchen and had been squeezed up as narrowly as they would go against the wall, propped tightly with three ironing boards and a clothesline tied to the refrigerator. This was probably the bed for the one with the weekend girlfriend. There was a long pole with a shower curtain leaning against the wall—the privacy for the kitchen. By the sink, he saw, was the phone, attached to the wall.

He dialed but got a sound and a recording in English. He did it again and got the same. He looked at the phone and puzzled awhile. This too would have to be shown to him. But he was patient; this was how it was. He stared at the phone even so. He was so close to putting his mother at ease. To have gulped beer and told stories, when Rafik and the others could have shown him how the phone worked. He did not think. The Egyptian situation had been the same. He had not thought it through.

It was the trap door, so familiar to him. The door was from childhood, from the first time he had seen a stage in Algiers, at a play his mother had taken him to, one in which the ladies wore stiff gowns and the men wore velvet shorts and carried swords. At one point, one of the men, who was fencing fiercely with one of the other men, was gone. A trap door on the stage had opened, he had fallen through, the door had snapped back up, and everyone on the stage was looking around for him. No one seemed to have the presence of mind to look under the stage. No one knelt and said, Look at this, there's a door here! Aziz remembered feeling his childlike sadness for the gone man, what it must have been like for his eyes to be locked with his adversary's, to be thinking about where to put his foot next and his hand after, and—*bang!*—to be gone, down a chute, out of sight, unheard of, unasked for, without name, loves, hopes, or memory. It had suited everyone that the spirited swordsman had gone.

Aziz sat on the school table and chair to take a look at his feet. The bandages of the wife were white like the moon under his socks. She had put a sparkled salve on him they use for burns. You must get these looked at, she told him; this is not something that can heal on its own. He knew she wanted to ask how it came to be that his feet were like raw chops in the market. Why didn't she? One thing he promised: He would hide his home from other Arabs. Or stay only with Algerians.

He must be awake to the Rafik situation. Perhaps he should sit here and think about what exactly could go wrong. First, Rafik was untrustworthy. That put everything on a provisional basis. Never believe anything he said; three-quarters was clearly not correct. Nothing, not one thing, could be trusted. The BMW, it would never ever turn out to be Heather's. Here was a better way to think about it: *He must always act as if Heather did not exist.* This was a principle. A principle, he reminded himself. If she walked into the room and said she was Heather, reserve judgment. Wait, see, listen, observe, consider.

Second, Rafik should be in a Tunisian prison for embezzlement, serving an eighteen-year sentence. That meant he must be vigilant and reject Rafik's deals, offers, opportunities, ideas, notions.

Third, Rafik would never change. This meant that Rafik was involved in some manner of wrongdoing this very moment. It was not conjecture, it was not possible, it was not probable, it was happening.

The front door banged. A face appeared. It was a woman in

an apron. She was old, short, and fat. She started talking to him quickly, in English, but he could not place the emotion in her face. Was it possible she was *not* speaking English? She was looking him in the eye. But she needed no cues, no nods, no nothing. He kept her eye. He offered an air of ambiguous concern. Then she banged on the wall: *knock, knock, knock*. She fell silent. She looked at him. A response was needed, but another door banged inside the apartment. This caught her attention and she was gone toward the bedroom. He heard her steps down the hall and then more talking, all hers, but this time she was talking faster.

He took his bandaged foot off the desk of the school chair and put on his sock. The old woman was back and there was another fat woman with her who was wearing a bathrobe, a velvety cream one made of silk and lace and ruffles. She was much fatter than the first woman, and much younger, and also much prettier, with long curls of soft blond hair. Her emotions were not difficult to read in the slightest, for she gave off the presence and command of an opera singer at the full bloom of her career and her powers. She was indignant.

The first woman was as unreadable as before, but she kept knocking on the wall, and every time she did, the robed woman kicked it. No voices were raised, no threatening gestures made. It was a pantomime that meant nothing to him, and the women performing it had no interest in him, their audience. They passed out of sight into the living room, and he followed, noticing as he did that someone was coming home, wearing a mechanic's uniform, his hands blackened, a bandanna around his head, and his hair in a ponytail. He thought it was the one Rafik had met in Paris, because he had a mole near his mouth, and from the night before Aziz remembered that he had thought this mechanic too self-composed, rude in some way.

The guy passed the women as if they were fish flapping on sand and said to Aziz in Arabic, "These whores run our lives." Aziz was not sure if this called for comment, but apparently the woman in the robe knew what he had said and she pushed him, saying in Arabic, to Aziz's astonishment, "Cocksucker." The old fat woman who began this episode was not privy to Arabic, because she smiled prettily at the mechanic, curtsied, handed him a piece of paper, and was gone.

The mechanic, still holding the paper, turned to the young fat woman, took the soft belt of her ruffled robe, and pulled hard. It came out of its loops and into his hands in the most masterful motion, but the robe remained on the woman undisturbed. She laughed. This provoked the mechanic. In Arabic he said, in sweet tones, as if he were speaking to his mother or his sister, "I would like to fuck you up the ass and make you scream with fear, you bitch whore." Apparently she knew the word *whore,* or maybe more, for she took the belt out of his hands, spit in his face, and kneed him between the legs. All the while, the robe remained on her person. The mechanic was on the floor. The young woman disappeared and a door slammed shut.

Aziz picked up a glass by the sink and filled it with water. He grabbed a roll of paper towels and knelt by the mechanic's head. "Here," he said, "here." The mechanic was lost to pain, doubled over. He did not look up.

Aziz waited. He could hear a stereo being turned on somewhere, the music so loud it seemed as if it were right there with them in the kitchen. He put the glass of water and the paper towels down and rounded the kitchen corner into a part of the apartment he had not seen before. There were two doors. By now it was raining or snowing, something was hitting against the outside windows, and it was dark for midday. But his sense of time was distorted; it could have been morning or closer to suppertime.

His feet, without warning, had switched to highest pain. He dropped to his knees to get off them, kneeling and rocking a little. Then he steadied himself with a hand on the wall. The music was coming from one of the doors, and he moved closer, very slowly, finally resting his ear in the place right by the doorsill as he had learned to do with his sisters, so he could hear them talking to their boyfriends who were whispering from the window outside in the tree. Sure enough, the woman in the robe was talking—on the phone, he guessed—and sobbing and straining and wheezing. In between the sounds, there were many other words in English, but Rafik was the refrain. This must be Heather.

He crawled toward the other door. It was the bathroom, but he quickly realized it was also someone's closet. There were shoes and shirts and dresses and suits, more clothes than he had ever seen except in a store. All he needed was a piss. He closed the door, got to his feet tenderly, and was relieving himself when the door pushed toward him. He heard a scream. There was Heather, or the woman he supposed was Heather, and here was he, with his dick in his hand, and there in the periphery was the mechanic, carrying the baby-blue lawn chair above his head.

4

"Aziz!" yelled Rafik, holding his hand over the phone's mouthpiece. Rafik was back from work just in time to answer it. "Aziz!"

Nothing.

"Where is he?" Rafik asked no one in particular. Two others walking in the kitchen shrugged.

That's when Heather screamed. It was a short sound, followed by crashing. Over and over this crashing went, and it was still going on when Rafik and the others ran back toward the bathroom and saw the Parisian mechanic hitting Heather's prone body, which Aziz, whose pants were down around his ankles, was trying to protect. It did look, to Rafik, as if Heather and Aziz had been—he knew this could not be so, but his eyes told him it was—grappling in some preempted rape, which luckily the Parisian had been able to hear and was now trying to stop. Heather's arms were in her robe, but the rest of it was twisted away from her, revealing her rose-petal voluptuousness in a haphazardly erotic way.

Rafik joined the Parisian, punching Aziz in the head repeatedly. Aziz passed out and rolled off Heather. But to Rafik's consternation, the Parisian was still whacking at Heather, who by now was saying, "Get that motherfucker off me. Get him off me!"

"Kamal," Rafik yelled.

Kamal continued.

There was nothing to do but punch Kamal too, which Rafik did. But Kamal did not go down as easily as a weakened stowaway. Rafik and he snarled into fisticuffs and kicking. Heather, robe flowing, began making her move; she planned to push her thumb into one of Kamal's eyeballs, but the appearance of Mrs. Massaquina made everyone, every last movement, stop.

"Police," she said, not very loudly. "Police." She paused, straightened her chest. "Police?" She enjoyed this word, its effect on them. Heather pulled her robe around herself. Kamal, bleeding from the mouth, wiped his chin. Rafik sprang up and took Mrs. Massaquina's elbow.

"There was almost a rape," he told her with sober respect. "But my friend here, he was able to stop it. There, on the floor, you see what we have done to the rapist."

Mrs. Massaquina looked at Aziz.

"He was here earlier."

"No!" said Rafik.

"Yes, I saw him, in the kitchen, looking at his feet. And this one?" she said, looking at Heather. "This *puttana* could not be raped."

Rafik made no objection. Heather was frozen in a posture of dignity, even though her left breast was beautifully exposed. Kamal was fingering his lip.

"More noise—I call police. Off to Pakistan for good."

Algeria was Pakistan was India to her. She turned her shoulders like a general and was gone.

"Rafik," wailed Heather.

Kamal knew he had little time. He got himself up from the floor. Grabbing the roll of paper towels on the kitchen floor, he was out the front door before Rafik had his arms around Heather and was saying, “My baby, my baby.” The others backed away, making no move to help Aziz. They knew he had not tried to rape Heather. Heather and Kamal had been at each other for weeks. Rafik was the only one who didn’t know—and Aziz.

There was the phone, still off the hook in the kitchen.

One of them hung it up.

5

Aziz came to and saw he was in a hospital. He tried to move, but he was tethered by tubes in his arm and his nose. A buzzer sounded: a loud one, he thought. He looked around and saw he was alone, surrounded by a curtain. Then someone pulled it back.

"Mr. Ricco?"

He stared.

"Xavier Ricco? Xavier Ricco?"

He kept staring.

"Do you know who you are?" The nurse had made the buzzer stop and was checking his arm and his nose.

"Xavier Ricco," he mimicked, hoping she had asked him his name and had been telling him his name. Her expressions were exaggerated, as if she were talking to a baby.

"Oh, good. Your speech is a little slurred, but that's expected. And you know where you are?"

He decided now would be a good time to appear to fall back asleep.

He put his head back on the pillow and closed his eyes.

"That's good, you rest now. I'll call your wife and your sister and tell them you've regained consciousness. They'll be so relieved."

Aziz understood nothing. His head was bandaged. His cheek was covered too, and when he touched the gauze it was tender. With alarm he discovered there was a tube up his penis.

His feet. Where were his feet? He pulled one up. It had been put in a new dressing and covered in blue fabric. He tried to wiggle his toes. He stopped abruptly. The skin was gone. He could tell, he had no skin. They were numbed too, his feet. He could feel them; he was moving them, but not very well. He felt sickened and had to force himself not to call out. Why did his feet have no skin? Suddenly his head was aching. He was sweating. Another buzzer went off.

A nurse came in. Then another.

"His heart rate."

"How can it be up that high when he's asleep?"

"I don't know. Mr. Ricco? Mr. Ricco?"

Aziz fluttered his eyes. He affected a groan.

"He's conscious. Are you in pain?"

It was morning. He was no longer in the curtained space. There was a window and two other people in beds closer to the door. They were sleeping. The sunlight from the crack in the blinds was a blue kind of gold. On the beach in Arzew, the rocks would get so warm. Lying on them, feeling their heat, he had often slept away an afternoon. He was very little then, and his sisters were still at home. It was usually Anissa who came to find him. It was because of her they called him Hmaam. This came about because they could never keep their eyes on him. You are always flying away, his mother told him. I turn my back for half of a moment, and you have wings. "He is a pigeon," Anissa said. And it stuck.

He tried to remember. There was a nurse earlier. He had said something. How had he gotten here? That was it, that was what was before this morning. The last thing he could remember seeing was the Parisian on the kitchen floor after the robed woman had kneed him. Could the Parisian have hit him? He must have been in a fight. He touched his head again. The pain was excruciating. The skin on his face felt very tight, stretched thin.

He heard a cart being pushed in the hall. A woman laughed softly. Another woman told her something. He glanced over at his roommates and saw that one of them, an old man, was awake and looking toward the door and the hallway sounds. Another old man, not as old as the other one, stirred in the bed next to Aziz. A phone rang, much louder than was needed to hear it. It was on the windowsill, right near Aziz's head. He tried to position himself so he could answer it, but this was surprisingly time-consuming. Then a nurse sailed in and picked it up. "Mr. Ricco," she said, "this is for you." She brought the receiver to him and gently helped him wedge it against the pillow and his ear. Then a dull bell sounded outside the room and she went away again.

"Aziz?"

"Rafik?"

"Thank God. Oh, thank God. I have been crazy."

Aziz looked at the two old men to see if they were curious and would hear him speaking Arabic. He yelled "Hey!" as loud as he could. They made no motion. They were sick and hard of hearing. "Rafik?"

"Aziz, listen, we are going to get you out of there, but we had to take you. Your heart—Heather thought it had stopped beating. And we could not find your pulse. And you were out. Cold."

"How—"

"You don't remember?"

"I remember a fat woman kneed your friend from Paris, and he was on the floor in the kitchen, and I was trying to help him."

"Mrs. Massaquina kneed Kamal?"

"Who is Mrs. Massaquina?"

"Landlady. Pain in the ass."

"Well, I think it was her."

"Listen, it doesn't matter. You have to know a few things. Your name is Xavier Ricco."

"I thought it might be."

"And you are a construction worker. Can you say *construction worker?*"

"Kunshukin wirka."

"Not good. Try again. *Construction worker.*"

"Kun-shuk-tan wirka."

"And your wife is Linda Ricco."

"Rafik, I cannot say these things. Just tell me when you are coming to take me home."

"I can't right now. This is bad. How—"

The nurse had come back in the room and was smiling at Aziz, saying something. She was black, and she had an accent that made him think she had been born in Africa. Nigeria, maybe.

"—do you, Aziz?" Rafik was asking something at the same time as the nurse.

"Yes," he said in English to the nurse, hoping that was the answer needed.

"You said *yes*!" Rafik was almost shouting.

The nurse checked to see if the phone was still in the right place and then left.

"I know I said *yes,*" Aziz said.

"Okay, okay. Look, this is the deal. We took you in there three nights ago—"

"Three . . . ?"

"Listen, just listen. Heather took you in with another secretary she works with, and this person, this Linda, said she was your wife, and Heather said she was your sister."

"I still have not met Heather."

"Aziz, I need you to listen."

"Okay. Okay."

"They only took you because Linda does have a husband, and insurance, so you kind of became him. We said you got mugged and beat up, and they took your wallet and all your identification."

"But—"

"But there was the problem with your feet. And they didn't fit with your being robbed and stuff, so we said you were a construction worker but kind of like a day worker, and you'd been out of work and been taking these day jobs, down in Chelsea where the men line up, and that somehow you'd gotten on a job where there was some dangerous shit, some acid, and gotten badly fucked up by this, and you were on your way to the doctor's when this asshole jumped you outside the house, and we found you passed out."

"Why do my feet have no skin?"

"What?"

"My feet, they have no skin. I can tell. Something is wrong, Rafik, very wrong."

"Goddamn."

"I am telling you. No skin."

"Didn't you ask them?"

"Rafik!"

"Oh, yeah, right. Right. Hold on. Hold on. Heather wants to talk to you."

"Aziz?"

"Yes."

"I talk Arabic no good," she said very slowly, in Arabic. "Rafik, come over here."

"Aziz, Heather is going to say something, and I am going to say it to you in Arabic, okay?"

"Sure."

"Tell him that he has to stay in the hospital for at least another week."

The voice of Heather was not a whine, but it was almost a whine. It was injured. She had a permanently afflicted kind of voice.

"Because his feet must have got badly burned when he was on the ship."

He listened to Rafik's translation and tried to think. When could that have happened? His life was breaking off, floating away from him in lazy circles. How could he not remember stepping in acid? But he did not remember why he was here. He had the story that the hospital had been told, but not the actual story. He remembered he had been in the kitchen, he had been telling himself not to accept anything Rafik said. *He must always act as if Heather did not exist.*

"Your feet have second- and third-degree burns."

"They do?" He knew the voice of this woman. She was insulted.

"Yes, Aziz. You do. It is bad."

"Wait. Wait. The skin?"

"She says that's because they had to take the old skin off. It's what they—there will be skin again. You have to have an operation to put skin back on."

Aziz was nauseated. He could not bear this thing, this thing that had happened to his feet. How could he have not known his feet had been burned? It would have hurt. It would have hurt.

"Aziz, are you there?"

"I—I—yes. . . ."

"Be strong, cousin. You must. This is something—it can happen. I think it was steam. On some of the ships, you can come on steam, sudden, sudden, and it probably knocked you out, and when you came to, because the burns cut off your nerve endings, you probably didn't know how bad it was, and the socks were still on, and—I don't know, cousin. I don't know. But it happened. It . . . it is happening."

He needed to talk to someone who was not Rafik. He needed to talk to the Nigerian nurse. She would tell him if this was so, if this had happened. He wanted his sister Anissa. He began to cry. For some reason, that caught the attention of one of the old men. He looked grumpily at Aziz.

"Tell him to be calm," Heather volunteered.

"Heather, I know. Look, let me talk to him now."

"He knows about Linda, right?"

"Yeah."

"Aziz?"

There was nothing.

The phone had slipped down the pillow, because Aziz had turned his head and was looking upward, straining to see how he was going to think. He remembered his near breakdown in the

Egyptian's bathroom and how he had willed himself away from it. It was realizing how bad off he was, that was the thing that edged him into—what? But now it was different. Now, he could not tell, by his own eye or his own ears or his own hand or his own nose or his own tongue, what was and what was not. He had only this Rafik, a devious man, and this Heather, who had been, after all, the woman in the robe who kneed Kamal, to bring him news of what had happened and what would happen.

The nurse came in and saw him, throat pulled taut, eyes upward, tears on his face. The phone was about to fall off the bed. She caught it up in her hand and said, "He will call you back."

"Aziz?"

"I cannot talk now, sir."

"Who is this?"

"This is Osana Jean-Batiste, RN."

"You are the nurse?"

"I have got to go," she said. She moved toward the burn patient, who was lifting his arms from the bed. It was the kind of trance she had seen as a little girl in Haiti; it was the arms that went first, before the whole of a man just went up off into the air, as easy as Lazarus. Levitating, they called it here. She crossed herself and did what her mother had always told her to do, which was to slide her arms around this patient, this bird of a man, and pull him close to her chest. "Peace, child," she said. "This child is all right. This child is all right."

6

His mother's voice had found him: *Tais-toi, mon enfant, tais-toi.* Her touch was his. *Ça ne fait rien. Ça ne fait rien,* she whispered in his ear.

"*Mes pieds,*" he said, "*mes pieds. Il n'y a pas de peau.*"

"*Vous êtes gravement blessé,*" Osana Jean-Batiste said. She did not know this patient spoke French. His arms were back on the blanket. His head lay on her shoulder. The danger had passed. The other burn patients were staring at her, old men with vinegar for blood. She gave them a look. What are you asking me about? it said to them. One closed his eyes. The other turned away—out of respect, she hoped.

She held on some. Not yet right to let go of this one. He had confusion in him; his eyes were still closed.

"*Monsieur? Monsieur?*" What was his first name? His last name was Ricco.

Then he opened them, those narrow eyes, kind of like a fox peering out of a safe place. But a big lamp shining in them. Face no wider than a broomstick. Not a pretty one, not an ugly one. A feather of a man too, just might not stay in one place.

"Vous parlez français!" she said.

"Vous aussi," he said carefully, as if he did not quite believe anyone did.

"Bien sûr." She smiled. There was something else now. Bad worry, she felt. Fear, too; it had been there awhile. She concentrated and said in French, "Tell me." She pulled back a little, to let him ease back if he found her too close. But he sank back entirely, and she could see he was ashamed. She put her hands in her lap and sat half of herself on the side of the bed.

"I thought I was dreaming," he said in French. "I thought you were someone else."

"Your wife?" She didn't know if he had a wife. He had just arrived from the burn unit and she had not yet read his file. He looked no more than a teenager, but one who had seen what a man knew by forty, at least. Could be he was born that way, because it didn't come from what she could see of him. Baby skin on that forehead, not a line.

He looked down.

"Girlfriend?"

Silence.

There was that bell again.

"I'll be back, I promise," she told him, and pulled close again to take his hand and hold it a beat.

He watched her, a thick-waisted woman with white-stocking calves thin as a schoolgirl's. Such a walk she had—a glide—and fast, yet quiet as a cloud. She smelled of plums. He wanted to tell her everything, he felt he *could* tell her. Mad longing, not thinking, he scolded. Think and wait and see and listen. He was already a mile farther down the road because she had held him. Something about her had slipped under him. He couldn't give her *gniin;* no, his lies would have to be true in some way, not hopping and light and false.

. . .

After the patient who needed her, she came back to the nurse's station and looked. XAVIER RICCO: AGE: 27. Married. WIFE: Linda Ricco. SISTER: Heather Montrose. OCCUPATION: Day laborer. So there was a wife.

He was admitted unconscious with lacerations to the head. Robbed and beaten outside his apartment in Everett. Second-degree burns on entire left foot, third-degree burns on metatarsal and toes of right and left feet. Wife and sister believe burns received on day job, construction site unknown. He had gained consciousness briefly yesterday. Gave his name.

Not a name for someone with French. But then his father could have been Spanish, his mother French West Indian. Catholic on both sides; Xavier works. But the accent, it was not Caribbean. She knew those, every last one. So what could it be? Maybe African, but not a black man, no. Looked Italian to her eye. Ricco: that was Italian, not Hispanic.

So he'd been just talking a little. No doctor had asked him a thing. Truth, they probably wouldn't, though of course they should. Should ask about how such burns came to be. Should ask about headaches. Should want to know if he was having trouble breathing. She put his file back in the clear plastic slipcase on the wall. He was going to have major surgery, scheduled for—let's see—tomorrow, and she didn't even have to ask to know that not a doctor or nurse had bothered to tell him or call his family. Nothing. He probably didn't have insurance. She pulled the chart back. No, he did. Wife had a job as a secretary in a pharmaceutical company in Cambridge. So did the sister.

She would call them. Worried sick, they most likely were, and not a doctor on any floor who gave a thought to them.

But first she wanted to take a look at those burns.

At the doorway to the room, she heard one of the old men trying to talk to him.

"Cat got your tongue?" he was shouting.

A pause. She looked in the room.

"You speak up, I can't hear a thing you're saying." It was the man farther from Xavier, right by the door.

The other man, whose bed was between them, said softly, "Good Christ almighty, would you keep it down?"

Then Xavier replied, "Keeptown."

"What?" bellowed the belligerent.

"Kweepown."

He was without a scrap of English. She had done the same thing when she had first come. They had called her *parrot*.

"Now, Mr. Richardson," she said, glancing at his wrist, "you need to get some rest."

"That fella speaks like a faggot, and I won't have it."

"Dumb as a post," said the middle man, who was speaking so softly, she was sure Mr. Richardson and Xavier heard not a word. He looked at Osana. "You're a good woman," he said flatly.

"I'm going to move you over that way, give you a little more privacy."

"That's nice of you."

"You comfortable?"

"No. I've got burns on my hand." He raised up a paw of thick dressings.

She made a show of adjusting his pillows, took five seconds with his IV. "Looks good," she said.

"Turn on that radio there." It was a weather station. "Keep the volume low," he said.

She pulled a curtain around him.

Xavier was asking her something, a thought she nearly guessed, but then it was out like a candle. He was looking toward the window.

Aziz looked at her again, willing her to know everything he wanted to say.

Lord, he's in love with me, Osana thought. Her hands went to her throat, then back on her hips.

"Child, you are not Xavier." She said this in English, to gain an upper hand.

"Xavier," was the word he said, but the tone was *You know*.

"Not Ricco either."

"Either," but really, *I know.*

"Let me take a look at your feet." She looked right at them, and he moved as if to peel the blanket back. She pulled over a stool and sat at the foot of the bed. Without her asking, he turned on his side, so she would be able to see the soles of his feet. His ankles were wan and the black hair of his legs seemed out of place, a man's, not a boy's, and this was only a boy, she told herself, one she could have mothered. She began unraveling, and then took the scissors, and then, when he did not flinch or speak or even move his hands, as so many she had done this for before had been unable to stop themselves from doing, she became careful on her own. But she didn't look up at him. She was afraid to, really, and that was out of her experience. She put down the scissors and looked at the last layer. It was good that whoever had cleaned and bandaged him last had been like her. Someone who was not stingy with the Silvadene, so that the flimsy grids of the bandage were not sunk into the raw of him. There was a whipped and glimmering froth still, and that meant she could take off the last of it without getting him more codeine or Demerol or both.

Gently, she lifted up the gauze on his left foot, the heel first. The salve came up with it, and she knew the moment the air hit his skin he would have to draw back. But he didn't. Those were second-degree, the most painful, because the nerves were intact. He was motionless. She got a shaky feeling then herself, and she could hear her mother back home saying, *He is not of this world.* She kept going and lifted the gauze at the arch, which was uninjured, and then the last, the worst, the ball of the foot and the toes. The salve was slick, put on with a ladle. God bless the one before her. God bless that one. She could not see through the white cream of the salve.

"Can you tell me," she heard him say in French, "why my toes have no skin?"

It was then she looked up at him, his cheek against the sheet, his hospital gown riding up his thigh.

"They do have skin," she said.

"They do?" His eyes were on hers.

"Yes."

"Why does it feel that they don't?"

"Wait here."

She went to the supplies in the bathroom. There was the salve, in its blue tub, like hand cream.

She brought it to him and knelt on the floor by his hands.

"Close your eyes."

He did.

She opened the jar, put down the lid, and stuck three fingers into the lightness. From the first day she became a nurse on this unit, she had never stopped being amazed by this weightless substance. It was not a lotion, it was not a cream, it was not anything but a suspension of micronized silver, and there was really no way, until you felt it, that you could even imagine the absence of its touch on your person. She took his hands, both of them, and smeared it all over; all five hundred dollars of the jar went on his thumbs and palms and every finger. She let go.

"Move your fingers."

He did. He was the trusting man she never thought would come to this hospital, to her unit. But here he was, and he moved his fingers, each against another, thumbs on the pads of all of them.

"They feel as if they have no skin."

"Yes."

"Your feet are going to be fine. Tomorrow, there will be an operation. And I promise you, after that, we will be able, not right away but in time, to stop using this on the burns, and when we do you will see that you have skin on your feet."

He opened his eyes. It was then she saw he was no child, and he was also not in love with her. She felt a twisting momentarily for having lied to him, because there was, in fact, no skin on his toes or even his heel. The black dead of it had to be removed, and when more of it coagulated, even into just red, or most often, that distinctive brick color, it too had to be cut away and discarded. To debride, at first, had been the one thing she was not sure she could do as a nurse. She would be light-headed from revulsion, examining burns catastrophically involved. Mouthing but not understanding her study tricks: "Fascia you should slashia" and the Four Cs—color, consistency, circulation, contractility. A mush of dead muscle, a jelly of fat. Dead muscle you cut. Fat you save. Fat protected precious nerves.

She was leaving people more maimed than they needed to be. At night on the bus going home she feared for her future. If she could not master this, what would she do? Where could she go? She realized after a while that she was giving little thought to the trusting burned-up ones she was hurting further than they were already hurt. As she left the room to answer the bell, Osana looked at this Xavier Ricco, or whoever he was, and wondered if he knew it was possible to care about only yourself.

7

The paint was white. But there were so many whites. He looked at the shapes on the piece of paper. What had he been told about how to say this word? He closed his eyes. *Beena. Beena.* Something-*beena*. He looked around the store, trying to sense, among all the many men he could see, which was a kind one. A man in a white shirt and white pants looked at him looking at him and turned, fast and sharp; it was not him. A small Mexican; his eyes were too dull. Another small Mexican; he spoke no English. Aziz could sense that because of the way he held his hands and by his hat, the way it was on his head. But wait, maybe he *did* speak English. He tried to get a better look at his eyes.

"Sir, may I help you?" It was a man in pressed pants, gold in color.

"I . . . I . . . need white, but—" Aziz started. He looked closely, without looking as if he was looking closely. He saw a young man with a ravaged complexion, so red and unsettled, it seemed impossible that he walked around with it, right there, on his face. Yet this bad face seemed nothing to this young man. His grass-colored shirt was stiff with clean. He was this way that Americans had, of being soft but hard; nothing difficult, nothing easy; nothing good, nothing bad. It was a way of being that Aziz had no words for yet. He knew one thing: It was not possible to predict which way it would go. Sometimes, talking to a person in such a state, they turned real, looked inside you closely, let you know something everyone knew but no one was saying. Other times, they snapped and hated. Most of the time, he was noticing, they just kept on with that thing that was not readable or nameable. But it was not safe to assume it would always be that way. Once, someone had laughed at him. Once, someone had hit him. He assumed there were many other things that could happen. There was only one thing to do, and that was to say what you could say.

"It is beena white," Aziz tried.

"Damn interior desecraters, so many damn-ass colors for a simple thing called white. Give me a look-see," the young man said. He craned over to read the paper in Aziz's hands.

"Verbena white. Jesus fucking Christ. Okay. How many?"

"Four gallon."

"Here we go."

Aziz followed him toward the mixing machines and stood to the side as the young man punched in the computer codes for the paint. The young man started talking with another like himself in the same exact pants and shirt. Aziz could not hear them over the sound of the machine. The coworker—who had not much backside and a big ball of a stomach—seemed to have more to say. His mouth moved quickly, his eyes stayed in no particular way that conveyed anything, and his impassive posture was constant. Aziz's salesman started pushing his chin forward and then drawing it toward his neck. He did this more than once. Aziz tried to do the same with his chin. Sometimes, if he did a movement, he felt something, and that feeling he was able to recognize, and know a little about the emotion of an exchange or of what someone was saying to him. But sometimes, when he imitated in this way, the person became furious.

Both of them were shaking their heads now. The paint was

done. Aziz's young man flipped a switch and kept talking to the other one while he withdrew the paint cans from the machine. By now there was a line by the counter, and Aziz could feel the anger behind him.

"Yappity-yap," a hoarse man said.

"This a talk show or a paint store?"

"Here you go, sir," Aziz's salesman said, smiling, probably, Aziz thought, because Aziz was the one he was satisfying, and the others were mice.

"Next," said the other one, his posture the same as before. He cared nothing for anyone.

Aziz produced a credit card.

"You got some ID?" the young man said. The not-readable aspect had returned.

"No," Aziz said. "I have this." He pulled out three pieces of paper.

"Oh, okay, no problem," the young man said, without looking at them. "Good deal." He took the credit card, pushed it on a machine, and gave it back. Then he started talking to the other one again.

He handed Aziz a box with the gallons resting inside. "Signature on file," he said. Aziz said "Yes" and lowered his eyes to see his feet walking on the cement floor.

At night, he kept his window open. Mostly he did this so the sound of the airport, the jet engines on their regular intervals, could put him to sleep. He loved them. They were going to places that existed but could not be seen. This made him feel that death, as he had been accustomed to thinking of it, was perhaps something of a mistake of thinking.

It was cold, so Heather and Rafik thought he was crazy. He didn't know how to explain to them that without that open window he would hear them, their loving, and because they had each other, he needed other sounds, and he needed sleep more than he sometimes could manage to have it. He told Rafik that he was so used to being cold on the ship that he was not comfortable being warm. Rafik knew this was not the way it was, but he left it alone. Now that it was only the three of them, a new careful began. Heather was particularly quiet. He knew something had gone on while he was in the hospital that they had not shared with him. When they picked him up, Heather had said to him in the car, "We've moved. Everyone else is gone." He knew there was a reason she told him this, but in the months that followed, he still did not know why, and he had let it rest.

The new place was a part of a house, but it was also partly underground. It had two bedrooms, and there was already furniture in it but it smelled, so frighteningly that they threw it out and, when no one came to take it, there outside on the sidewalk, they pulled it to the chain-link fence at the end of the street. But it bothered them there, a pile of things that when they came home they could see and, as if it were right near them, remember the smell. It could never be melted away or rained into the ground, so one night they set it on fire.

The fence went on for blocks in both directions and contained an empty parking lot. It belonged to the airport, Rafik said, but no one ever parked there, because the terminals were so far away. The furniture burned slowly, and they had to keep lighting it again and again. Finally, Heather said she would go to the gas station, and she drove off in her BMW, coming back with a red watering can of gasoline. And then it burned. Aziz worried that someone would surely come running. But the neighborhood stayed dark and closed.

Kamal, the friend of Rafik's from Paris, the one who had hated Heather and tried to knock her to the floor with a chair, left the afternoon of the fight. He had an apartment in East Boston but he drove a taxi, he had a Brazilian girlfriend, and Rafik had confided to Aziz that under no circumstances was Heather to know that Rafik and Kamal still got together. Aziz knew Rafik and Kamal were not right. He just hoped Rafik would never tell him the details. The two friends of Rafik's from Germany had flown back to Munich, promising to be back. That was all, in total, that Rafik would say about them. And the friend of Rafik's from Tunisia—whom Aziz knew for certain was a holdover from the main calamity of Rafik's life—Rafik said he had been arrested for shoplifting some tampons for his girlfriend and ordered deported, was released on bail, and had boarded a bus to California.

There were other messes. Aziz learned of them in pieces, and sometimes those bits changed. Linda had been touch and go. The insurance company accepted that her husband, Xavier, was in the hospital, but Linda had to be talked to and calmed down almost every two or three days. Heather took care of that part of the situation. She told Linda no one would ever know.

But it was wrong, Linda said. Heather told her it was fair when you thought about it, because these were just big insurance companies with plenty of money. Someone was getting saved by this; it was humanitarian.

Linda never met Aziz, so he was more of an idea than a person, and a suspicious one. Rafik and Aziz were interchangeable in Linda's mind, and Rafik, in her view, was too calm and too friendly and talked too much Arabic with his friends, saying just about anything, which for all she knew was "Linda is dumb" or "If only Linda knew." But she didn't want to let on to Heather about these worries, seeing as Heather had only ever done right by her, buying her groceries one time when she was broke, giving her an airplane ticket to get back to Texas because of a bad mix-up, and listening to her in the ladies' room at work while she cried and cried about her crush on their boss, who had carried on with her as long as it suited him and then dumped her and taken up with his boss's secretary. The name *Rafik* threw Linda. Not *Brad* or *Rick*. That's who Heathers dated. The only time Linda'd heard the name Rafik was when a Filipino, who turned out to be Indonesian—or was it Malaysian?—moved into the apartment across the hall. Somehow this woman's son, who happened to be named Rafik, had been in trouble and got put on a boat by those who didn't like him and drowned. This son was Muslim, went away, came back different. Muslims, the ones who make nuns out of their women. Heather with that? But then

Linda saw Heather and Rafik together when he picked her up from work one night, and there was this *muy rico* one with bedroom eyes. That's when she saw the BMW too. Rafik said Heather's dad got it for her.

Heather came from money, and you never knew when something might come of that. Heather's father in Virginia was a basket that Linda hoped she could get closer to, and it was more likely to be in reach someday if she did this thing with the insurance. So she didn't tell Heather that her husband, Xavier, had been out of the house, out of the state, and, for all she knew, out of the country since the summer. She played it so Heather would think she had risked a lot, that Heather owed her much. She would ask Heather, "What if my husband gets sick? Then what?" Another time Linda told Heather he was home sick from work. Heather offered to take him to the doctor, to pay for it out of her own money, but Linda said, No, no, that would be too much; he'd be fine. When he "got better," Linda started asking, "But what if he gets hit by a car?" He won't, Heather kept saying. He just won't.

Then there were the hospital bills. Insurance paid most but not all of them. Rafik assigned Aziz to go to Linda's house every day and take the bills from their mailbox, so she would never see them. He instructed Aziz to toss them, but Aziz kept them under his bed. Eventually, even with Aziz removing the bills, there would be trouble about that, and that was why they had moved and why Heather had quit the job at her dad's company, which luckily, it turned out, was *not* actually his company. The calls to Linda from collection agencies began long after she and Heather had had four glasses of wine and a tearful two hours at a bar near their office. Heather told Linda she would be going back to college in the fall, and in the meantime her father was taking her on a tour of Europe, Africa, and Asia. It was going to be hard to go without talking for six months, but Heather promised Linda she would call her along the way.

8

It was early for the club, not quite ten. The music was still low enough for talking. Rafik looked hard at Aziz. "You are not telling me the whole story," he said.

"Another one?" A waitress pointed to Aziz's empty bottle.

"Two," Rafik told her. "There is a woman in this story," Rafik continued. "There was one for you."

"There is no story." Aziz did not want another beer. He did not want Rafik's blunt to have any chance at the intricate of Soumeya.

"Your brother is coming soon enough. He will tell me why you came. And—"

"We are lucky American immigration has this lottery," Aziz interrupted. "It is—what—nine months since I came? And the prize, the lottery for green card, my brother has won."

"You enter both your names in the lottery, and he, who does not want to come, wins. You, who wanted to come, lost. God hates us."

"My parents are happy."

"One less to feed."

"Mourad is hungry, and there is no work for him, and my father cannot take him and Latif and Bilal and my mother and her sisters. Oh, and of course my aunts, my father's sisters. He cannot feed them all. It is not possible."

"Mourad should have found a woman."

"He is depressed."

"He is ugly."

Aziz laughed. His youngest brother, Mourad, was no uglier than any of them. But he was apart, pitied. Yet he was the only student in the family. Unlike his three older brothers and two older sisters, Mourad learned some English, not just French. He was dour, he said little, and, because he was the youngest, was often ignored. But this forgotten one would have a green card from the start, which would mean a real job. They would start sending home money. After nine months, he had not sent any. He had not paid any hospital bills either.

"That is a beautiful woman." Rafik was looking at a table near the dance floor.

"You should try to know her," Aziz said.

"I am in love with Heather. We will be married one day."

"Then why are you here with me, while she thinks you are working in Providence to make more money?"

"No, seriously. Do you see her? Her friends are not like her. Over by the other bar."

Aziz looked across the dance floor and scanned the tables. "Right by the dancing?"

"One sort of back, behind the table with the two couples. She is American. Blond. Small, very small. Her eyes, they are like Djara."

Djara was a singer from home who had big eyes, very blue. Aziz believed they were fake. He knew about contact lenses that changed your eye color. No Algerian woman would have eyes that deeply blue. Maybe an American. He looked.

She was small like him. He would be able to carry her. She was wearing something that did not show her shape; maybe it was a dress, but it was hard to see from where he sat. Her friends were laughing, and they were leaning into each other, and she was too. She laughed in a way he had only imagined someone could laugh, but not actually seen. She did not think anyone anywhere would be watching her. She did not feel that her face had to be any one way in particular.

"I am not sure she is American."

"Aziz. She is American."

"No. Look at how she is looking."

"Looking?"

"She does not have that thing the Americans have. Being soft but hard; nothing difficult, nothing easy; nothing good, nothing bad."

"*Matter-of-fact* they call it."

"Rafik, she is not American."

"You make no sense, cousin."

"I cannot explain it to you. I just know this."

They sat in silence, watching the table of women. There were four of them. There was a tall woman; she made him remember giraffes. Her hair was extremely short and spiked up in the air, and she had tipped it with orange. She had a beautiful smile. But she had no chin, and this robbed her of being beautiful. But he liked her immediately. There was a woman smoking, but he could not see much of her from where he was sitting. Every so often he glimpsed her hands, because she was waving them, fluttering them like a fan, but no, that was not right. She was also rising up in her chair a little, then down, then up a little. Then there was another blond woman who was also small and had blue eyes—Aziz realized that she could be described as the Djara woman could be, and yet somehow Rafik had not noticed her, nor had Aziz. And she laughed a lot too. Why was she so hard to see?

They were having a wonderfully happy time. He had never seen women in this place laughing like that. Mostly women here were nervous. They looked around and looked around and then they looked down. Others were so sexy, he almost feared them. Once, he had taken one of the sexy ones back to Brooks Street. She was naked before they were in his bedroom. She wanted to go down on him in the living room. This was something no one had ever wanted to do before. He had let her. He liked her. She liked him. She told him he was sexy. Sexy, what did it mean? So many women and so many men saying *sexy,* everywhere he went. It may have been the word he learned first, after *yes.*

"Ask her to dance." Rafik always said that.

"I like to watch this one."

"Her friends are not beautiful."

"I don't know. They are too small for you."

"Small? That one, she is an ostrich."

Yes, the giraffe was more of an ostrich. Aziz sensed she knew she was an ostrich. She did not care. She was a happy woman with happy friends.

"You like women who are pillows," Aziz said. He often thought of Heather's skin and her breasts, which were unbelievably full. Such softness, so easily given to Heather for no reason, and all hers, to have and to offer if she wished. But Rafik? How, why, did she want Rafik? They said he was handsome.

"I don't see why the other blond one is not good for you," Aziz said.

"That one? That waitress?"

"You! A man who moves boxes!"

"She is a waitress," Rafik insisted, laughing.

"She is just like the other one. The Djara."

"The Djara." Rafik said this dramatically, swaying back and then left.

"Look, both blond, both dark blue eyes, both small."

"Not the same, my uncle, not the same."

"I know. But why?"

"Aziz, you are mad. Who cares why? Who knows why? Just—not the same."

"I tell you," Aziz said, "not one man here will talk to them."

Rafik looked around. "No."

"Who?"

"That one."

There was a boy in a suit. Aziz picked up his chin to see. "Him?"

"Him."

Aziz ordered another beer, and Rafik ordered a shot of rum to go with his.

"That is a boy," Aziz said.

"In a suit."

"And what are we—I am wearing this one you gave me, it—is what?"

"It is Versace. A jacket."

"Very fine. Very much like this boy."

"He is Saudi. And he is wearing a suit."

"You know him?"

"No. But I know some who do."

Rafik probably did. And it was bad policy to be wearing the clothes Rafik loaned him. Rafik stole them or got them from someone who stole them. When his brother came, he would end this habit. It was a few months off.

The Saudi could not have been more than eighteen.

"He goes to university," Rafik was saying.

The Saudi was walking now. He walked three feet, then more, more, toward the table of the Djara and her friends.

"Uncle!" Rafik was triumphant.

"Wait, wait. Patience," Aziz whispered. The Saudi was perhaps going to another table. Another one was near. But no, he addressed the one with the cigarette, but with overweening gestures and expressions.

"He is a boy!"

"A boy!"

"Look at them!"

"They are confused!"

Rafik grabbed Aziz's arm. "I cannot watch this."

"He is asking for a cigarette," Aziz said.

"You are right, uncle, you are right. He is begging. He has a warehouse of cigarettes. He owns every cigarette in the world. See that man—he is snickering, he has a cigarette in his mouth!—he is the bodyguard."

Rafik was standing up. He pulled a pack of cigarettes out of Aziz's pocket.

"I am going to help him."

"Rafik, this is a bad idea," Aziz was saying, even as Rafik was moving across the dance floor, briefly holding a woman's arm who had spun into him and then started touching his face. Rafik was handsome. This was something that was most likely true. The woman was dancing with another woman, and she briefly delayed Rafik, but not long enough, because the woman with the fluttering hands at the Djara's table was rummaging around in her purse when Rafik arrived at the table, and she was drawing out a cigarette as Rafik began speaking. Aziz could not hear. But he could see the Saudi was rabid, mad, rabidly mad. The bodyguard was moving in, another one was following, and the Saudi was developing into a smallish figure as the ostrich woman stood up to her full height and put her hand over her mouth. Aziz looked around to see if anyone else was paying heed to this tableau. Yes, they were. A semicircle of tables around the scene had fallen silent. The bartender was just looking up. The woman who had flirted with Rafik on the dance floor was standing still, watching.

So Rafik was now an Algerian without papers who had consumed five drinks and taunted men in a club. It fell to Aziz, if he would only do it, to pull Rafik back, to apologize to the Saudi, to explain deferentially to the self-important guards. Or he could let Rafik get punched by one of the guards, kicked by the Saudi. All Aziz would have to do was get his friend off the floor and into a taxi. They could not afford a taxi. But this would be a special case. He looked into his wallet. He had enough to get them home.

The guards each had an arm of Rafik. They were bitter, lips pressed tight, while the Saudi said something to Rafik with utmost urgency, close to his face, hands and body in great disturbance. He was a boy, and look what he could do. The ostrich still had her hand over her mouth, but she was sitting back down.

It was then that the Djara leaned her head against the Saudi's forearm. Aziz felt it was intentional; she did it in a way that was tired but gratified, as if they were brother and sister, which of course they were not. It was as if she was communicating to the Saudi that this kind of scene often happened, and by her familiar way of putting her head on his arm she was reminding him of its ordinariness. Don't get excited, she was saying without saying it. As if by magic, or because he felt something resting on his forearm, the Saudi looked down at her, and when he did, the guards loosened Rafik's arms a bit so that they could follow the Saudi's gaze. Rafik turned to her too, and so he did not angrily pull out of the guards' grasp but just relaxed his arms. By her gentle forwardness with a man she did not know, this woman had changed the temperature not just of the Saudi but of all of them. Aziz let out a breath, amazed. They were now standing as if in a family photograph, arms linked, smiling for the ostrich's camera.

She did not have one. But someone else did. A flash popped at a table. Then another flash. It was someone famous. Someone Aziz did not know. Or a birthday. People were knotted around a table, raising their glasses.

The Saudi somehow had put his hand under the Djara's chin, tilting her face so he could see her. It was clear that he had not noticed her before, Aziz felt, because the full force of seeing her made the Saudi lose his footing by a degree. Aziz could see her perfectly from where he sat.

Her civilizing effect was not yet over. The Saudi began making introductions, bowing a little, as did Rafik, and the guards—they too were made affable. They pulled up an empty table, they politely asked around for chairs, a round of drinks was ordered, and soon there were four men and four women at a pair of round tables. Aziz knew this was his cue to slip out. It was late; he had to get up at five to get to work. Rafik could spend the entire night at these places. How he got up and went to work, Aziz did not know or ask. It would stop when his brother arrived. They would get a place, the two of them, and he would be done with Rafik. He had not come here to fall in with him.

9

When he came home, Heather was on the couch in the living room with a face made sour from hours of rage.

"My daddy's coming," was the first thing she said. "This place is a dump."

"Kitchen?" he asked.

"Wet. Bucket on the table."

"I do that."

"I saw Linda."

He turned around. "Linda Ricco?" he asked.

"She's calling somebody she knows at Customs."

"Customs?"

"Yes. Customs."

"Rafik home soon," he said in jackass English, storing *Customs* for later.

He walked into the kitchen. The blue bucket was overflowing on the table. A sheen of plaster-flecked water covered the floor and was fingering into the hallway. *Kus tums, kus tums,* played in his mind, set to the last song in the club. The illuminated face of the Djara in the Saudi's hand flicked into the back of his head, making the pulling of all the sheets from his bed into rote. *Kus tum kus tum kus tum.* He played the scene in which they were introduced, and the Djara asked, *So what do you do?* and he said, *I am a gas station attendant. Kha sim ta mim. Kha sim ta mim.* No, a painter; he could say that, he had been one. A painter is similar to construction. He threw the sheets on the kitchen floor. They were transparent in an instant, their effect on the water invisible.

He redid the meeting in the club, with *Yes, I am in construction.* He saw her face dull. *Construction management,* he revised. He went into the bathroom and started gathering towels. He could not possibly get away with management past one conversation. On the floor the towels went, and he stepped on them and skated them around some. That was all he wanted. One conversation with her, and done. If he held himself to one conversation, she would not know how little English he spoke, where he lived, what he did, how he had come, why he had come, and why he stayed. He stopped pushing the towels. They would dance. Nothing was asked for in such a thing as a dance. One conversation and one dance. *Kha sim ta mim* rocked in him.

He looked up at the ceiling, exalted. A widening brown and gold aurora now reached to the refrigerator. He followed its markings and saw that one wall was wrinkling, like the skin on a child's fingers during a long bath. On the wall were framed pictures of poetry with waterfalls and bears. He had never looked at these before. Could Heather have just put them up today? He looked closely—one of them was bubbled. He pulled it from the wall and saw its brown paper backing was pocked with wet. He took all of them down and carried them into Heather and Rafik's room.

It was a cave of clothes. He tripped and landed softly on the bed, which took up so much of the room. He lay there for a moment, replaying his memory of the Djara. He smelled it then, the soot of hash. He sat upright. He looked for the foil by the bed; there was none. He paused, listening for sounds of Heather, but there were none. She wanted nothing of cleanup. She wanted Rafik to see her on that sofa when he walked through the door. She would wait there, he guessed, until he did.

He promised himself he would confront Rafik. But he knew he only would if it were—what? More than a shoe box? More than a pillowcase? He crunched into the bed, already not wanting to know. Under him were Levi's and Armani and pink panties and more. He pulled up one and then another. A tie in pearl yellow, label: Missoni. A brocaded camisole: La Perla. A boot, its leather like the inside of a new lamb. Small black felt pouches, almost like velvet, dozens and dozens of them. What were these? He checked many of them, but they were empty.

A dozen or more suitcases, their handles threaded with a clothesline, hung from the ceiling. He had never noticed them when he came home from work. This was, for as long as he could do it, eighteen hours a day, seven days a week, until he got sick and then got fired, because if you were sick you had to go; you were no use. Sick he would be, his weight down too far, his sleep so foreshortened he could not be trusted to paint, or to man a register, without his head slumped—so. He touched his chest. And then it was, Find the next job. Sleep came between jobs. It was the only way. And after that, it began again. So why were you out drinking? his brother asked him in his head, not angrily. How is it you find time to wear this jacket, which is stolen, and go to these nightclubs?

He ducked beneath the row of suitcases and around to their other side, tapping one to see if it was heavy. The first two were empty, but the third was tight. He pushed the next one, a mustard vinyl. It was cement. The line swayed dramatically. He imagined a body, in its requisite pieces, inside the suitcase. He burrowed under the bed's clothes and hoped nothing would give. The smell of hash was once again unmistakable.

"What are you doing?"

Heather was in the doorway, her voice a stunned whisper.

Aziz stayed still. Heather, always Heather, he thought, wondering if he should pretend to have passed out. He lifted his head up to see her.

"Sorry. Sorry."

"You pervert."

He understood only *You*.

"Sorry," he repeated, extricating himself from the cape of assorted clothing that covered him, backing himself onto the pile on the floor, standing up, as best he might, while he pulled down on the hem of his borrowed Versace jacket, which he had never had a chance to take off.

"Wet," he said, pointing toward the kitchen.

"That's disgusting," she said, in the same whisper.

"Kitchen," he added.

"Where is Rafik?" Suddenly she was screaming. "Where is he? Where is he?"

Her lips were quavering, her eyes bloodshot. Did Heather smoke hash? He looked around again for tinfoil, but all he could see was clothes.

"That stinking sonofabitch!" she was screaming. "That goddamn whoring piece of shit!"

"Heather," he tried, attempting to maneuver in such a way that she might come toward him, thereby freeing the doorway. "Work."

"That motherfucker is not at work!" she screamed.

"Work. Providence."

"You take me to the motherfucking dog-sucking nightclub that asshole is at right now!"

"Heather," he tried.

"You were with him!"

"Heather."

He wished he could understand more of what she was saying. He heard *nightclub*. He tried to see if he could dare her into the room. He put his hand on one of the suitcases.

"Don't touch that!"

She moved toward him, just as he had hoped. He slipped past her and out the bedroom. But she was after him.

"Look, you cocksucking douche bag, you are telling me which club, or I kick your brains all over this apartment. *¿Comprende?*"

Spanish, this was bad. She was out of herself.

"I take you," he tried.

"You what?"

"I . . . take . . . you," he said slowly.

"Tell me. Don't take me. Tell me."

He began moving past the kitchen, where his efforts had made no impact on the lake of water, except perhaps to postpone its advance into the living room. He listened. It was raining outside.

"We go."

"No, you dickless shitheel. Tell me."

He could not let her find Rafik. He decided to keep pretending he did not know what *tell* meant.

"My daddy is coming tomorrow, and Rafik is out drilling some whore. You stupid sack of shit, tell me where he is. Now!"

She had backed him into the living room.

"Take you. Take you," he said.

"Fuck!" She looked at her watch, then flew back to the bedroom and slammed the door. Aziz looked at the front door and began fumbling with the dead bolt, the steel floor guard, his pockets for keys. At last he pulled the door and closed it as gently as he could behind him. He would run around the block. She would think he was gone. He would sneak back later.

It was pouring. His jacket was as wet as the towels on the kitchen floor. He started back, then thought of a porch. It was close, he knew it was. It seemed the choice, nothing was open in East Boston at 2 a.m. Everyone here worked; everyone here had never been to a nightclub; everyone lived out their lives in spoons and napkins, trying, trying, trying. There were corner bars, which closed at eleven. A Schlitz neon winked at him through the downpour. Why did he have that last beer? Why? Work, he said to himself, you have to be at work, up at five; you cannot live like this. His brother's face looked at him, wordless, mystified. He thought of the Sikh family that lived next door, the wife in embroidered chiffons, the boy in that head sock with the bun on top. *They* were asleep, holding on to one another.

The horn jumped him. Heather was in her BMW, dressed in

black leather, eyebrows dark, lips spooked to an eggplant matte. Her hair was cascading everywhere in Niagaras of coppered blond. She rolled down her window. "Get the fuck in," she said.

The club was dialed high when they arrived. There were lines. There were bouncers. There were cars and motorcycles on the sidewalk. Women in fur coats were slicked down by the storm, their hair and their minks shiny as seals. In an alley near the club where they parked, a woman in a pink plastic dress was spread-eagled, a man between her legs. Lighters bobbed in the rain.

Heather parked. Aziz opened a lime umbrella and held it over her like a suzerain's slave. The rain had already drenched him through, but she was untouched. It was as if he had capsized desperately while she, queenly, had floated down a river on a canopied felucca. She handed one of the bouncers a hundred-dollar bill, and when this failed to move him she handed him another. They were in.

The crush inside was harsh. Heather pushed forward, and he straggled, hoping she would forget him. Work was only three hours away. His shame was exquisite, flowers and more flowers of it, multiplying across fields and fields, covering the world. He winced.

She pulled his hand and dragged him on. He could see she was saying something, but the music was so loud, the drinking around them so thick with glasses and voices trying to outshout the music, that all he made out was her grape lips and every so often, when the strobing shifted, her teeth.

They reached the edge of the dance floor. Heather never drank. She had only one thing on her mind, and that thing was there, right before them: Rafik and the Djara, dancing slowly, while the music scissored fast.

Aziz pulled Heather back toward him, so he could better shove her into the crowd. Then he rushed himself between Rafik and the Djara and turned his eyes hard and fast into Rafik's.

"You, my friend, are fucked," he said.

"Heather?"

"Heather."

The Djara looked at Aziz. There was the blue that was her eyes. There were the narrow shoulders. But his disgrace made her less. He wanted nothing of the dance he had imagined.

"Sorry," Aziz said impatiently. He would not come here again, not ever. His brother would find nothing of this.

"Wow, you're really wet!" she shouted. She was the Djara's twin sister, Aziz suddenly realized, not the Djara. Identical, but not. How her voice grated; he almost pushed her away. But wait. His mother's hand rested on his shoulder. *We are to be kind.*

"Please, miss, my friend goes now; no dance is possible. Sorry. So sorry."

Maybe she could not hear him. He shrugged and opened his hands to the ceiling, then pointed to his ear. She touched hers and smiled, nodding.

He tried to see where he could make his way through the dance floor and out again. The music was loud; one thought began before another one could finish, so he moved blind. He got to the edge and began pushing around a standing couple, past a girl's mouth against another girl's ear, a wineglass nearly empty in a hand. Someone pushed into his back. He felt the crowd move around him in a reaction, and then another elbow came, and he had to hold on to the back of a chair to stay standing.

It was the chair of the ostrich. He saw the tipped orange of her hair just before he saw the Saudi was no longer there, the bodyguards gone too, and there, looking as if she wanted to leave, unlaughing, was the Djara. Not the lesser version he had spoken to on the dance floor, but her, the actual one, with sapphire for eyes. She was looking right at him, and a sympathy—where was it?—passed between or around or inside them. He wanted to pull her by the back of her head to his mouth. To see what it was to have her against him with kissing that overcame her. He sank then, almost as soon as he felt the relief of her possible understanding. How was it he could tell these twin women apart, but Soumeya, when it mattered, he had not recognized?

. . .

He worked. He saved to pay the hospital bills in the cereal box under his bed. He called home and told his mother he was happy. He sent money to his father, who begged him to send less. He told his brother he would love it here, and they counted the days until his arrival. He told Rafik to get rid of the hash and the suitcases and inspected his room every Friday night, with Rafik nervously watching. Using Heather's talk of Customs as a threat, he made Rafik take him to this job he supposedly had at a moving company in Brighton. There was a boss and three workers who spoke Russian. He knew it was most likely theater, staged only for him, to be closed down soon as he left. As part of the show, Heather informed him that she had made up seeing Linda Ricco. Customs was not on their trail. He wondered if the invention was earlier or now.

He thought often of the visit from Heather's father. His BMW, a much larger and newer one than Heather's, parked out front, left much of Brooks Street to conclude that drug dealing was the only anomaly that could explain it. He was a tall silver-haired man in a camel coat and tasseled dress shoes. He came into the still damp that was their now-mildew-fragrant kitchen and seemed to think everything was more than great, that Heather and Rafik were "a hell of a fine couple," and that Aziz had "a future ahead of him." When the father took them out to dinner, Aziz marveled at Rafik in a restaurant with walnut walls and table roses. His English was a dazzle. Sentences were long. Words were many syllables.

"He thinks you are a contractor!" Aziz said to Rafik in the men's room.

"Not the same," Rafik said. "Entrepreneur is different in English."

So here was a Rafik who knew that *entrepreneur* in French was *contractor* but something else in English. But what was that else? Aziz could not tell. He could see that raging Heather disappeared near her father. There was honey in her, soft he'd not seen before. Her father was lit up, shining with being pleased at Heather. The mother of Heather; she was hated. The expression on their faces was like Aziz's mother talking about Ghaleb, the son-in-law with snobbery in him, the one they called Peahen. The riddle of Heather's father preoccupied Aziz, but after trying to solve why a man of such seeming stature would speak ill of his wife in front of strangers, and allow his daughter to live in a dwelling so ragged, on a street so dismal, with a man so underhanded, he realized there was so much of his new existence that was unknown to him, outside his English, or kept from him deliberately, or not yet anything he had ever experienced, so that recognizing it would have been like remembering a man he had never met. He felt as if he saw only a percentage, and a small one, of what was. Mostly, he had no one to discuss most things with, so their weight and importance were all too often equal. Anything could matter. Anything could be anything.

He became a student of windshields and the couples beneath them, scenes he followed for signs of how to live. Once he took a credit card from a woman's hand, and her diamond ring, big as a marble, fired with light. Her husband on a cell phone had a little computer on his lap. She never looked at this husband, nor he at her. Straight ahead she stared, her chin level. There was nothing to see where she stared. Suddenly, she took the cell phone away from her husband's ear and slammed his computer shut. Aziz thought the husband would get angry, but instead he calmly reopened the computer and starting typing. Almost instantly, the automatic window on her side came down. She threw out the cell phone, just missing Aziz's knee.

He saw that he was unseen. Days—no, weeks—went by without a person speaking to him, and longer still, without someone's eyes meeting his own. His place in the order of things was not a place; maybe, as he came to think of it, it was an insert, a scooping out, into which he belonged, but if he were to die or to quit or not be there for some reason, another, not like him but adequate to his function, would be fitted in and, like the tab in his cereal box, would keep it neat and closed.

But lucky, that was what he truly was, if only he could feel this luck. How often did he hear from his father that a soldier on leave had been found with his throat cut on a road from Algiers? How often did his father call to say that a friend's son had been taken for questioning by La Sécurité Militaire and had not yet, after months, come home? Compared to those entering the draft now, his tour of duty had been well timed. Daily the press ministry printed Algerian newspapers that said the massacres—boys mutilated, mothers decapitated, bodies plowed in ditches—were the work of terrorists, the ruthless, fanatic, always increasingly desperate Groupe Islamique Armé. His father reading these words tried to see what was true and what was not. But how could his father know? He could not be everywhere in Algeria at once. He was one man running a hotel where a flute played by the sea. In Boston, uncensored papers from Cairo that Rafik brought home described an Algerian civil war. A fairly elected Islamic government had been overthrown by a corrupt military backed by France. The GIA was armed resistance to tyranny: tyranny that tortured defenseless women for information on their brothers and sons.

Aziz's father told him of any massacre he knew of even slightly. It was stories incomplete, half wrong, made by ones boasting or guessing or wishing they knew. Aziz rejoiced each time he knew none of the dead. He saw this as cowardice. One day he forced himself to remember. Sitting by the cash register in the glass box, he willed the massacres into animation across the street, trying to see their Boston version. He imagined a sidewalk exploding, a handbag flying, a baby's hat plopped on a manhole cover. But these dioramas melted in the radiance before him: the metallic of cars, the kid of a caramel glove, the creamy red of brake lights. The pretty new nothing that was America—he wanted to watch that.

The day came when he did know some of the dead. It was almost exactly a year after he had first arrived in Boston. His father called on a cold January morning before work, and through the stumble of sleep he listened to the story of his cousin Fouzia. She was from the side of his father's family that was odd, and so in some sense he was able to make what happened into a little less, a little more distant, than what it was, which was 98 dead and 120 injured, as the government had it, but from a friend at the hospital, whom his father trusted, it was 400, all dead. By his father's telling, the terrorists spared the old mother of Fouzia's husband, and from her Aziz's father learned how the terrorists slit the throats of the others, since the bomb they had thrown into the house had not worked. Fouzia was dead, her husband Ali was dead, so also Ali's sister Fatima, and her son Moussa, only seven, and daughter Nadia, only twelve; though it was a mercy she died, since Fouzia's daughter Amina, also twelve, the killers took with them. All of the furniture in the house burned to nothing; a car and a truck were stolen, jewelry too. They had been a not-poor family, and while Fouzia was excitable and had ideas about raising children that included nursing them until they were three, it could not be said that she or her husband were anything other than what they were: a plumber and his wife who kept a household of mother and sister and three children in a good part of Raïs.

His father was stricken. "Perhaps she died, mercifully, and the burning meant they could not find her," Aziz offered.

His father made a sound of doubt. "No, because her grandmother saw them take her."

There was a pause because of the phones. The echo adjusted into a loud click and then was gone.

"Her mama was so old. Maybe—"

"True. But not blind. She saw," his father said.

"Amina, had I ever met her?" Aziz got this said, but too fast. If only Rafik would call for him, so he could beg off the phone. But Rafik this early was asleep.

"No. We did not see them. We"—his father's mouth moved away from the phone but then was back—"Fouzia married into this family, and he, your uncle Chadli, he felt it was not the best. So I respected his thinking. I never saw Amina."

"Does anyone know of this besides you?"

"Your mother."

"You told her."

"I could not not tell her. It has been news here. They could not make this quiet. It was—so many."

"And how is *gemmi* Chadli?" It was the natural question.

"He says he is going to kill himself."

"He says that all the time."

"Yes, he does. This is his way."

"Had he cut Fouzia off?" Aziz tried a turn to family spites.

"No, he was not so hard. He saw her and Amina, but not the way it would have been if he had loved the man she married like a son. But Amina, she was his only granddaughter, and in her he saw only good. He said to me, 'Brother, she was a beautiful child. Nadia was not like Amina. Nadia was the plain one. And for her beauty, they will do unspeakable things to her.' "

"Amina."

"Amina."

That day, Aziz saw girls in the cars and wondered if they were twelve. After he ate lunch, toward evening, he threw up in the wastebasket below the cash register.

10

After Amina, more came. Rafik called them *ṭarā'id*. Later he corrected himself. Game were hunted. They were worth pursuit. But no one chased ants and beetles fleeing a dry well flooding. You step on them without thinking. We, he told Aziz, are catching the crawling before the heel comes down.

Like prayers, the tankers came every Friday. Through the spring and into the summer, Aziz and Rafik kept watch at the docks. They talked about how, when they had come, they swam alone. The new stowaways waited for committees. They drew up out of the water and were comforted by their kind.

Aziz avoided Friday services, so waiting for *ṭarā'id* never bothered him. As for Rafik, his view was firm: Mosques cause problems. But others did mind. They complained, saying the shipping company timed the arrivals for Fridays as an insult. They brought prayer rugs, and bottles of water to wash their feet, and were impatient when Rafik and Aziz seemed ready only to pass the night smoking Marlboros. Sure, Rafik told them, we can pray. But Aziz would not bare his feet. They were still the color of poppies. His toes were a luster of pure scar. Rafik washed his feet, to mollify the prayer boys. Aziz worshiped dirty. "That was ridiculous," Rafik told Aziz later that night. "Next Friday, we go around the other terminal."

No one jumped in daylight anymore, as Aziz had. Stories were plentiful of how the tankers had too many men on deck, armed, hating, tense. They were not even Algerians, these guards. They were French and undercover, snakes in ship uniforms. It was said if they saw you they shot you. But Rafik disputed this. The natural gas had to be cooled into liquid. It was explosive. Guns would pierce the containers. Aziz thought the containers were bulletproof. Rafik said yes, that could be. They discussed the tankers' condition, the men who might come, the prospects for hope. Here was a Rafik with a purpose besides scheming, a Rafik who honored their vigils without complaint, no matter the tedium or lack of profit. When Aziz came home from the gas station at nine, Rafik was ready. Aziz had the new pack of cigarettes, Rafik the extra clothes and towels and blankets. They drove to the Everett terminal and waited until midnight, sometimes later. Some weeks no Arzew stowaways showed. One week, three did. Once they saw dawn.

They stayed far from the prayer boys, but in the beginning, at least, they hoped to meet other Algerians. There were young men from all over: Blida, El Harrach, Telagh, Aflou, Keddara, Chlef, Tizi-Ouzou, Saïda, Ain Defla, and more. Rumors ran like thieves. Someone from Bentalha said the prayer boys were wanted. This someone knew another who recognized one of them by his missing finger. A man with a missing forefinger, this one said, had run a knife from the corner of an old man's mouth, from cheek to ear, deep into the back of the neck to the other ear and the mouth's other corner. The one without the finger tore the flaps of the old man's cheeks from his face. His white hair was lathered in his own blood, but they would not finish him off. They watched him die, slowly—while they talked, ate, prayed; yes, they prayed—and made the old man's sons and daughters and grandchildren witness this at gunpoint.

Rafik scoffed. No matter what story, no matter which teller, no matter the atrocity devised or described, Rafik interrupted every pause with "Show me proof of this." He told every storyteller, "A big story does not make a big man." You are with them, one teller accused. Rafik's voice stayed easy. "I am not one to believe," he advised. Aziz, eyes down, encouraged peace to his chest, his belly, his eyes, his ears, repeating a word of one kind or another to still himself. "Believers," Rafik said, "love death. I would rather wonder, my friend, than believe."

They used to call any Algerian in Boston *brother.* In this new time, they were only *friend*. Soon enough, the ground near the harbor on Fridays became as riven as the home country. Here, Aziz trusted only those from his hometown. He or Rafik knew the families, knew boys they grew up with, knew someone who knew someone. But what did Aziz know of men from Chlef, Blida, El Harrach? Men from these places could be anyone or anything. It became too much work to separate the killers from the killed or the relatives of the killers from the relatives of the killed. Stories had to be remembered and details of maimings compared—names, dates, places pieced into a coherence. That, at least, was what he told Rafik.

Arzew produced stowaways, but some who were said to be coming never seemed to arrive. They learned from Rafik's father that three brothers would come at once. Risky, Aziz thought. Stupid, Rafik said. They waited months for them. The timing was wrong. They feared a neighbor's tattle. They heard of traps. The Three became part of Brooks Street talk: "I'll get that money back from you when the Three come"; "She'll fall for him when the Three come."

So on the Friday when the Three came sodden up out of the harbor, Aziz was giddy. He called Rafik at Brooks Street and babbled about the feasting that must be had, the food to be started, the bedding arranged. Rafik cooked, and cooked more. The kitchen counters were squeezed full of bowls and bags and jars and cartons. While he worked, Heather laid out blankets and pillows on the living room floor. By each, she arranged a flashlight, an orange, and cookies wrapped in a paper towel. Aziz was assigned the shower.

Now he was the Egyptian. He showed them how the hot water worked. He helped find them shirts and pants that fit. He saw in their faces his previous self, and he knew Rafik saw his own.

The Three were younger than Aziz and Rafik; they had barely known them in Arzew. Aziz and Rafik had grown up with their older brothers; an older sister had been Aziz's first crush. Like her, the youngest brother was serious. He was slight, so thin that Aziz worried the rich food might sicken him. He watched how he picked at it and how worry shaped his movements.

It was amazing that they had made it together. Rafik asked them, How, how had they done this great thing? Heather smiled and said, "They're strong, I know that much." But as she was saying these words, Aziz read in their faces such tremors that he blurted, "Tell me of your sister."

The youngest brother, whose name was Lahouari, looked behind him, then down on the floor, his full plate suddenly plain to everyone. He was wearing Aziz's black T-shirt, and it hung from him. His arms were pencils. The apple of his throat was a basket that rose and moved and fell.

"We paid money," one said, putting his hand on Lahouari's back. He had decided to answer Rafik's question and ignore Aziz's about their sister. "My father, he was ready to pay with his life. But he was able, because my mother has a brother in the oil ministry, to speak to him, and together, man to man, they were able to send the money in a way that ensured our safety."

"This is not for others," the youngest brother said. "This stays here."

"Never," Rafik said.

"No, we would never," Heather whispered.

"And your sister? Zahra?" Aziz reminded them. Zahra had married a man Aziz respected, Ashraf Frarma, a philosophy professor. Ashraf's mother was a doctor, and all their family had been college-educated in Algiers or Paris. Ashraf's sister was a novelist in London. This family, Aziz knew, was superior to his own. But they were not proud. Ashraf's father treated Aziz's father with deference.

When Zahra and Ashraf were married, it was in the hotel Aziz's father managed. They spoke of the poetry of the place. It was a hotel, thanks to Aziz's father, that resembled the words of the wind; Aziz remembered them saying that. The last he had heard, Ashraf and Zahra had two daughters. They lived in one of Arzew's best homes, with a view of the sea. Their daughters were Fellah and Fatima. They could not be more than babies—but no, they were older. Or were they?

"My sister had a son last year," the youngest brother said. Aziz searched his tone, but could hear too little. Dread barreled through him.

"What a gift!" Rafik exclaimed. The two older brothers' heads were bowed. The youngest brother gave his one smile. It too was impossible to read. His eyes closed, a laugh threw back his head, and then he shook it, almost desolate. "You cannot say that," one of the older brothers said to Rafik. "No," said the other.

Rafik's eyes dropped. "It is not a gift?" he asked softly. "To have a son is not a gift?"

"You know my father," the youngest brother said, his eyes on the floor, still shaking his head. "Daughters, more daughters. He has been saying this as long as I could make out words to hear him. When this son came last year, do you know what he said?" He paused. "I will put this one on a boat, like the Chinese do with their girls. What use are men who grow to be killers? I want sweet songs for Algeria."

"You can't answer a question!" Aziz heard himself yelling.

They all looked up. He did not care. Something had happened to Lahouari's sister, and Lahouari was ashamed to tell it. "Answer me! Is your sister okay?" Aziz was louder. And still this Lahouari said nothing.

"Aziz," Rafik said, pulling down Aziz's right hand, which had flown up in the air.

"I just want to know if your sister is okay! Can you tell me that? Tell me!" Aziz was standing up. Rafik held Aziz's hand to the table.

Lahouari raised his eyebrows, the rest of his face fixed. "Is there a problem?" he said, in formal Arabic. What, Aziz fumed, did he think he was in a classroom? No Arzew patois? This Lahouari was empty of feeling, a haughty baby. Or maybe, Aziz thought, this Lahouari had betrayed his own sister.

"Lahouari," Rafik intervened. "I think Aziz is worried about your sister's safety. Is she well?"

"My sister is safe."

Rafik let go of Aziz's hand, and as if on a spring, it went with the force of a gust to Lahouari's left temple. Lahouari crumpled on the floor, along with most of his uneaten food. It smeared on his face and lap and chest. It was lamb, cardamom, raisins, and rice. It smelled unaccountably to Lahouari of women's perfume. A pain in his head made him woozy, so confused he could see his mother screeching at his father in the garden back home, an embarrassment so acute he was crying himself to sleep, because no father allowed a mother to berate him out of doors where all the neighbors heard. "You let her," Lahouari said hotly to his father. "You did not defend yourself." He remembered his father's reply: "As long as there are men and women, they will scream at one another. There is no disrespect. There is the flame of love."

Then the past was gone and Lahouari was in Boston again, but the food was still sickly sweet to his nose. His tongue pushed some of it from his lips so he might speak, tell Aziz that he was sorry, there was no disrespect, and it was only then that the taste of stew betrayed how wrong he had been. It was savory lamb. It was the lamb of his grandmother's house. His nose was not working correctly; he had been all wrong about this food, and this place, and this kitchen, and Aziz and his questions. Lahouari, right then, was hungry. More than hungry, famished.

Aziz was kneeling on the floor, watching Lahouari talking to someone who was not there, his eyes fluttering shut and open. Aziz's knuckles ached. He had become Kamal, batting down a weakened one. Aziz tried to clean stew from Lahouari. His two brothers were cradling Lahouari's head and shoulders. Rafik and Heather were about to get washcloths. But then Lahouari said, "This is delicious."

They saw he was not only alert, but also actually and finally eating. Aziz looked to the brothers to judge how mad at him they were. They were not, he saw with joy. Lahouari was saying he was sorry. Rafik placed the pot of lamb on the floor and all the plates came down near the table legs. They sat there cross-legged, and the three brothers, whether from weeks in the hold or Aziz's outburst or both, pushed back tears. "Troubles buried only sometimes sink," one of them said. Aziz worried; what did that mean? Did they know of his story? But then the oldest, Hamid, put his arm around Aziz and said, "Thanks to God for Rafik. And for you."

They were knitted to the Three, and the Three to them. Heather tended particularly to Lahouari. It was something of mothering; he was a tadpole. He had bones like straws. He looked like a fourteen-year-old, not his recorded eighteen years. His voice was a man's but he did not shave. Aziz could tell Lahouari had not yet been with a woman.

Unlike the rest of his family, Lahouari had not made it to college. There was no point by the time his turn came; Algeria was violence and bad stupid jobs. Lahouari told Aziz he had wanted to be an engineer. Now he aimed to be a mechanic. He worked on Heather's BMW to learn the English words, studying her owner's manual and an Arabic version Rafik found for him. Heather and Lahouari spent long hours on her car, and as the months went by they carried on in a sign language and then in words of their own creation. Watching them, Aziz found himself rearranging his ideas about Heather. There was room for gentle. She could be patient.

The other two were older: Ali was twenty-one and Hamid twenty-two. They were bigger, in size and attitude, and they had been to college, and then the army, as Aziz and Rafik had. They wanted to tell Aziz stories of their tour, but he would not let them.

"He is ugly."
"Well . . ."

"Admit, my friend, your brother is ugly."

Rafik and Aziz were in a lounge at Logan Airport, watching Aziz's brother from a distance in a cordoned area near Customs. It was late fall, turning into another cold winter. Soon it would be two years since Aziz arrived.

Mourad had a green card. He had checked luggage. He had a one-way ticket on Air France. His aisle seat was next to an empty window seat for the entire eight-hour flight. He had slept comfortably with three pillows and two blankets. He looked disconsolate.

"He does not want to be here," Aziz said.

"If I were that ugly, I would not want to be here," Rafik responded. "Back home, he would not get laid, but some poor female would have had to face his bed in marriage. Here, women feel no compunction about rejecting such a beast."

"He is more of a rodent than a beast," Aziz observed.

"Yes, too small by half to be a beast."

"He will make good money, though."

"Yes, there is that."

"He will send my parents more money in a month than I sent in a year."

"True."

"He will not be drafted back home."

"Yes."

"He came on an airplane, like a diplomat."

"Yes."

"Look at him. He is not even happy to see me." Aziz waved and smiled broadly. Mourad looked up and pushed his hand in the air, then dropped it and turned his back. "Then again, maybe he will take Heather from you."

"Maybe I will saw off your dick."

Mourad got a security job at the airport. This was cause for manic amazement at Brooks Street. Mourad made so much money, Aziz told him to tell all the other Brooks inhabitants that he made only a quarter of his true salary. Mourad went to work in a black uniform with an obsidian billy club and a lightweight stun gun waggling from his belt loops. He was considered an enormous asset because of his French, Arabic, and acceptable English. The owner of the security company told him he had a future that was bright if he "kept his nose clean." When Aziz explained this expression, Mourad said, "I am not Rafik."

After two months on the job, Mourad purchased a television. Rafik and Heather had a television in their bedroom, but as if by bad charm, when Mourad walked into the apartment after being picked up from the airport, it stopped working. Rafik had planned to "find" another television, but Mourad told him that if he did he would report him to the police. He told Rafik this in uniform although, as a concession to Aziz, Mourad refrained from strapping his club and gun to his side until after the delivery of this news. Mourad, to Aziz's shame, bought the largest available television and a home theater system with speakers the size of a bathtub. It took four men to deliver it, and four others to set it up. It was placed in Aziz's bedroom, which was now also Mourad's bedroom. Aziz pleaded with him to put it in the living room, because after all, Heather and Rafik as a couple could not be asked to pile into their bed along with Lahouari and the other two, all of whom were still sleeping in well-tended pockets in the living room. Mourad refused.

11

Mourad liked nightclubs but rejected dancing. He talked little. His drinking, to make up for both, was extensive. No one could match him, beer for beer, and not show it. His pleasure in going out was in solidifying this reputation. He decided to start a mustache, and before long he was not so much well liked as he was recognizable and respected. His club of choice was Reach. He was often pointed out and referred to in conversation there. As Aziz had hoped, after a while, when it became standard to say, "He could drink—not like Mourad, of course—but he could drink," Mourad allowed the television to be moved into the living room.

Aziz was unemployed. His jobs were many, his time at most short. His jobs, he realized, lacked titles. He was not a painter, just someone who scraped or hammered when told. He was not a janitor, only someone who hosed sidewalks or emptied trash. He was a busboy who never made it to waiter. He was someone who raked leaves or watered grass, not a gardener. Gas station attendant was a title, but one he mumbled when asked.

It was forever a hard thing, looking for a job. With Mourad paying for things, the incentive to go for interviews and be turned away was smaller than ever. This backsliding had no consequence. His mother and father were overjoyed. They finally could afford to buy a car, ten years old, to replace the always failing motorbike. His mother went to the doctor for the first time in years, and they discovered she was in perfect health, even though they had worried for so long about her shortness of breath. They were informed she needed exercise. She began walking down at the beach every morning. She is singing again, Aziz's father told him. These respites came and more followed. Soon Amina and the one with no finger folded away into drawers Aziz stopped opening. Rafik's and Aziz's fathers no longer called about stowaways from Arzew. Rafik stood watch less and went to Reach more.

Luxury—Rafik could not have it at Brooks Street. Mourad tossed one of Rafik's stolen cameras, then a week later its replacement. He disposed of gold lighters, fine wallets, Italian sweaters, even a set of kitchen knives they all loved. Mourad took the phone out of Rafik's hands if the talk was suspicious. Now the entrepreneur took most calls on a windy cell phone outside the front door.

The only thing that suited Rafik was Heather's innocent love for Lahouari. It freed him to do a new wrong, finding a new woman almost every night. He went to these women's beds and was home before three. He never gave them phone numbers. He never told his true name. He had only one rule. He never saw the same woman twice. Heather and Lahouari were not lovers, but Aziz knew Rafik, in his own mind, pretended they were, so he could love his own lies. Mourad had not uprooted the wrong. The weeds were still in the ground.

How had he thought Mourad would make Rafik leave and their lives straighten? Many nights he listened to his brother's alcohol-stiffened breathing in the bed next to him and wondered when a certain kind of punishment would come.

. . .

"Her breasts were like buds," Rafik said, joining his fingers into a compact blossom. "I feasted on them for hours. She could come this way, I swear to God."

"Rafik."

"You don't believe me."

"I believe you, I believe you."

"The small tit is underrated."

"Can we talk of other things?"

"The smaller, the more feeling."

"You are crazy."

"Aziz, look, look." Rafik was motioning with his cigarette toward the door. Mourad was arriving, for the first time with friends. "He has brought someone!"

"It is that shithead from work."

"Which shithead?"

"Bob something."

"An American?"

"Of course an American."

"He has a woman, this Bob."

"Rafik, I swear to God, on my mother's grave, if you go near to this Bob's woman, I am not helping you when he comes to kill you."

"Look at her. She is not beautiful."

"No, she is not. So leave it alone."

"But she has the small tit, I believe. Yes, look at her. I am sure she yells like a cat. I would love just to hear her. Just once."

"On my mother's grave."

"Oh, I will not have this one."

"You are sick."

"I won't have her."

Mourad and Bob and his girlfriend were almost at their table. Rafik got up and pulled out a chair. In his own head, Aziz hit him. He watched Rafik bounce down and up to the ceiling and back, smile gone from his smirksome face.

"For the lady," Rafik said grandly. Mourad glanced. Bob shrugged. "That ain't no lady." Bob was still in uniform. The pink of his neck peeked out over his collar, and the soft of his waist did the same over his belt. He turned away from his girlfriend, who looked at Rafik appreciatively. Rafik was dark and slim, and he was now sitting himself next to her, a woman so unremarkable that she was speechless at Rafik's intensity. He was particularly gifted with the plain. Lately he had been saying that it was nothing to love a beautiful girl. It was something to make a plain one believe she was loved.

Mourad and Bob ignored Rafik. They were men's men, and they would leave games with women to this peacock. Or that was what Aziz first read. But he felt uneasy. He got up and walked to the bar. As usual, it was five people deep. He put down his head and felt himself sinking. He should leave. But he didn't.

"I am lost," Aziz said the following day. He and Mourad were eating dinner, alone for a change. The Three had gone to Wal-Mart. Rafik was at Kamal's, which Aziz was not supposed to know. Heather was still at work.

Mourad looked at him, but not closely. "You are fine," he said.

"I am not fine," Aziz said.

"You worry about things that don't matter," Mourad said.

"You have changed," Aziz said.

"I have. Praise God."

"No."

"No?"

"God does not want this for you."

"You are a boy. A baby boy. Go play with Lahouari and Heather."

"I am going to speak to Father."

"Go ahead."

"You think our own father can be bought."

"See. Go see."

Aziz did not call his father that night or the next day. A week went by, and he knew his days had become the same and that he would not ever call. He was hung over in the morning. He watched television in the afternoon. He went to the club at night.

. . .

"There is one, she has bewitched me."

Rafik was on his third drink, and he was, if it were possible, better-looking that night than ever. It was a mystery, Rafik's appeal, where it came from, but Aziz thought, through his own third drink, that it came from the wrong. Women came to their table every night. Even the beautiful women came.

Aziz wondered who this bewitching one was. Was she one of the gorgeous ones, one of the ones with boyfriends, one of the ugly ones? There were weeks when the ones who were hideous, whom no one had ever wanted or looked at—these were the ones Rafik pursued.

"Her name is Rita."

"Rita?"

"Rita Alicanda."

Rafik was silent. He put his head close to Aziz.

"I want her again."

"That is normal."

"No."

"Rafik, I beg you, stop this—"

"I know she will be here tonight, and I want her again."

"Why only once? Why? Be with her. Tell Heather the truth and be with this Rita." Aziz looked away from his friend. This was no way to live. He said it again to himself. Then he ordered another drink.

When the waitress left, she was standing there.

"Antonio," she said, the name Rafik had apparently given as his.

Rafik looked away from her and said, "I don't want to see you again."

"Antonio," she said.

Aziz looked at this Rita. She was small and dark. She reminded him of someone, but for now he could not place her. She was not beautiful. She was not ugly. She had one thing he wanted, so badly, to touch. It was her hair. It was like the hair of girls from home. It was blue-black. He started to feel his eyes moisten. And she was not agitated. Like the girls from home, she was unruffled, made out of stillness.

"Rita," Aziz said to her.

Rafik turned to him and said, "This is not Rita."

Aziz could not believe Rafik had said this. "This, this—is not?"

"This is not."

She was walking away from their table.

"I want—" Aziz began.

"You can have her."

"You have had this woman and you do not want her anymore?"

"No, I don't. I want Rita."

"Let us think of something else," Aziz offered.

"You need a woman," Rafik said.

"Rafik."

"Seriously. The last time was what? When that whore blew you in the living room. A year. More."

"If she was a whore, what are you?"

"A man who takes what he wants."

"A man who has forgotten his mother's love."

It was then they saw the Saudi. A shirtless man in black vinyl pants was removing the reservation sign from a round table next to the dance floor. Beside him were Americans, but boys again. There were chunks of watches on tan wrists. One of them had on a white button-down and had rolled up his sleeves. He looked like an Italian sailor Aziz had seen once on a yacht in Arzew. The Saudi, as always, was in a suit. There were ten or more of them. Within moments, bottles of wine arrived, though it was clear they had already been drinking. One of them was quickly asleep with his head on the table. He was chubby.

"Fuck."

Aziz looked at Rafik. "What?"

"One of them will have Rita."

"I would think that all of them will have some kind of Rita."

"Yes."

"Which may affect your prospects. But then, pickiness has not plagued you."

"They are from Harvard."

"What is this Harvard?"

"It is the Sorbonne of America."

Aziz stared, interested now.

"They are smart—even this Saudi?"

"Rich."

"So it is the school of playboys."

"Those are the playboys, at that table. The smart ones do not come to Reach."

They were godlike. Aziz saw that Rafik was a tailless hound to their imperial. Their eyes were like skies or lakes. Their hair was wavy, not nappy. Their smiles were glacially white. One had hair burnished like a scabbard. Another had a jaw from conquering Sparta. A third sat with one leg crossing the other, leaning back, a forearm lazily in the air behind him, to take a drink or toss a comment to another table. Like the Italian sailor Aziz had never forgotten, they had the look that only people who have never suffered possess. As if the prevailing confusion of Aziz's inner moments were instead, in their civilized interiors, harmonized into a quartet played for a czar.

"I'm going home," Rafik said.

"No, please, don't go."

"You want to stay? You?"

If he told him he wanted to watch these ones, Rafik would leave.

"I am thinking you are right. I am in need of a woman."

"Aha!" Rafik exploded.

"I was hoping I might see the Djara," Aziz said, not entirely fibbing.

"The who?"

"You have forgotten."

"That singer would not come here."

"Not Djara in Algeria. That woman we saw one night, the night Heather came to the club."

"That night. Shit. I remember."

"She looked like Djara. You called her Djara."

"Fuck Heather. Just fuck Heather."

Aziz thought of his shame that night. It was now far below, in a seabed.

"I think the Saudi knew her."

"The Djara?" Rafik frowned. "She would not touch his oily ass."

"I think mine is at least as oily."

Rafik laughed. "True, true."

"It is oily, and it is not rich."

"But your brother; you could present him as rich."

"And I am able to say I am no longer a gas station attendant."

"Energy business," Rafik mused. "Say you used to be in the energy business."

"Not a lie."

"Not a lie."

Rafik was alive. He ordered drinks, he pulled a napkin and a pen together on the table. "Let me explain something about women."

Aziz looked at the round table. He was curious about the Saudi's stature among these Olympians. Surely they thought him a goose. His bodyguards were at a nearby table for two. They were playing cards in their sunglasses. They looked like the sullen hotheads who played dominoes in the alleys in Oran. How could they see the cards?

"The American man, he thinks a woman is to be ignored," Rafik instructed. "They tell them this in magazines."

Already the table was divided. Four boys were on the dance floor, and they were dancing with no one but themselves. He had seen women do this, never men. Two others were making paper airplanes from matchbooks and throwing them at women at other tables. Three others were drinking and loud, though the club's din absorbed their raised voices. No one was talking to the Saudi. He was tapping a foot on the floor to the music. His leg looked like a goldfish on a carpet.

"All women believe they are ugly. They believe this, I tell you. The more beautiful they are, the more they believe this. They want these American idiots to tell them how beautiful they are, but because of these magazines, they do not."

Why was it that these ones had come with the Saudi?

"So as you can see, an enormous opportunity is created." Rafik had been drawing triangles and lines on the napkin to illustrate his points. Aziz looked down at it. Rafik started drawing some more. "See, this circle is the number of women who are beautiful."

"Rafik, this is excellent."

One of them had fallen down on the dance floor. He sat there, smiling and patting the cement with his palm. His companions bent over, slapping their knees and laughing. "Waiter, I say, waiter! Bring me a Pimm's!" he shouted from the floor, as if he might stay there. Another boy slid next to him, put both elbows down, propped chin on palms, and stretched long legs across the floor. A woman tripped on his ankles and just missed falling. Soon a waiter delivered a nickel mug with celery and oranges flopping at its lip. Then a tall woman, slender, wearing patent leather boots past her knees, approached the Pimm's drinker from behind. She lifted her boot and rested it on his shoulder so he could see it to his right, the high heel over his chest. One eye was smudged black as if she had been hit and her straight hair shadowed the other eye. Without looking up, the Pimm's man closed his hand around her ankle and said something to his friend, who nodded. The woman knelt behind the Pimm's man and put her cheek against his neck.

"On my cock."

"She must know him," Aziz said, not taking his eyes away from them.

"I think she does not." Rafik's voice was monotone. He sounded drugged.

The Pimm's drinker had now taken the woman's head in both

his hands and was kissing her mouth. The force of him pushed her head back.

"Surely they will not fuck before us," Aziz said.

"No," Rafik said blankly.

But the kissing continued; the man wanted her like one starving. Her hands were helpless at her sides. The friend was still beside them, but he had turned on his back and he appeared to be studying the moving lights on the ceiling.

"This woman, she is—" Aziz lost his words. He looked at Rafik for help.

"This woman is Rita."

Before Aziz could speak, Mourad was upon them. He shoved his cell phone at Rafik. "Heather is calling. Someone has come to the house. Someone who says he knows you."

Rafik swung his eyes up to Mourad's face. "You told her I was here?"

"You are." Mourad's face was rigid.

"Aziz," Rafik began.

"Let me talk to Heather," Aziz said to his brother.

"No. He will." Mourad lifted the cell phone to his ear and said, "Here is Rafik." A pause. "He thinks you are stupid." He handed the phone to Rafik. Rafik took it and looked at it for the longest time. Then he threw it across the dance floor, where it bounced twice and disappeared into the crowd.

12

His name was Taffounnout Belghazi. They called him Ghazi. Mourad took to him. From the first, even on the cell phone, Ghazi had made the wood goat smile. While Rafik was running home in a taxi fearing Heather's wrath, Mourad was nodding and bobbing like a boat in a sunny sea. By the time Mourad and Aziz got home, Heather and this Ghazi were drawing pictures on the kitchen table in place of language. She already had taught him how to say *fox bitch*. Mourad laughed so hard that Heather touched Ghazi's shoulder to make sure he was real. How had it been that Rafik had never mentioned him? He was not like the others. Heather had to drop her eyes; his looking at her was searching. Rafik said something in Arabic, and Mourad and Aziz and the Three and this Ghazi laughed and shook their heads.

"Aziz," Heather kept on, "you never said anything about this Ghazi."

Aziz upturned his palms. She turned to Lahouari.

Lahouari's eyes were lit. "He is one who might win," he answered.

"Win?" Heather cocked her head.

"The rules," Lahouari tried.

"Ghazi finds ways where others find walls," Rafik helped.

Ghazi had had fifty-eight days in the hold. No committee greeted him. No one called in a tizzy of worry to wonder if he arrived. He had shoes, socks, shirt, dry pants in a plastic bag, and American dollars in the pockets. He came in January, swam through ice, and hailed a cab to Brooks Street. He was older than all of them. He had served in the army long before Aziz. He was an architect, educated in Oran, the only one in his family with a university degree. His father was military intelligence. His brother was a high-ranking officer in Algiers. His mother and Aziz's mother had been close friends since girlhood.

Ghazi was his mother's favorite. The last few years, arthritis that had plagued her as a teenager and then subsided had flared. She was in bed more than not. Her husband, Ghazi's father, was cold, often gone; it seemed odd to Aziz that Ghazi would have left her side. As they drank and talked longer into the night than usual, Aziz kept waiting to hear Ghazi's story. But Ghazi was more interested in all of them. Aziz could see that Heather, the Three, Mourad, even Rafik—all were telling Ghazi more than any of them had told the others. There was something in him that loosened them, left them unstrung and breathlessly alive, wanting morning to come so they could tell him more.

Aziz and Ghazi were at Del Fuegos, a Mexican restaurant. Heather had clipped a help-wanted ad and driven them there at lunchtime. Ghazi was wearing pressed jeans and a new sweater. Aziz was wearing a suit. There were two dishwashing jobs open. The owner was a John Hill; there were no Mexicans on the premises. "You two look Mexican," Hill remarked. "You work hard, I move you up to waiting tables."

Aziz spoke humbly and respectfully. Ghazi repeated, as they had rehearsed the night before, what to repeat. Hill put them to work on the spot. Their pay was $4.95 an hour. Aziz's best suit pants were drenched in the first thirty minutes. Ghazi was whistling and dancing like a cartoon bear from the start.

Del Fuegos did a fast business, and when they finally stopped at 1 a.m., they had not moved from their stations beside the industrial dishwashers. Aziz's arms felt like mashed apples. Ghazi was grim.

"They intend to kill us," he observed.

"Yes, that is the plan, I believe."

"But it is good to work."

They were waiting on the sidewalk for Rafik to come get them. Aziz imagined him at Reach, forgetting.

"It is good," Aziz agreed, rubbing his hands for warmth.

"You have talked to your mother since I came?" Ghazi asked.

"No. I talked to my father."

"And he says?"

"He says your father tells him you are dead."

Ghazi nodded. "I expect this."

"Ghazi, what happened?" Only two of them. Maybe Ghazi would talk to him.

"You know my father."

"Yes," Aziz said, sad. Ghazi's father and Ghazi were closed to each other.

"He is what he is," Ghazi said. Aziz waited. He could not read Ghazi's face. It was a face of one with something behind his back. Ghazi's father was military intelligence; he might know of Aziz's tour of duty. So could Ghazi's brother, some lieutenant colonel, though where, Aziz could not remember. Had they sent Ghazi?

"Your mother?" Aziz finally said.

"Was better."

"Really? When you left she had improved?"

"Yes. You should speak to your mother. She will say how much better."

"I will."

"Ask her to find out for me."

"That your mother—"

"Is still okay."

There was a pause. Aziz stomped his foot. The night cold bit at his ears. How to touch here and not there, to nudge Ghazi where he could get a better look at him without Ghazi noticing. He thought of hinting at Soumeya, but no, not yet. Besides, Rafik would be driving up soon. Or maybe not. Rafik with his women. Aziz guessed Heather knew and no longer cared. But Rafik—it might help to find where Ghazi stood on him.

"Listen. Rafik, he—"

"Tunisia," Ghazi said quickly.

"So you know," Aziz said, surprised.

"Yes," Ghazi said.

"Do they know back home?"

"Who, his parents? No."

"You learned of it from—?"

Ghazi's face was blank. "One who was with Rafik in Tunisia," he said.

Aziz knew it would be strange in Ghazi's eyes to ask more. He veered instead.

"He is still . . . Rafik." Aziz shook his head. "I worry. I have smelled hash. The clothes. The suitcases."

"Suitcases?"

"Heavy. Locked. Maybe hash. Maybe something else. I know he is stealing suits. And underwear."

"Underwear?"

"French and Italian. Steal here, sell somewhere else."

"Underwear," Ghazi mused. "An opportunity I had not imagined."

Aziz had to laugh. Ghazi shook his head and smiled.

"Goddamn," he said.

"Kamal is in it with him," Aziz said.

"Kamal?"

"Kamal Gamal. He knew him in Paris."

"Not from Arzew?"

"No."

"Where?"

Aziz had no idea. He raised his shoulders and shook his head. It worried him, now that Ghazi asked, that he did not know.

"Kamal—how can I tell you?" Aziz said. "He lived with Rafik. Went after Heather with a chair. There was some fight long between them. Hit me by mistake trying for her. After that, he left." It was too much to tell of the hospital, the burns, Linda, the move.

"For Paris."

"No, somewhere in East Boston. At a girlfriend's place. Brazilian one. He drives a cab."

Ghazi blew on his reddened knuckles for warmth. "So Mourad made Rafik get rid of the hash."

"No, I did. But now I think he rents a storage."

"A storage?"

"Here they have businesses where you rent a small room and get a key and put things in it. Rafik has one."

"We will steal the key and find out what is in it."

"Cousin, we—" Aziz began. Ghazi made these jumps.

"I think we will do this."

"But he will know."

"He will not know."

"*I* do not want to know."

Just then Aziz saw Rafik approaching in Heather's BMW. "He is here," Ghazi said, as if that settled it. Aziz felt stiff. He had turned wrong in the conversation. Fixing it was unlikely.

Rafik opened the car door and the radio blasted into the coldness. He turned it down and gave Ghazi a slap on his back, saying, "You need the kind of hot I just had." Ghazi did not grin, as Rafik wanted him to; Aziz could tell Ghazi was calculating.

"Hot can always be found," Ghazi finally said. "It is getting close enough to warm, without burning, that matters to me." Rafik was unimpressed. Aziz wondered if that was meant for him. If so, what did it mean? He could not see Ghazi's face in the dark. Aziz twitched. His eyes hurt. His toes hurt. He sat on his hands, hoping for warmth; soon he was asleep. When they got to Brooks

Street, Aziz woke to see that Ghazi had worked up a closeness with Rafik. They were making plans to go shopping the next morning on Newbury Street. This was a street of minted perfect Rafik could not, unemployed or employed, afford. Had it been Rafik's idea or Ghazi's? Aziz cursed his sleeping.

Inside the gloves, his hands were sweating. The rubber was thick and black. The cuff of one was torn, and Aziz worried it might split further. Should he take it off and turn it inside out? Dropping a plate would be bad. A stoned Cuban with a deep tray of dishes came toward him. Behind him, John Hill was upbraiding an elderly busboy, black-skinned, silver-haired. Aziz looked at Ghazi. With the water rushing and Hill barking, talking was impossible. Ghazi looked back, then directed his head toward Hill and mouthed, "Shitbag."

John Hill was on them. "You boys keep good time."

"Thank you, sir," said Aziz.

"We like," Ghazi contributed.

As John Hill walked back out to the floor, Aziz closed his eyes. John Hill would hate them soon enough, no matter how they bowed.

Ghazi tapped him. He spoke in Aziz's ear.

"Rafik is in shit."

"Tell me."

"He charged over five thousand dollars on a credit card this morning."

Aziz looked around, afraid someone had heard. Not a one could care. He was embarrassed. "Are you sure? Do you know this new money?"

"Aziz."

"Okay. Okay."

"He bought two suits."

"Two?"

"Only two. I swear to God."

"He is crazy."

"You say he does not work."

"No. Not now. He did."

"What work?"

"A moving company in Brighton. Russians."

"When did that stop?"

"When Mourad came, he had not been working. When the Three came he was not. He took me there after the Djara. So he has not worked since the Djara."

"The Djara? Took you where?"

"I met—no, I *saw* a woman, she looked like Djara. We were at Reach, and that night Heather made me take her to Reach—"

"Reach?"

"A club."

"And Rafik took you where?"

"To the moving company."

"Where he worked."

"He said he worked there."

"But you think no."

"The men seemed fake to me. Called in for show. It was that night I found the smell of hash in his room. He had these suitcases on a rope—"

"A rope?"

"Across the ceiling of his room. His and Heather's."

"Is she—?"

"I know nothing about the true nature of Heather."

"The suitcases."

"They were cement."

"Concrete?"

"Heavy. The bed was covered in clothes, expensive. In the bathroom too."

"The underwear caper."

"And more."

"This here a tea party?" It was John Hill. He shoved Ghazi hard against the sink. *Tea party* was not available to them.

"Yes," Ghazi said agreeably, straightening.

"No," Aziz said, hedging.

"No dishes, you grab that mop, see?"

"Yes," Aziz said.

"This floor is a roach toilet."

"Yes."

"I pay you good money to work. To talk, I pay with this." He kicked Aziz in a shin and walked away.

"He could have cut off your ears," Ghazi observed, as they saw John Hill busy scolding a waitress.

"Or foot."

"Or your finger."

"Or my nose."

"There is always your dick."

They were laughing. But they could not talk of Rafik until they were waiting for the bus home at midnight. They were alone in the cold, composed of aches and insults.

"This is how it is," Aziz said, lying on his back on the bus-stop bench.

"A little different from home," Ghazi said, lying with his head next to Aziz's on the same bench. "No. Better than home."

"Worse. And better."

"Remember Tariq?" Ghazi spoke of a bully.

"He kicked."

"Always the kick."

Aziz nodded, remembering.

"They have their ways, these ones."

The air was like a freezer. Rafik had declined to get them tonight. Business, he said. Heather had the flu. She did look sick. But Rafik, naturally he was lying.

On the bench, they moved closer. Ghazi needed a winter coat. He was wearing three sweaters and a knit hat. "My friend, this is good," he said. "Aziz, you and I, here. We are here! We have made it to this place!" Ghazi was off the bench and throwing his hat to the stars. "Soon I will marry John Hill's daughter!"

Aziz had to laugh.

"I will have John Hill's grandchild!"

Ghazi was standing on the bench, making steps and curtsies.

"I will take him to the park in a fur coat the color of summer clouds! My son, the grandchild of John Hill, will be a general in the American army! Meanwhile," Ghazi said in mock melodrama, "Conniving Rafik . . . will be . . . in jail!"

"Ghazi. He saved us." Aziz could not let go of Rafik's rescuing him from the Egyptian and so much more. Ghazi too. And the Three. Ghazi sat down on the bench. Aziz was still lying down.

"I will not be the one who sends him," Aziz whispered.

"Nor will I, my friend, nor will I. He will send himself."

Loyalty lodged hard in Aziz. Going to the storage, which he had hoped Ghazi would forget, would be a mistake. Seeing—he did not want to see. He had done enough getting the hash out of Brooks Street.

The acrid of bus bellied up to them.

13

Ghazi, wearing headphones, was at the kitchen table. Aziz could hear him from his bedroom. *I. You. He. She. It. We. You. They. I am. You are. He is. She is. It is. We are. You are. They are.* It had been a week since their conversation about Rafik's storage unit. Each day gone meant Ghazi might have forgotten. Luckily, Mourad had lent Ghazi language tapes. Now Ghazi's chief obsession was English. Aziz looked over the bed at his brother. Mourad was dressed, shoes on, asleep. He had been at Reach late again. The mincing one at home was the prancing one here. It was the green card.

Status had taken the rigid out of Mourad. Back home, Aziz had never considered confiding in him. His older sister Hazar was the one he trusted. Here, he was forever shifting his mind about who it should be. His reasons for unburdening himself changed daily. One day confession was needed for protection, in case Ghazi had been sent to entrap him. That meant he must tell Mourad. Aziz glanced at Mourad's stun gun near the bed. Mourad would defend him anyway, no matter what he knew about Aziz's army days. Besides, did he think Ghazi would kill him sleeping in his bed? It was ridiculous. His mind was stew. He had lost how to think clearly. No, thinking was the problem. Thinking too much, that had always upended him. Yet trust irked. A pin stayed stuck in his heart. Hadn't his army tour shown he had a talent for befriending his enemies?

He sat on the edge of the bed. A few times he had thought of disclosing enough to Heather so she could help him apply for asylum. She helped Lahouari get a social security number, a triumph none of the others had achieved. Asylum meant safety, a path to the green card. Asylum, he had gathered from listening to Rafik dispense advice to the Three, was for those who were persecuted, physically in danger in the home country. The Three would not qualify; they had left because there were no jobs. Economic reasons were not enough.

He stopped. Asylum: Rafik? Rafik knew specks about asylum. It was the Three Aziz should rely upon. They were apart from all wrong. Through their father back home, maybe they could find out Ghazi's reasons for coming. But wait. Their father had lost touch with Arzew. He lived in Algiers. Or was it Constantine? He tried to remember. He lifted the sheet thumbtacked to the windowsill. He could see the same thick icicles that had been there for months. There was even a layer of ice like mica on the windows inside. Maybe Lahouari, in that unknowing way he had, could ask Ghazi and get an answer. But Lahouari would miss too much. Simple himself, he would bring Aziz only a simple version of what Ghazi had said.

He got out of bed and walked down the hall. There Ghazi was, at the kitchen table. It was so cold his headphones were under a wool cap; he was wearing mittens. The kitchen, because of the never-fixed leak, rarely got warm in winter. There was the blue bucket at Ghazi's elbow, catching slow drips of water. It was the only place to sit, apart from the bathtub, because everyone else was sleeping. Ghazi was trying to say the word *refrigerator.* He missed syllables and tried again. It came out *refugator.* Now it was *oven.* That was worse; Arabic had no *v.* He seemed to be saying *oben.*

There was silence. Then *sink*. Aziz felt a sudden eddy of sorrow. Let this be. Let Ghazi be what he appeared: the smartest one who had not stopped hoping. He thought of his father's words over the phone on Ghazi's motives. "An architect forced to sell vegetables on the sidewalk? Of course Ghazi left."

Ghazi was studying a cookbook. "You know this word *marinate?*"

Aziz had no idea.

"*Combine?*" He said it like French: *Combien.*

Aziz thought. "Maybe for hair," he said. "In English there is *comb.* It sounds like that."

Ghazi frowned.

Heather and Rafik were gone. Mourad had the day shift. The Three had gone to see someone from Lahouari's garage who said he had a minivan, very cheap.

"Fuck this."

Ghazi threw down the book and disappeared down the hall.

Aziz picked it up. It was thick. There were photographs and drawings. Many pictures of hands holding a knife and an artichoke. Pictures of a fish, a knife cutting away the tail, then the head, fingers lifting the backbone out like lace. He felt awful and curious at once. There were photographs of kitchens, with silver counters and silver ovens, big shining slicers and grills. This was for restaurants: how to run them, secrets for cooking. They had made a radish into petals. There was a fan made from a carrot.

Ghazi walked into the living room. Aziz looked up. Something was wrong. Ghazi was excited or scared, or—no, not those things; he was proud.

"I have found it," Ghazi said, bringing a silver key into Aziz's line of vision.

"Three tries—under bed, first drawer near bed, under pebbles in aquarium—*bang, bang, bang,*" Ghazi said. "The aquarium is the one."

He had not forgotten about the storage.

Aziz's mouth was dry. "The aquarium. I would have left that alone."

"Rafik's mind, easy. I see how he thinks."

Ghazi picked up a phone book from the floor. "I will find where this keys goes," he said.

"Uncle, why? This should rest. We find out, then what?"

"We know for sure what he does."

"Yes. Then we are in it."

Ghazi was paging through. He stopped. "The hash. You let that rest?"

"That was here. In the house. Different."

Ghazi began turning the pages again. "Maybe I am curious."

Maybe you are already in it, Aziz thought. It didn't fit, though. If Ghazi were in it, he already would have a key. No need to tell Aziz, to make a show of finding it.

"Rafik could come back," Aziz said.

"He is with Heather." Ghazi's head stayed down.

"You know how they are—they could be back early."

"Heather and he, I have fixed," Ghazi said.

"Fixed?"

"I told Rafik that Heather confided things to me."

"Things?"

"That she knows of his women."

"You did not."

"That she forgives him. Because she knows she has not loved him as he deserves to be loved."

"She said this?"

"That he lives in her soul, lives constantly."

"Heather does not talk that way."

"That she will wait until he is ready for him to come back to her bed. And when he does, she will pleasure him to distraction. She will submit to him body and heart and mind and spirit."

"He did not believe this."

"He wept."

"He what?"

"Cried in my arms. Said, 'Ghazi, I love her more than life. I am only hers. I have defiled my love and her. God sees. God knows. He sent you to me.' "

"He was playing."

Ghazi shrugged and dialed a phone number from the yellow pages. "Storage Planet? Yes. This is Muhammed Ghezil. My father, he has a storage. . . . Yes, in Boston. . . . No, yours. Maybe yours. . . . No, no, he died. Yes. Last week. I have a key . . . yes . . . yes. Yes, his estate. Absolutely. His name was Rafik Ghezil."

He would never find which one. There were too many in Boston. His English was still too bad. But *absolutely*—how did he have that word? After two months and a few language tapes?

Ghazi drove Mourad's new Escort. They spent an hour being lost. Aziz begged him to turn back twice. But now, at the U-Stor-It in Everett, Ghazi was jiggling Rafik's key at unit 523.

The door opened.

They peered.

"There must be a light," Ghazi said.

They patted the sides of the wall for a switch.

"Mourad has a flashlight in his car," Ghazi said.

"He does not."

"I believe Mourad does." They opened the trunk. There was a first-aid kit, a gasoline canister, a blanket, four bars of chocolate, and a flashlight. Aziz meekly followed Ghazi back to the unit.

The suitcases Aziz had seen in Rafik's room a year ago were in the front. Behind them were enormous drums, corrugated and metal. Then there were boxes—Minute Maid, Ajax—making a barricade. Ghazi took a suitcase and tried to open it. It was locked. He tried another. Shut. He knelt before the third. "Smell this," Ghazi said. "Here, on this zipper." Aziz's nose touched the cool metal.

"Hash," Aziz said.

"No."

"What then?"

"It is not hash. I know from university too well the smell of hash."

"But this is old hash. It has been here for months."

"Maybe."

"So what is it?"

Ghazi shook his head. "Check every suitcase. He may have forgotten to lock one."

They tried each one. All had combinations or tiny locks made for tiny keys.

"Next time, I bring a knife," Ghazi said. "We slice here." His finger traced the narrow band of cloth against the teeth of the zipper. Aziz lit a cigarette. He looked at his watch.

"Ghazi," he said. "I swear to God, we have to go back."

"He hides something here."

"This is Rafik. You know this."

Ghazi sat down on a suitcase. "I should have brought something for these locks. I could open them easily. I brought nothing." He went back to Mourad's car. Aziz watched him rummage in the glove compartment. "He has no woman. So there is no hairpin."

"Please," Aziz said. "It is better not to know."

"I want to move a barrel," Ghazi said. "To see how heavy it is."

Aziz stubbed out his cigarette. They moved aside some suitcases and two of the boxes and positioned themselves around a drum.

"Don't hurt yourself," Ghazi said.

They braced and hoisted. It went over their heads in a swoosh. It felt like a foam cup.

"Empty," Aziz said.

"Maybe," Ghazi said.

They placed it back on the floor. They tapped it. The metal gave up no sound. Aziz backed away.

"Let's get out of here," he said.

Ghazi laughed. "Relax."

He started putting the suitcases back. He put a blue one next to two black ones. Aziz put a brown one next. "No, that one was here." Ghazi motioned to the far right.

Aziz tried to think. Why this urgency? And yet, not urgency, because Ghazi came unprepared in a way. The key, but not the hair-pins. The Rafik and Heather reunion, but not the knife to cut open and really see. Was it a show? Something to convince Aziz that Ghazi was upright? Something to say, I will not tolerate wrong-doing? Or did he want to control Rafik, by knowing his wrongs. If so, he still did not know them.

When he had confronted Rafik about the suitcases long before Mourad and Ghazi came, Aziz had seen hash. In plastic. In one of the suitcases. But only one suitcase. The rest of the suitcases, obviously, Rafik had brought here. Maybe these suitcases had no hash but something worse. Ghazi said the smell here was *not* hash. They were both thinking *chemicals.*

Ghazi's words were not the words of a man posing. Ghazi's words belonged to someone puzzled, who wanted the truth. Ghazi had been outraged at Rafik's buying two suits for five thousand dollars on Newbury Street. Ghazi could have kept that from Aziz. Ghazi had talked of sending Rafik to prison. It had been Aziz who had defended Rafik. Ghazi had been intent on finding out what was in the U-Stor-It. It was he, Aziz, who was acting like Rafik's accomplice.

When they got back to Brooks Street, Rafik and Heather were still gone. Mourad was watching television with the Three. "Where is Rafik?" Aziz asked.

"Heather told me they went far," Lahouari said.

Ghazi was back in the bedroom, his hand in the fish tank. Aziz looked at Mourad, not understanding Lahouari.

"They came back. Left again. For days," Mourad helped.

"They are in love," added Hamid.

"No more whores at Reach," said Mourad.

Ghazi was back in the living room.

"They go to a place called Maine," Lahouari said.

"Romantic getaway," Mourad said in English, getting up from the couch to give Ghazi a mock punch. No one understood him. He gave an approximation in Arabic. Ghazi laughed. So did Aziz. Lahouari was a stone.

"I get their room," Ghazi said.

"No way," Mourad said.

Hamid said, "If anyone should, it is us."

"He can have it," Lahouari said. "I will not stay there." Aziz and Ghazi exchanged looks. They saw Lahouari's crush on Heather. So did Hamid. "Ali and I will stay there," Hamid said. "You take the sofa here," he said to Lahouari. That left Ghazi where he always slept, on the floor.

"I am blessed with this floor," Ghazi said. "A most inviting floor. A beautiful floor. I have loved her many nights."

14

The chef quit. It was an hour into dinner. Ghazi's hands were in the sink, washing a baking tray. John Hill was at his elbow, sharing falsified details of the calamity. After nodding without comment, Ghazi said, "Let me cook."

Ghazi had charmed Hill. Ghazi's English was better after only six months than Aziz's after two and a half years. Ghazi's English had ushered him into two waitresses' beds on a regular basis. He could watch cooking classes on television. He could quiz the now ex-chef before work about how to prep for the day.

"Listen," Ghazi said to Hill. "Search your bag. Who is there besides me?"

"Fucking Christ, you're right," Hill said. "Go on, then."

Aziz watched as Ghazi put on the apron and replaced the bandanna around his head with a knotted towel. Four waitresses were leaning on the counter, one tapping her pen. Ghazi tilted his head to the first, and she read out, "Taco Sunrise, Old El Paso Mix-up."

"Merci," he said taking the ticket, which he stuck on the string

with a clothespin. "Gail." He called her back. She returned impatiently. One of the other waitresses huffed and one hissed.

"Remember, I live for you," he told Gail.

He turned to the second in line. "But you, I give my life for." He traced his finger along the chin of another.

And so it went. John Hill drank too much and fell asleep in his car. The waitresses smiled. The food was fine. People paid for it. After closing, instead of rushing home, the staff stayed and Ghazi passed out platters of enchiladas, stuffed peppers, and hickory catfish. When Mourad came to pick them up, he parked the car and joined them. Ghazi served them beer and tequila. "You waited on these shitheads, now I wait on you," he said. They turned the radio dial away from the Latino station and stopped it at Classic Rock.

Ghazi took a waitress in his arms and held her while the music pounded and the rest of them ate. He had one hand around her waist and the other in her long hair. Aziz, too tired to eat or drink, watched them. Ghazi was a wide man. He was not a particularly good dancer. Nothing about him was good-looking. Yet what Aziz saw of him was not what he sensed in him. His jet hair was cut close, and his short beard, instead of softening him like beards did most men, blackened his face. His eyes were tar dark. He had fair skin; the charcoal of hair and brows and eyes and beard were bolder because of that pale setting. He would have looked frightening, Aziz thought, except for something in his unhurried gait, the slow way he used his hands, and, the strangest thing of all, the mournful downcast of his eyes, which were also unaccountably merry.

They worked. There seemed to be nothing but that. They knew there was, but it was not for them. Heather was a secretary at a law firm. Rafik said he was at the Brighton Moving and Storage Company. Aziz assumed he was over at Kamal's, on a cell phone to Munich, haggling over stolen suits, plotting shipments of nothing good, stalling someone with variations on words like *margins, deadlines,* and *overnight express.* Lahouari worked at the Old New

England Body Shop. One of his brothers, Hamid, delivered pizza in Cambridge. The other, Ali, fried doughnuts. The Three sent money home. Mourad sent money home. Aziz sent money home. Ghazi, now chef at Del Fuegos, sent money home; his father sent it back. The Brooks Street kitchen leaked. Repairs were infrequent; they didn't last. The ceiling was many browns.

Ghazi's latest girlfriend waitress was his third romance at Del Fuegos. She knew an immigration lawyer. His name was Charlie Stone. He spoke Arabic. Charlie knew Algeria. No one before Charlie knew Algeria. The first girlfriend waitress thought it was near Panama. The second one thought it was Nigeria. But Charlie, he knew the Groupe Islamique Armé, the Front Islamique du Salut, the Front de Libération Nationale. To make Ghazi happy, Aziz went to Charlie's office. It smelled like insecticide. They spent a long night drinking bad tea and talking. Charlie said the GIA were terrorists; Ghazi said the GIA were terrorists but the FIS was not. Aziz was quiet. Charlie pounded on his desk. Says who? Says Ghazi. Every so often Aziz smiled at Charlie approvingly. He did the same to Ghazi. Mostly, Aziz looked around.

The top of Charlie's scuffed desk was empty. The shelves had cardboard boxes but no books. He had no secretary. His phone was on the wall, not the desk. Ghazi had gone gullible. Maybe this Charlie was a spy from home. Maybe he was the secret police of the Americans. His name and talking Arabic did not match, of that Aziz was sure. He looked Arab, but his Arabic was sometimes Lebanese, sometimes Egyptian. Textbook Arabic, Aziz believed. Charlie's explanation for his name was from a book too. Had to change it, he said; his real name was hard for Americans to say.

When Aziz told Ghazi the office was fake, Charlie untrustworthy, Ghazi laughed and patted Aziz's cheeks. "I am playing him," he said. For what? Aziz's expression asked. But Ghazi ignored the look.

"He does not use the Algerian word *khandji,* or even *irhabi.* Always *mujahideen.* Always *jihadists.*"

"*Irhabiya, khandjiya mujahideen, jihadists, terrorists.* Same, same, same, same."

Aziz knew they were not the same. Even the smartest one, he concluded, could act like a grasshopper. When Ghazi started filling out the forms Charlie gave him, Aziz knew it was Charlie who was playing Ghazi, though for what, Aziz could not exactly imagine. It was an application for asylum. Apply, Ghazi told Aziz. Charlie knows how to word these things. He knows the home country. He has made a story about me the Americans will like. With asylum, we get the green card. We become like Mourad.

Aziz said the same thing he said all summer when Charlie Stone came up. "How do you know he is an immigration lawyer?"

Aziz and Ghazi were waiting for the bus after work. It was past midnight, the street emptied except for a traffic light's green, yellow, and red. They heard nothing but crickets. Something felt sad to Aziz. Ghazi was inside himself, his clowning put away.

"Aziz," Ghazi said. "Did you ever believe you could leave?"

Dread would have come a few months ago. But Ghazi had shed mysteries all summer. He was as hapless as any of them.

"To be honest, no," Aziz answered.

"Three times," Ghazi said. "Three times you tried to leave."

"Yes."

"Me, just once."

"You never talk of why," Aziz said.

"We are here," Ghazi said. "That is what matters."

Still the deflection.

"Could you marry an American girl?" Ghazi asked. More deflection.

"That is hard to know. I am alone." Aziz paused. He was preoccupied with what he might safely say of Soumeya. To delay, he reached for any question. "Perhaps you will marry Carol?" Carol, the third girlfriend waitress.

"Carol? Goddamn. No."

"Because she is American?"

"No. She is not enough. To me she is—"

"Ghazi. Have you ever loved a woman?" There, Aziz thought. That was the question he wanted to ask.

"No."

"Never?"

"I hear in your voice that *you* have."

Aziz had set the table. Yet still he hesitated to sit down. "Yes," he said finally.

Ghazi turned. Aziz felt his eyes but could not look back. "There was never one for you at home."

"There was," Aziz said. "No one knew of her."

"Who?"

Aziz thought he could feel Ghazi studying length of pauses, inflection, the muscle that betrayed or hesitated.

"You did not know her," Aziz began.

Ghazi said nothing. Aziz felt him waiting.

"She is dead now," Aziz finished.

Ghazi made a humming sound. A silence lasted until Aziz moved his foot against the sidewalk.

"I saw her killed," he said, scraping his shoe on the concrete.

Ghazi, who had been sitting on the other end of the bus bench, moved toward Aziz and sat next to him. For a while, neither spoke. There were no cars, no highway noise, only the even call of crickets. The night air was cooling. Wind lifted a page and dropped it behind a fence. Aziz remembered the newspaper that had warmed him the day he swam. He was easily as lost now. But there was this: He had expected Ghazi's shock. Ghazi's quiet—that was ease.

Ghazi put his hand on Aziz's shoulder. "I am sorry, uncle; I am sorry for this. You, your suffering—it is too much. Words for this"—Ghazi put his head against Aziz's ear—"I have none." They heard each other breathing. They stayed that way until the wheeze of the bus came down the street.

Ghazi took the jelly of chicken strips in handfuls and dropped them in the oil. Bubbles coated the strips. The sound was like roof rain. To his right were heads of lettuce. He took his knife and began: first in half, then in half again. The quarters made a long row. He began the slicing. Dominoes of lettuce tilted left. He looked at the chicken and stirred. With a strainer, he fished out meat and spread it on the grill. Up went the flame. In seconds it was time for paper towels. He spooned the lettuce into bowls, and bowls went in refrigerators. He palmed the cooling chicken and decided to dust it with salt.

Aziz sat watching on a bar stool. "It will be hot today," he said. They had not spoken of Soumeya since last night. Aziz was grateful for Ghazi's not asking questions. It would be explained in time, Ghazi's attitude said.

"Here, give me some of this," Aziz said. "I will chop."

"To really help, do this." Ghazi demonstrated taking the chicken out of the oil.

Soon they would come. First John Hill. Then Aderley, the old man. Then Mariah, who had two babies, twins. Then Ramona, who loved Marco, the headwaiter. Then someone whose name Aziz could not say: Birgin. Birginia. Some called her Ginny.

"There was one for me," Ghazi said.

Aziz sat up.

The raw chicken roared up in oil.

"Her mother was sick," Ghazi began, after the chicken quieted. "They sent her mother to France. She was living there for medical problems, and the one for me, she was in Arzew." Ghazi's face was turned to his chopping. Aziz was lifting chicken from the second pot. He could barely see this chicken. His heart drummed.

"Her father was dead, but her uncle, he worked in the courthouse and had known my father, though not long. That was the connection, how it was arranged."

Aziz nodded. "Was she—to look at, something good?"

"She is not, but fuck that. She is private, modest. Her voice is young. If it pleases my father, who favors my brother and kicks me, I am happy. It worked. My father, I swear it, softened to me."

Aziz nodded. Still Ghazi was chopping. Still Aziz kept at the chicken. It was important to act ordinary. Everything typical.

"I go to college. I go to the army. I come back. There are the usual things. We get along. I see she is always talking about her mother, so I give her money to give to the mother, to send to France. This money I get from security work; there is nothing for architects."

"Security?"

"At the navy base. Then taxi. Then vegetables on the sidewalk."

"The uncle of her, couldn't he find something at the court?"

"He says no."

"And your father, at military intelligence?"

"DRS? Hell, no."

"Nothing?" Aziz asked. Ghazi's father had joined Direction du Renseignement et de la Sécurité long before it had that name, back when it was called what many still called it, Sécurité Militaire. Someone as proud as Ghazi's father would let his son sell vegetables?

Ghazi had stopped chopping. He leaned toward Aziz.

"I would not throw myself in with such soft hens."

Aziz was jolted. This was opposite to what anyone said about DRS. It was feared, hated, vicious. Military intelligence—soft?

Ghazi was talking. He was explaining how his intended told him the uncle was sending money to the mother in France. Aziz could not quite follow why this mattered. "And a friend from university comes into Arzew," Ghazi was saying. "He has a bride he has come to claim, and he says to me, 'So, my friend, when will your bride be yours?' And I say, 'My bride is soon to come, she is Djamila.' And this one, he says, 'Djamila Yasin?'

"And I say, 'Yes, it is that same Djamila.' And he pulls my head to his head, and he says, 'On my mother's grave, and by God I swear, that Djamila has been with your brother.' And as if he knew I would hit him, he takes my hands like this and holds them here, and I know, in that holding, that he is sure."

Aziz made a sound. He could not help it. Ghazi seemed flat, almost automatic.

"She had been with him before my father settled on me," Ghazi said. "I do not know if my father knew about Djamila and my brother. If he did not, still, my brother said nothing when my father—"

"He let your father make this for you."

"Yes."

Aziz looked at the bowls, chicken to the brims. Ghazi had stopped chopping.

"I find out, soon, that her mother is not sick. I find that this mother is not in France. I find that her father is not dead, he is in Turkey. My brother knew all this. I tell my father; they call me liar, my brother innocent. It has been that way, uncle, I swear to you, from when I was born.

"I prepare. I get clothes, plastic bags, American dollars. I watch the tankers, I ask the routes, I find Rafik's number, and the night before the wedding, I pay one I have known since soccer days to hide me on board. When the ship leaves that morning, I am in it, thinking of Djamila waiting, hour by slow hour, for me who will never appear."

They took cover in the desert. No one hid land mines in blowing sand. Aziz's unit was camped south of Biskra. They were forbidden to leave at night without written instruction. Another unit had been called up to defuse the mines, but they had been attacked on the way. CONSIGNÉ À TOUT LE PERSONNEL MILITAIRE: *Ne sortir sous aucun prétexte. État d'alerte. Communiquez toutes infractions à cet ordre.* Aziz had seen the bulletin himself, because he was trying to find Ramdane Benane: Benane, who served under the intelligence chief Zahaf. Benane reported to Zahaf, but it was said that he was not Zahaf's man. To catch sight of Benane, Aziz had poured tea for the officers all afternoon. *If only Benane, if only Benane* . . . was the song in his head.

But the day had given him nothing. Perhaps Benane had not come to the camp, as the rumors had it. Now the sky was ink and the tents quiet. Near the foot of his blanket, Aziz made out the outline of Mohammed Nazzar, a soldier in his unit. Nazzar was dim; Aziz in his mind called him *turnip.* Nazzar was from Belcourt. He

bomb in Belcourt. Today, he
t blood, lines of it on pavements,
valk on the blood of your brothers,
a sin. Go get some water to wash this
zzar was mad or meant to make him mad.
oked asleep, but Aziz moved and rustled to test

asleep. It would be more Belcourt.

Aziz, are you awake?"

He had heard that they put people beside you to test you. That his commanders, and some soldiers, spent most of their time and their energy finding out where you stood: FIS or FLN, *hizb esserqa* or *hizb frança, le clan réconciliateur* or *le clan éradicateur*, Islamist or secularist, *khandjiya* or patriots, crazy or practical, bad or good, dumb or wise. Could this turnip be crafty? Not so far. Nazzar had no nuance. Or was that to lull? Then again, he could be a man near ruined by bombs and death. Or, most innocently, he could be a simple comrade, unaware. Perhaps Nazzar had not felt the disappearance of Ahmed and Fawaz and Bahir, soldiers in their unit Aziz had known well. Perhaps Nazzar had not wondered, as Aziz had, why it was that Ahmed and Fawaz had been close to a tight-faced soldier named Wahid, who died in a training accident. Perhaps Nazzar did not lie on these sand floors in the heat, thinking, made restless by thinking. There were times when Aziz believed he was the last man who thought or noticed or knew what it was to imagine something wretched or remember something fine.

"Yes, have to piss."

Life was a series of commonplaces leading to reasonable events. He had once thought that. He could not believe he had ever been someone who thought such a thing. Life was a series of dramas in which the goal was a place where you could talk, truly talk, and say whatever it was that haunted you at night alone. He would get to that place. He would get to that place, but Nazzar was not going to get him closer to it, no matter who or what he might be.

"I can't sleep," Nazzar bleated.

"Jerk off, you'll sleep."

"They are *harki,* all of them," Nazzar said. Aziz kept walking as if he had not heard him.

Harki, the old word for French collaborators. Now it was for anyone hated, and for Nazzar those were the Belcourt bombers. Bombers who despised the French. Who said the FLN who fought the French had become the French. Given enough time, Nazzar would be *harki*. Every last man in every last place would be *harki*.

Aziz opened the flap of the tent and felt the night coming at him in a cinnamon smell. What was that? He looked behind him. Sometimes the whores who visited the camp seemed to smell like candy; did they sprinkle cinnamon on their clothes? They were miles and miles from whores. He crouched. He put his ear right on the ground and lay down, just feeling and not thinking. He heard nothing at first, just an indeterminate abstraction of sounds. He relaxed all his muscles, starting at his forehead, and with each one, shoulder, ass, thigh, heel, the sound began to give way into its parts.

There was someone walking. Not close by. He estimated: maybe the next tent. He swiveled microscopically and considered the sound again. It was someone who was walking incredibly slowly. Or perhaps someone who was hitting the ground very slowly. The space between the hits—he decided to count. One. Two. Three. Four. Five. Six. Seven. Eight.

"Aziz."

He felt electrocuted. He suppressed a scream.

"What the fuck are you doing?" Nazzar demanded.

"I feel sick," Aziz said, not far from truth this time.

"Fuck. Barfing?"

Aziz lay immobile. "Yes."

"Listen, Aziz."

Aziz could not believe this. He tried to imagine that he loved him, that he was a good friend from home. He did not want to radiate hatred. He willed himself to float a little in a happy state of loving Nazzar.

"My brother, I am not well," Aziz said weakly—or so he hoped.

"I will get help."

"No. No. I beg you. No."

"Aziz, you will feel better in the tent."

"Brother, sleep. I will lie here. It is not that bad."

"I cannot sleep."

Aziz made to retch and tried again. "Leave me, I beg you."

A voice from the tent said something.

"You wake others," Aziz said.

"You will come in soon?"

"I will. God willing."

"God willing."

Aziz heard the tent flap whoosh. He stayed on the ground, waiting for the sound he had heard earlier.

He waited. And it began again. He counted the intervals between what he believed were footsteps. Sometimes it was eight seconds. Then it was three. Then two. Then eight. He rested and counted and then he decided to pretend to piss, to see if he could see where this walking was. He rose up quickly, as if he had just come free from the tent flap. He looked around and of course saw nothing. The tents were walking height. All he saw was the one next to his, the one behind his, the one ahead of his. To walk onto the joining footpath would be madness. There was a significant chance of finding the night patrol. But he had not heard their footsteps, had he? They would have walked in intervals that were regular. They were *just walking*. No, they were not here. He felt a rush at his own deductions. It pushed him out onto the path. Pissing would still be his cover.

The moon was exceedingly small, and even though his eyes had adjusted to the twine of light by being outside for so long, he was shocked by the darkness the tents created. He could smell the canvas, its fabric faint petroleum. He was looking down a corridor whose ending vanished beyond his eyes' capacities. The air was silent.

Down far but not the last row, he saw a figure. But no, there was another figure. Or was he confusing the first; had he merely moved? But now there was a third, and as quickly as he had appeared, there came a fourth. He held his breath. Like the first sip of wine that warms, he knew it. This was no chance meeting.

If he moved, they were certain to see him. If he did not move, there was a possibility they might not see him, but it was a small one. If he could see them, they could see him. He was racing inside to accommodate his raging surprise. Not patrol. He felt a slick sensation in his stomach. His rectum went hot. He felt his bowels loosening, a wretched insufficiency of control. He pulled up on himself. And the memory busted into him then. He had caught his cousin with a magnifying glass. His cousin was holding it above an ant. It was noon. The ant began to smoke. First its fluttering kickers and antenna and filigree sparked. Then there was a mute flame—so small. What was left was a crinkle. And then his cousin found another one.

The reek of his intestines drifted away. He shook there, unmoving, and not quite still.

They moved toward one another.

Then they were gone down the side of a tent.

He dropped to the ground.

Still, still, still, still. He said this inside.

Still, still, still.

He didn't even want to put his ear to the ground.

They were upon him quickly.

One took his ankles. One took an arm. One took the other arm. Someone kicked his head, but softly.

They began to argue, in whispers.

"It is too early. He should not be here yet."

"Wait. This is not so easy."

"You are a woman."

"You are a whore."

"Think."

"He is DRS."

"He is not."

"Ask him his name."

Aziz lifted his head. "What if I belonged to Tahar?"

An informed gamble, but instantly someone said, "Prove this."

He had no idea.

"How many know of Ben Aknoun?" Aziz asked. He knew of this place from overheard conversations. It was where Aziz believed this Tahar, a DRS colonel, hid the shock troops of military intelligence. Perhaps these ones were they. Ben Aknoun was also rumored to be the stronghold for torture. By mentioning Ben Aknoun, they could think he had been there, tortured there, and was, like them, a militant.

Someone let go of his ankles.

"Wait. Wait."

"No one knows of Ben Aknoun!"

"I told you to wait."

Hands held his ankles again. It dawned on him: These must be the *irhabiya* that had attacked the nearby unit trying to defuse the land mines.

"Where is Ben Aknoun?"

He had no way to know where in Algiers this hidden DRS place could be. Even Benane did not know of Ben Aknoun. How could he? Benane was worthy. He had no truck with someone like Tahar. Tahar's men were the ones Aziz feared had taken his fellow soldiers or killed them, and it was Benane he had hoped to tell of it. He had pictured their rescue: Benane's gratitude. Their mothers' weeping joy.

Boy dreams. A brutal imagining, that was all there was now: imagining how these ones on his ankles think. Imagining how they talk. Imagining he was they. But which *they* were they? How to tell an *irhabi* from a secret soldier? He hardened his voice. As if they, if they doubted his answer, were the impostors, not he.

"On my mother's grave, I have sworn I cannot say."

They pulled him up. A bearded one clapped Aziz to his chest. Bearded: the sign of Islamists. They were *irhabiya*.

"Brother," said the bearded one.

"We feared you would not come," another said. "That slipping away—"

There was a crunching sound.

All of them dropped to the ground.

Aziz could see Nazzar straining to see, his hand on the tent flap. Had they come for Nazzar? It couldn't be. And yet, Nazzar had been checking if Aziz was awake. He had been aggravated by Aziz outside the tent. Yet none of these secret ones seemed to recognize Nazzar. Maybe they didn't know who they were looking for by sight.

The bearded one's face was near Aziz's face, their eyes were locked. The eyes asked the question—Aziz could feel it—*Who is this?* Aziz shook his head. As if he did not know this was Nazzar. The bearded one nodded. He moved his head right and at the same time lifted his smallest finger, almost imperceptibly.

They watched Nazzar turn to the right and hug along the tent's side in a crouch. He looked left and right but not behind him, where five men lay. He vanished behind the back of the tent. In time, he returned on the tent's other side, but now he stood upright. He made a tapping by knocking one fingernail on his right hand against another fingernail on his left. One, two, three, four, five.

The bearded one looked at Aziz again, asking something else. This time, Aziz nodded, as if to say this man was not to be trusted. The bearded one looked grateful. He put his tongue against his palate. One, two, three, four, five. Nazzar began walking toward the clicking from the bearded man's mouth.

When he was right upon them, the bearded one whistled low and soft.

"Here, here. On the ground."

Nazzar knelt, slowly, as if afraid the ground might break.

The knife they used was the length of a finger. The carotid was an instant bleeding out, but apparently not fast enough, because another knife caught the thin moon's light before Nazzar began his cry for help.

When he was completely still, all of them, like puppies, began to dig in the sandy dirt with their hands. No one spoke. They paddled in contented unison. Soon it was just enough to cover him, and they crawled away, five men slithering from the massing of tents.

Aziz was now Nazzar to these men; that much he understood. He had not known until now what fear would do to him. It was this coolness. Ahead, he saw what he thought were two tanks. One was gleaming. It was black without chrome. Then the smell of new rubber made him think it might be a van or truck. The other behind it was old. Its black had been ground by sun to gray. Its windows were down or gone.

The unit's camp was a distant formation under an unhelpful moon. All its tents from the overlook where Aziz now stood were one blackness on bone sand. As they made to get in the trucks, one of the men put his hand on Aziz's neck and said in his ear, *"Vite, mon frère, Benane attende."* Hurry, my brother, Benane waits. These ones meant to assassinate Benane, the Benane he had wanted to find all day.

Someone kicked his head, but softly. This one was barefoot. His feet were ulcerated and stank of festering. Aziz looked up. The trucks were gone. The wounded one stood over him. No uniform on this one. He was dressed like an Afghan. The sun-thickened skin on his face was the color of cedar. Aziz got up from the esparto grass he had slept in. He saw brushwood and juniper—it was possible he had been taken somewhere near the Aurès Mountains.

"As-salaam aleikum," the wounded one said.

"Wa aleikum as-salaam," Aziz said.

"Allah Karim," the wounded one said. He spoke with a solemnity Aziz had only heard from old men. *"Kaif halaq?"*

"Bi-khayr. Al hamdu-lillah," Aziz said. *"Bi-khayr."*

"Anaa Antar," he said. He looked at Aziz with intensity. Maybe this Antar had heard a description of Nazzar. Maybe he was thinking Aziz did not match this description. Aziz could have been wor-

ried, but instead he gave Antar a disembodied stare and said, *"Anaa Nazzar."*

They walked for days, and then the days were weeks. The man in front of Aziz was wounded. His balls were bleeding; when he walked, he fell down, and when he was down, he tried to get up again, because stopping was lying in blood. "Dog," the man said. "Dog," he said again. Aziz tried to carry him, but the man called him dog and pushed him away. Aziz wondered where the man had been. Was it right to wonder? Up above the sun shrank.

Night was coming. He knew this, and yet he wished he would be burned into ash, before anything else. They had a woman.

The mouth, the saliva, the pulse of the lip under her other lip.

Someone had torn it. There is no *e* in the language.

So say *evil,* they told her. Say *evil.*

She was lost in *alif* and *wa* and then the sun made his left knee into reddened raw.

Kill her, go ahead.

She wanted nothing but to show herself, so that is her way.

One of them put his thumb on one part of her, then the heel of his palm into her softness below the carriage of her throat. *Literally: A wife possessing them.*

A prostration is to be performed here.

He leveled himself in body and mind.

She died easily, as it turned out. Antar began with his knife to cut back her hair between her legs. She was still breathing, because she jumped. He took the knife in her, cutting left and right, and then up, but still she would jump. So he put his boot on her mouth and, covering her nose, stomped once; pushing the knife again, she jumped, so he stomped harder; and still, after the knife, she jumped, so he played with the knife, feeling the jittering of her.

Then we took vengeance upon them; so look into how was the end of them who cried lies.

Still, she was not still.

Someone had a shovel. He put the blunt of it on her collarbone. Her eyes were open and she said, *All merciful, all merciful.* He pushed into the sand. The head came in one part, away from the shoulder. And still she said *all merciful.* They began to push the knife into her stomach and out through her under her heart.

The jitter stopped. The eyes stopped open.

16

Ghazi, without Aziz, went back to the U-Stor-It. He hid and watched. Rafik and Kamal sometimes came together, sometimes separately, but always in a Brighton Moving and Storage truck. Others came in a white Econoline van. Once Rafik brought beer boxes. Sometimes there were metal drums like the one Aziz and Ghazi had lifted like a plastic cup. Sometimes there were wardrobe boxes. There was no sign of suitcases.

Ghazi wanted Aziz to come with him. To be lookout, so Ghazi could open boxes, pry apart containers. Aziz turned it over in his mind. Not to know was not to be responsible. To be loyal was to not try to know. He must always act as if Heather did not exist. These rules had been good the last two years. But new facts were plain and stout before him. Heather did exist. There was a U-Stor-It. Something wrong or nothing wrong—or many things in between—was in it.

Why not do what Ghazi wanted? Since they had made their confessions, Aziz realized Ghazi's motives were better than his own.

Djamila's betrayal was every reason and more to leave home. It had carried away Aziz's last doubts. Ghazi was not DRS sent. His father may have been military intelligence, a DRS loyalist, but he was mostly to be condemned for how he treated his own son. Soft hens, Ghazi had called DRS. Ghazi knew nothing of DRS if he could call them that.

The plan was complicated. They would have to wait until Rafik and Heather, still in their Ghazi-made bliss, had one of their Saturday dates. They debated involving Mourad. Ghazi argued for it. A stun gun was good. Mourad meant police were certain, countered Aziz. He has changed, said Ghazi. We lose control, insisted Aziz. Ghazi conceded. Maybe just take Mourad's stun gun. Especially if Mourad was at Reach that night. Aziz agreed.

Ghazi bought two cell phones. He made two copies of the key hidden in the aquarium and gave one to Aziz. Ghazi would enter the unit. Aziz, down at the main entrance in a rental car, was to call if he saw the Econoline van or the Brighton Moving truck. If some vehicle Aziz did not recognize went by and Ghazi's key was confiscated by Kamal or one of his cohorts, they would still have Aziz's key for another attempt later. And this time Ghazi had bobby pins, razor blades, packing tape, pliers, crowbar, and three flashlights.

For weeks Rafik and Heather seemed to go only to the movies. And two hours was not enough time. When it wasn't movies, it was the bedroom door locked, the expected sounds. "You have made them love too much," Aziz complained to Ghazi. "It is bed, bed, bed." Why no dinners out and *then* a movie? Why no more getaway to Maine? Aziz was a jump rope in a schoolyard. Ghazi counseled patience.

The night finally came in late October. It was also a night Mourad went to Reach. The stun gun was tucked in Ghazi's waist, Aziz was parked by the entrance in a white subcompact, and the first downfall of a storm was spattering the windshield.

"The rain is best," Ghazi said on the cell phone, from inside the storage unit. "Not a good night for loading."

"What do you see?"

"No suitcases."

"Barrels?"

"None."

"None?"

"Boxes. Boxes. Boxes."

"Beer boxes?"

"Fuck."

"What?"

"Stun gun."

"What?"

"Nothing."

"Your dick. You shot it."

"Cousin, I call you back."

Aziz pushed a button on the phone and put it on the dashboard. He considered turning on the radio but worried it might distract. It would be risky to run the engine; he was the only one in the lot, and the exhaust would draw attention. He slumped down to see if he could still see the entrance. He could, but not all of it.

It was not really an entrance, it was a turn. There was a highway, not much of a shoulder, then a strip of graveled tar instead of grass. After that, a speed bump. Not many cars on this suburb highway. He shifted his ass. No, he could not stay down. Too hard to see, really. He sat up and molded himself to the seat. After a time he realized he was thinking about Rafik, and Ghazi finding chemicals, and, yes, he was staring at the entrance but not seeing it. He focused. A car on the highway went by, fast, a blue one maybe. Orange was the color here. The U-Stor-It had a squat office with backlit orange walls. The roof was orange. The pole sign, lights on, shined orange.

When the cell phone chirped later, Aziz jumped and something slid to the floor. He fumbled. He felt his lap. Behind the seat. The phone's tweeting seemed to come from the steering wheel. The dashboard! That was where he put it. It was still there. He pressed the button Ghazi had shown him. He put the phone to his ear. Nothing. He tried again. Nothing. It was dark, quite dark. Had he hit the wrong button twice? He tried one he hoped was far from the wrong one. Still nothing.

The phone had stopped ringing. He brought it close to his face. This was impossible. There was not nearly enough light. He had to open the door. There was a handle but it was sticking. No, that was part of the armrest. Maybe start the car. The keys should be in his pocket. The ring started again. Fuck the keys. His fingers found the handle and the door jutted out. With the light came rain, but not that much. It must be blowing from the north, hitting hardest on the windshield. Finally he could see the buttons. There was the right one: TALK. He pushed TALK.

"Okay, bogeyman." Ghazi was almost laughing.

"You okay?"

"Me? Yeah. But you. What's wrong with your phone?"

"Nothing. I could not see it."

"I gave you a flashlight."

He had. It was right there on the passenger seat.

"I forgot."

"Okay, uncle. Okay. Look, I opened some."

"And?"

"Cigarettes."

"That—that makes sense."

"And Batman," Ghazi said. He was laughing.

"Batman?"

"Lots of little plastic Batmans. Thousands of them."

"What is a Batman?"

"For kids. Toys."

"Toys. How is there money in toys?"

"I crushed one with the crowbar, just to make sure. There was nothing. Pure plastic. Solid. I have cigarettes for you. Cartons. You smoke Marlboro?

"Not Rafik Marlboros."

"Cousin, last half hour I open thirty boxes. Batman. Cigarettes. That's it."

Aziz looked at the windshield. The rain was pelting it. Wriggles of the parking lot were all he could see. He realized he had not been watching, not even half watching, during the phone ordeal.

"Ghazi."

"Uh-huh."

"I better come up there."

"Why? Stay there."

"The rain. Hard to see."

"A truck? A van? You would see them."

"I . . . I do not think so."

"Relax."

"I will just drive up there. To make sure."

"But that is when they *will* be at the entrance. And you—gone."

"Ghazi. I have a bad feeling."

Aziz turned for a better look out the driver-side window. There were only a few drops on it. The way the rain was falling, this was the way to keep watch. Ghazi was saying ". . . the thing is . . ." when the Brighton truck's high beams rose on the speed bump at the entrance. They swept like searchlights in an arc across the parking lot until they rested on the subcompact, exposing Aziz's narrow face a bleaching white. He was blinded. He ducked.

"Ghazi. The truck. The truck."

"The truck will not come. It is pouring."

"It has. Just now. I swear it."

"At the entrance?"

"Yes. Yes. I am here. It is here."

"Oh, my cock."

Aziz peeked and saw the truck lumber past the turn for the driveway that went to the storage units.

"It is not turning," he said.

"Not turning?"

It was almost at Aziz's parking space.

"Leave. Leave now," he told Ghazi.

"How? Get up here. The back entrance. Like we said."

"Me. Me. He is after me."

"What?"

Kamal jerked open the door. He grabbed Aziz by the arm and pulled him into the storm. He was screaming, but gusts swallowed most of his words. He pushed Aziz down on the subcompact's hood. "Answer me," he was saying. He put his mouth on Aziz's ear. "What the fuck are you doing here?"

They had not thought of what Aziz would say. Ghazi had only worked out his own lines. He planned to claim a friend gave him this key and this address and asked him to get a box from the unit and bring it to him. The friend swore him to secrecy. Rafik would find out eventually, but Ghazi would have gone to Mourad by then. Explosives, stolen property—confiscated. Police notified. Rafik on the run. Instead, it was only cigarettes and toys. And Aziz with no story.

"An hour from East Boston! An hour!" Kamal was screaming.

Aziz felt himself cool. His mind arranged itself into smooth grooves.

Kamal lived in East Boston.

Kamal was an hour from East Boston.

Just like Aziz.

"What the fuck is wrong with you?" Aziz screamed into Kamal's face.

"What the fuck!"

"Fuck you!"

"Fuck you!"

"I have a fucking storage unit here!" Aziz spit the words.

"In the parking lot?"

"I was waiting for the rain to let up!"

Aziz felt Kamal's brain starting to go into reverse.

"What the fuck are *you* doing here?" Aziz shouted.

Kamal let go. He pushed wet strands from his ponytail out of his face. He was saying something the wind sucked away. He started toward his truck.

"You stole Rafik's moving truck!" Aziz hollered.

. . .

For weeks, they waited for Rafik to say something. Ghazi hoped Kamal had been at the U-Stor-It behind Rafik's back. Maybe he is cheating Rafik, doing his own deals. If he tells Rafik of you, he told Aziz, how does he explain why *he* was there? Aziz hoped Kamal believed Aziz had a unit at the U-Stor-It. One bad scene worried Aziz. Say Kamal tells Rafik that Aziz was there. Kamal and Rafik try to figure out what Aziz being there means. To help Rafik figure it out, Kamal tells about Aziz yelling about the stolen Brighton Moving truck. Rafik realizes. Why hasn't Aziz tattled on Kamal? Rafik would know Aziz had been playacting.

Ghazi now feared the U-Stor-It. "Too close," he said. "Over what? Toys." They recounted the night many times. At first Aziz could not understand how Ghazi had taped back all the boxes. Ghazi explained he had sealed each one almost as soon as he opened it, to make a fast escape easier. He had tripped and slid down the back exit on the wet macadam with his trash bags of gear. The crowbar broke through one, spilling bobby pins, pliers, and Mourad's stun gun. He saw lights coming behind him and ran. When it got dark again, he crept around the chain-link fence until he reached the front parking lot. The Brighton Moving truck was gone. The subcompact was there. When Aziz told him what he had said to Kamal, how Kamal had driven off, Ghazi was amazed Aziz had not panicked. Aziz could see Ghazi had trouble reconciling the cell phone bumbler with the quick thinker who scared Kamal.

There was one other mystery. Mourad never mentioned his missing stun gun. Ghazi had never found it on the wet driveway. Then one day Aziz saw it, or one just like it, in their bedroom next to the billy club.

Kamal was scared, but not about Aziz. Aziz could wait. Kamal's girlfriend had flown to São Paulo in May and never called. Kamal by June had put her social security number to work. He succeeded in spending more than $250,000 over the summer, with the help of an experienced identity thief of Guatemalan heritage named Freia.

Credit under Freia's capable hands extended and extended. Treasury agents came in navy blazers to arrest Freia at dawn a day after Kamal's U-Stor-It encounter with Aziz. Freia, in federal custody, told them about Kamal.

Kamal was easy to find. He had been greedy. He had been sloppy. He scolded himself as the cuffs closed on his wrists. But in time he got another chance. It came from a treasury agent named Hank Bridges.

17

Aziz, always the busboy, usually the dishwasher, now was a waiter. Ghazi had wheedled John Hill like an old woman. "Give him a try. . . . A fighter, this one. . . . Look at his hands. This man is a waiter." One day in November, Hill agreed. There was no raise. That would come if Aziz did well. With Ghazi in Hill's ear, Aziz felt luck was with him.

If only Ghazi would let the asylum thing rest. On the way to Del Fuegos, on the way back, it was Charlie Stone, Charlie Stone, Charlie Stone. The third waitress, who was still Ghazi's girlfriend, who had introduced Ghazi to Charlie, was Aziz's shadow. "Charlie's good people," she said to Aziz, while they waited for their margaritas from the slow young bartender. "Charlie's been asking about you," she said, when lunch was quiet on a Monday. "Charlie wanted you to have this," she said, pressing an envelope into Aziz's hand as he headed out the door for the bus and home.

It was a conspiracy. Mourad said applying for asylum was the thing to do. Heather, prodded by Ghazi, took Aziz aside on a Saturday morning and said, "Lahouari, he can't apply. Ghazi says you,

you suffered, you can. They're still after you. Mourad was telling me it hasn't been easy for you. You go home—" She moved a finger across her neck in a line.

Aziz explained how Charlie Stone had no secretary, only a phone on the wall and a desk with no papers. "You work at a law firm," he said. "This—is this a lawyer?"

She looked worried. "Don't go through him," she said. "I can help you get the forms. I go by the federal building all the time for work. I'll help you fill them out."

Lahouari, coming from the bathroom the next morning, said, "They tell you asylum. Listen."

Hamid that night said, "Make the wrong done to you help you."

Ali the next morning said, "If I could, I would try it."

Rafik passed Aziz in the kitchen, sat next to him on the sofa in the living room, bumped his arm in the hallway coming out of the bathroom. He had nothing to say. All he asked a few days later when Aziz was leaving for work was, "So, you closing up Del Fuegos tonight?"

"Go home," Ghazi said.

"I want to wait." Aziz was putting Sweet-n-Low in the table holders.

"You take the bus now, home before one. Stay with me, two."

"We have to talk. This asylum. Charlie."

Ghazi shrugged. As if he had not been banging that hammer. "You need sleep," he said.

"Hill told *me* to close up," Aziz said.

"What does Hill know who closes? You. Me. Me. You. The same."

When Ghazi set the alarm and locked the three deadbolts, it was already two. The streetlights were flashing red. It would be a long wait for the bus at this hour. It was cold too. Another November in Boston. He started walking toward the stop. He smelled a cigarette. Had Aziz come back? He looked up. There was a man smoking on the bench at the bus stop. He was looking directly at Ghazi. He was in shirtsleeves.

"You have a woman?"

The man in shirtsleeves was driving. Ghazi was in the passenger seat.

"Hell, yes."

"Free Boston pussy makes you forget Allah real quick."

"Free. That is the thing. Free."

"You gotta pay with your left ball back home, eh?"

"Absolutely."

"I don't get it."

"It is like this. They have mothers. And the mothers tell them, This is the way. And we have fathers. And they tell us, This is the way. For fathers and mothers back to time beginning, it has been this way."

"Much as I'd like to talk about how pussy gets managed around the globe, I have a few things I need to go over." They were on a highway now. Ghazi did not know which one. The black Expedition was showroom clean, and for long stretches no one else was on the road.

The man in shirtsleeves slammed on the brakes. The seat belt around Ghazi snapped tight and he was crushed, fighting for breath, by the dashboard. All he could think at first was that his body must have broken so badly that he was in parts. He could hear laughter. He tasted blood. He tried to bring his hand to his face, but he was trapped between the seat and the windshield.

"Don't try to move. Just makes it worse." The man in shirtsleeves chuckled. "Never seen an air bag, I guess. You're getting a first-class introductory lecture."

Ghazi realized he could open his eyes. Through the windshield, he could see they were stopped in the center of five lanes. The highway was deserted.

"Oh. By the way. You're in trouble."

Ghazi tried to speak, but his breath was not enough for it.

"Not much to say, I see."

The man turned on the radio. He hummed along with a song. Then the weather report. Lows in the teens, chance of flurries in the morning. Another song.

Once before in his life, Ghazi had been through a wait like this. The sickest of the sick liked these waits. They wanted your fear to root in you like a burning stick. Your helplessness was their honey. They could suck on it for a long time. He had thought in some cases it was better to succumb, to plead crazily, because that was what they wanted and expected and had crafted for you to do. To remain inside himself, untouchable, serene, was to invite rage and worse. He considered the possibilities. This man, who was obviously some kind of secret police, could kill him, because Ghazi, asylum application or not, was an illegal, a nonperson. This shirtsleeve one liked very much that this was so. Ghazi was certain he had killed many, though he could not do it too often, or his ability to keep doing it would be threatened. So the question was, when was the last time this one had killed another such as Ghazi? If it was long ago, Ghazi was soon to be joining his predecessor. If it was recent, Ghazi might be spared. Now he was singing with the radio. He had turned up the volume.

but on the other hand
is a golden band
that reminds me of someone
who would not understand

Ghazi decided it was safe to look. The man's eyes were closed, his chin jerking in the air as he sang. This was outside anything Ghazi knew. This man had no interest in Ghazi's pinned chest and blood-wet mouth. He didn't enjoy his suffering. What was he thinking? Ghazi felt a needle of panic. The weather came on the radio. The man pressed a button, then again. Another song came on. After a bit, he turned up the volume.

like a circle in a spiral
like a wheel within a wheel
never ending or beginning
on an ever-spinning reel
like a snowball down a mountain
or a carnival balloon
like a carousel that's turning
running rings around the moon
and the world is like an apple
whirling silently in space
like the circles that you find
in the windmills of your mind

It was so loud the windows were vibrating. Ghazi tried to look to the other side of the highway. How could it be that not one other car was here?

like a tunnel that you follow
to a tunnel of its own
down a hollow to a canyon
where the sun can never show
like a door that keeps revolving
in a half-forgotten dream
or the ripples from the pebbles
someone tosses in a stream

Ghazi began to cry. Quietly at first, the tears came. His chest had been replaced by pain.

where's the jingle in your pocket
where's the jangle in your head
why did summer go so quickly
was it something that you said
lovers walk along the shore
leave their footprints in the sand
is the sound of distant drumming
just the fingers of your hand

pictures hanging in a hallway
and the fragment of a song
half-remembered names of faces
but to whom do they belong

The radio announcer's voice came on. The man turned off the radio. Ghazi's heavings filled the car.

"Hey. Hey. Let's be reasonable."

Ghazi heard only the music gone.

"Shut the fuck up." The man took him by the hair and looked him in the eye. "Shut the fuck up."

Ghazi pulled up on himself. There was some sound from his chest and the back of his throat, subsiding.

"Your buddy Kamal sang a very interesting song for me the other day. About how you're a big man. Identity thief. Trafficking in fake IDs. Credit card fraud. But the best thing about you? You're a stowaway. You don't exist. No record of you coming here. No record of you leaving the shithole you crawled out of. So basically, this here Hank Bridges, United States Treasury agent, Secret Service Financial Crimes Division, is in sole charge of your pissant existence. I'm expecting that right about now, it's sinking in just how worthless I consider your continued habitation of this planet." He paused. "Thoughts? Recommendations?"

Ghazi swallowed.

"Excellent. We are off to a ripsnorting start."

Still he held Ghazi's hair in his hand. Ghazi tried to look at his eyes but not into them.

"Since you owe your existence to me, you are the man who will do what I say. You will wipe your ass with barbed wire if I say so. You will cut off your pencil dick with a butter knife if I say so. Clear?"

"Yes."

"All right then. All right."

He dropped Ghazi's head. He pulled a knife out of his boot. He began cutting away the thin nylon bag pinning Ghazi. Puffs of powder like cornstarch settled on Ghazi's bloody lips and chin.

"You look like shit." Hank Bridges balled up the bag and threw it in the backseat.

Ghazi did nothing.

"Now. Tomorrow. I pick you up at eight. We start talking about what you need to do to get out of this pickle. Kamal, see, he's all straight and clear now. He gave me you. You give me some of your associates. Everybody's happy."

"Yes."

"I know where you live. I know where you work. You run, and your mug, your prints, your dick size, and every last name you have ever used, stole, or even thought about pilfering will be at every airport, border crossing, and falafel stand from sea to shining sea. Now get the fuck out of my truck."

Ghazi ran toward where they had come. When he finally looked behind him, the Expedition was gone.

The highway was empty, he learned, because it was under construction, and when he reached the barricades, the signs were draped and hidden. It wasn't until he ran down a ramp and onto another highway that he saw where he was. Downtown Boston was in the distance, and East Boston was another long way.

Aziz woke up thinking about asylum. It was not even six, and Mourad was up for work. Aziz could smell the syrupy coffee his brother liked to make.

Aziz glanced at the blue bucket when he walked into the kitchen. The leak was off today. There had been no rain since the U-Stor-It night. "Brother," Mourad began. "The asylum. My green card, it gives you a 'legal family member.' Stable. Working. My supervisor will write a letter. And you have a safe job now. Ghazi watches for you."

"Mourad, that Charlie Stone, he is not a lawyer."

"What is he then?"

"Con man. Or police."

"What would police want with Ghazi?"

"He's illegal. Stowaway like me."

"Aziz, there are ten million like that in this country. They have no time to watch all of them."

His army tour—it had bent him, Aziz thought. Mourad was right. No one here cared or watched or noticed him, never had.

They heard the front door, one of the locks. Then the second lock. Mourad screwed up his face in a question. They were pushing back their chairs to see when Ghazi came into the kitchen. The blood on his face was a scrim the color of mud. His lips' deep cuts had clotted and frozen and broken, then bled and clotted again. He started pulling off his ski jacket, undoing his shirt buttons. His chest was a black purple where the air bag had exploded against him. Aziz shuddered. It was as if someone or something from his army tour had walked continents and found him.

Mourad was helping Ghazi off with his things. "I need hot water and I need towels," Mourad said to Aziz. "Here, here, sit here." Mourad guided Ghazi to a chair. He cleared the kitchen table and put the blue bucket on the floor.

"Get me clothes," Ghazi said.

"The hospital is what you need," Aziz said, turning on the hot water in the sink.

"You do not understand," Ghazi said.

Something in his voice halted them.

"Get everybody up," he said slowly.

"Everybody?" Aziz said. He meant, Even Rafik?

"Yes. Everybody. There is not much time."

Aziz woke the Three from their living room mattresses. Lahouari looked at him with questions, Hamid and Ali too. "Hurry. Hurry," he said.

They stretched and yawned into the kitchen, wearing blankets like capes. Heather was in a bathrobe, her hair in tangles. She was dipping a towel in a bowl of soapy water and daubing Ghazi's face. Aziz's eyes flew around the little room. Where was Rafik? As if he heard his thoughts, Ghazi said, "Rafik never came home last night."

Heather's hands were unsteady. Aziz noticed tears down one cheek.

"Last night," Ghazi started. He spoke English for Heather's sake. "Aziz was to close Del Fuegos. I told him go home, get some sleep, I do this."

Aziz remembered Rafik. *So, you closing up Del Fuegos tonight?*

"Outside Del Fuegos, a man waits." Ghazi continued. "He tells me he is secret service."

Ghazi looked to Mourad, who looked puzzled but said, "Did he say he was federal?"

"I did not hear that word."

Mourad shook his head. Heather looked as if she was searching for an answer too but couldn't find any.

"Okay. This secret service, this police." Hamid urged Ghazi on.

"He says, 'Please step into my vehicle, sir.' " Ghazi imitated an official voice. "He takes me to that highway they are building, and"—Ghazi motioned to his face and chest—"does this.

"He says a snitch says I am a credit card fraud. Illegal. Stowaway. Now I must snitch also to fix my problem."

The U-Stor-It. Rafik and Kamal had done this. Rafik thought it would be Aziz, not Ghazi, closing Del Fuegos. Aziz remembered boasting about the new duties he had, using the register, taking credit cards, closing up. "My first night to put on the alarm is tonight," he had said. This was their revenge. This was to get Aziz deported, so their schemes could grow. Ghazi had walked into the rigging meant for him.

"This police comes here this morning," Ghazi said. He looked at the oven clock. "In one hour forty-five minutes."

"Aaberdi," Lahouari whispered. So little time.

"Wait. Wait," Mourad said. "Who is this snitch?"

Ghazi looked at Aziz. Aziz shrugged. There was no reason not to tell.

"Kamal," Ghazi said.

"Kamal?" asked Heather, her voice nasal. "The Kamal we lived with? Who hit me? That Kamal?"

"Who is Kamal?" Mourad said over her.

"He was before you," Aziz said to his brother. "The first place, in Everett. There were many there. Kamal hit Heather with a chair. Hit me also. Kamal is—"

"Violent," Heather finished.

"He is scheming with Rafik," Aziz said, using Arabic so he could explain quickly to Mourad. "They have been selling stolen goods. For over a year now."

"You knew this? And didn't tell me?" Mourad turned to Aziz, then Ghazi.

"We were not sure," Ghazi said. "We tried to find out. Kamal last month discovered Aziz trying to find out."

"How?" Mourad was not pacified.

"Tell me," Heather kept interrupting. "In English. In English."

"There is no time for this," Ghazi said.

Mourad dropped his shoulders.

"This is the thing," said Ghazi in English. "Eight, this morning. This police, this Hank Bridges, comes to take me. I won't be here. But if I am not, he will take everyone."

Aziz understood Rafik not coming home last night. Rafik would never come home. Aziz looked at Heather. Tears still, no sobbing.

"He will not take me or Heather," Mourad said. "But everyone else is a stowaway. And he will take them."

"I will go to another city," Aziz said quickly. "The rest of you: away for a day, then back."

Ghazi shook his head. "He will not go that easy."

"The thing to do is Canada," Mourad said, after a moment. He was back in Arabic. "And a bus, that is the thing. At the border, Ghazi, you ask for asylum and use your real name. They won't be looking for your name. They will be looking for Aziz's name. Aziz, you take a bus to New York. There are many Arabs and Muslims there; it is easy to get lost in them. Ghazi, at the border, you say you were in the Algerian military—bring your army papers, your real passport—and say *irhabiya* killed your family and you fled. In Canada, they will let you in. If you do this by the end of today, Hank Bridges will not have had time to figure out you are not Aziz, and your true name will not be on the list. You cannot go to airports. Airports have too many checks. Hank Bridges may even go right to the airport."

Ghazi nodded. "Good. That is good. Aziz and I will go to the bus terminal. And the rest?" He looked at the Three.

"We will find places. There is always someone."

"There are five from Arzew in Revere," Lahouari said. "They will take us."

Mourad looked at his brother. Aziz wondered if he remembered saying, "You are hunted." That night back home, the rest of the family was frantic. Mourad had been granite cold.

Mourad hung his head for a moment and Aziz saw the place where his hair had already thinned to a fuzz. It touched him lower than tears to see it. A rasp of grief came from Mourad. "You," he said in Arabic to Aziz, "for you to have this. Just as good was walking toward you."

Then Mourad glanced around and into the hall.

"We have to make this place look as if only two live here—the American girl, Heather, and the green card Algerian, Mourad," he said.

"But it is a two-bedroom!" exclaimed one of the Three, who thought no one would believe such wasting of space.

"This is not a problem," Mourad said. "We will be lovers," he said to Heather. "We met at Reach. The other room is the guest room. I want these mattresses and the rest on its way to Revere before eight." Mourad pulled out his wallet. He counted out several bills. "Take this," he said to Aziz.

They began moving.

18

Hank Bridges sized up Heather, this girl answering the door at 6A Brooks Street. But all too fast there was Mourad, his boots a shellacked black. He was wearing a large jacket that said AIRPORT SECURITY in white block letters, and his angle of a jaw looked as if it needed to be unhooked and unlatched before he spoke.

"Can I help you?" Mourad said.

Bridges put his hand up to flash his badge, but Mourad put a finger inside the billfold, tilted the cover back up, and read it—slowly—making Bridges hold it for several beats too long. Mourad tilted his head and withdrew his index finger. He raised his eyebrows. His eyelids still looked heavy; they were hoods, really.

"I'm looking for an Aziz Arkoun," Bridges said. "Please step aside."

Mourad stepped aside. He said nothing. He put his arm around Heather, who was just behind him.

Bridges walked to the back of the apartment into the bathroom and pulled down the shower curtain. Then he was in the bedroom, which was in fact Aziz's bedroom but was now adorned with a ruffled yellow bedspread. He upended the bed and it rested on its side while Mourad and Heather sat in the living room. There was nothing in the closet, but he tried to kick in the sliding plywood doors and they made a splintering crack: once, twice. Then it was Heather and Rafik's room, which was now Heather and Mourad's room. There the closet was crammed full, the doors open, and Bridges pulled dresses and skirts and pants off all the hangers, *whoosh,* in a destructive abandon that reminded Heather of ripping paper off packages. They heard him pulling up the greasy, flattened wall-to-wall carpet from the floor and pulling it, like a giant canoe, out of the bedroom and into the living room where they sat, holding hands.

Bridges pulled the carpet past them in the living room and out the front door. It grabbed onto things and toppled other things as he went. Heather wanted to get up and look out the window to see what in the world he was doing with the carpet, but Mourad whispered *no*. Mourad could not believe they would be so lucky as to have this be all that Bridges would do. He concentrated on reminding himself to say as little as possible when he came back. Those who talked too much, he knew from work, always talked, after painful-to-hear meanders, into lies.

Bridges, outside, was wadding up the carpet into the back of the Expedition. He pulled out a black metal shelf and took down a suitcase from which he got a camera lodged in gray foam. He photographed the carpet. He photographed the front door of 6A Brooks, the hallway, the bathroom, the bedrooms. He was about to photograph the kitchen when the phone rang. It so surprised him, and Mourad and Heather, that Bridges dropped the camera and Mourad instinctively pulled his stun gun. When it rang again, Heather was breathing so fast she felt Bridges must be able to hear her, and she put her hands over her face to make herself quiet. Mourad had almost slid into the kitchen with a gun pointed at a police officer. He was so shocked by his own self-destructive foolishness that he deflated, mind and body, and clung—as he had as a schoolboy to the teacher who once protected him from a parent intent on caning him—to Heather, who, he was unhappy to realize, felt like a single thin leaf.

Would Bridges answer? Someone, somehow was calling, they just knew, to ask for Aziz. Their thoughts pushed and shoved against one another and fear kicked up around them.

Bridges picked up the phone. They heard it. It was suddenly elaborately quiet. It seemed at least one hour passed between his "Yes," and his reply, which was, "Who? A who?" And then they heard their rescue, because he said next, "Oh, Heather." He walked into the living room and looked at them. Mourad was cowering, still not recovered from his dread of his runaway instincts.

"You Heather?"

She nodded.

"Talk to this person then."

She got up like a woman in a home for the elderly and made a dazed shamble toward the kitchen. Her departure woke Mourad into a greater insecurity. He simply sat. He heard her say, "I know I'm late. I apologize. . . . Yes. I'm sick. A little sick. But I will come in. . . . No, not that sick. Just sick a little."

Bridges considered Mourad. Here was a man with a job, a job that required a background check. He was suited up to head to work. Here was his gash, all set for work, and work calling because she was late. There was no sign that anyone else but these two, who worked, who could afford this shithole, lived here. And how had he thought that Aziz Arkoun lived here anyway? From that cocksucker Kamal. He suddenly saw that his own appetite to keep this off the books, to not check anything on this Aziz because he was not sure he would not end up wanting to waste him, had led to this mistake with two people who, he could see, were respectful of law enforcement, put up no argument, did want to see the badge but made no fuck-assed shit about warrants. Any guy who worked airport security knew that mentioning warrants was for people who were going to be very fucked over, very soon. So it all tracked. The girl was about what a guy like this guy could get, this guy was on the right side of things, and shitheel Kamal was going to pay. He clapped Mourad on the back.

"So you work over there with Miller and those other losers." To his discomfort, Mourad didn't respond. He tried again. "It's just like some scumbag to give the address of a cop who hassled him at the airport. This is why they need to crawl up the asses of those statehouse donkeys and get all our addresses sewn up shut. I mean, any dickbrain doing card fraud knows how to get an address. Shit."

As if through a curtain, Mourad felt the hand on his back. He completely misread these tries at conciliation. He heard insults, he heard cursing. Here was how it ended, he thought. Here was how. He had no idea how he was going to feel, but he knew one thing; he was thankfully beginning to feel numb.

"Miss," Bridges said, looking at Heather as she walked in, "I owe you an apology. This has been a terrible mistake."

It was the sound of Heather's voice that brought Mourad back. She was saying, "What? What did you? Are we? I—and he—"

"Heather," Mourad breathed. She really should not talk. Might set him off.

"It's cool, really," Bridges said.

Mourad awoke a little to the possibility that Bridges was being friendly.

"She's shook up is all," Bridges said. "I don't count it as disrespect."

"She shouldn't be asking questions," Mourad said, feeling his way into his role.

"Ah, that's Miller-think. That motherfucker makes you guys into some kind of commando unit. I told him he was crazy."

"You know Miller," Mourad said, as if he revered his ultimate boss Captain James T. Miller, whom he did not know, had never met.

"Miller and I came up together. Listen. You—uh, the carpet, I just have to take that to the lab, no real reason, just dotting *i*'s and what-have-you."

Mourad nodded. He had recovered himself sufficiently to remember his original charge to himself to say as little as possible.

"I'm not even gonna write this one up; I mean, take down your names, and the whole thing. The carpet—I mean that will go under a number with an unnamed CS."

Confidential Source. Mourad nodded again.

"Good, then."

Mourad nodded.

"So. I'll just let you people go about your business."

Mourad and Heather nodded.

"No hard feelings."

"No," Mourad said.

"No," Heather said.

Aziz and Ghazi said little on the bus to the bus. Aziz had a shopping bag and one suitcase. Ghazi had nothing. He looked awful. The wounds were behind a ski mask, but a cut on his eyelid too small to bandage was seeping. Passengers tried to sneak looks at them. Aziz knew his expression was the one that made him look like a crazed lying pickpocket. He guessed Ghazi was thinking something close to what he was thinking—that better, upward, was over. Aziz's mistakes tumbled in his mind. He should not have gone to Rafik at the start. Having gone, he should have left after weeks, not stayed for years. He should have never visited the U-Stor-It the first time and certainly should have left Rafik after he did. He could have told Mourad about Rafik. He should have ignored Ghazi about going back to the U-Stor-It. And he should have never fucked with the belligerent Kamal. Having provoked him that night in the rain, he should have left Brooks Street the next day.

Ghazi was not blameless, but that was hard for Aziz to see, looking at his gummy eye and raw red lips, injuries he had saved Aziz from by kindness, his everyday constant concern for how Aziz was doing. Aziz needed a better job, so Ghazi pestered the boss. Aziz was tired, so Ghazi closed Del Fuegos. Aziz imagined John Hill at the lunch shift, and no sign of them.

. . .

Mourad believed Bridges was out there watching, or, more likely, had sent someone to watch. He looked everywhere when he came home from work and when he left for work, and he could see nothing, but he knew these were not baboons like back home that you could see plain. These were Americans, and they knew how to watch without bringing attention. They may have even bought the house across the street—he had heard from talk at work that the FBI did this, that they bought houses and waited and watched for *years*.

He insisted Heather sleep in the same bed with him. They could be watching. Or, worse, when Bridges was in the bedroom that morning, he could have planted a tiny camera. Heather said Mourad had seen too many movies, and there was no way she would crawl into his bed, no way at all. She allowed that it would be best to go into the other room only at night, and only with all the lights off. Then one day she came back from work and said a girl who worked for one of the lawyers had a case where somebody, she wasn't sure if it was the FBI or state troopers, had in fact used "listening devices and micro-cameras" and they had *everything* on tape that was said or done by these people, who were just trying to make a living and were not really criminals, just doing what everybody else does anyway.

So Heather slept in the same bed as Mourad.

At first Aziz tried to live alone, away from Muslims or Arabs. He rented a mean room without a bathroom, except for one shared with a Nigerian and a Chinese. The Nigerian spoke English, but he was not well. He had some kind of disease, and every time Aziz went into the bathroom the stench from him was overpowering. It was not puke or shit, it was something worse. The Chinese spoke no English. Every so often Aziz would look at him when they passed in the hall and try to say with his eyes how worried he was. But the Chinese never once looked up. Then one day he was gone. A little later the Nigerian was found dead outside the front door of the building.

Aziz, who had only a radio and an extra pair of shoes—everything else had been stolen—put them in a grocery bag and took the subway to Coney Island Avenue. He had gathered by his second week in Brooklyn that Pakistanis lived there. He could disappear among them or perhaps find others—Moroccans? Tunisians?—who could at least help him find a job. The money Mourad had pushed in his hand—about a hundred dollars—was running out.

On Coney Island Avenue there were strollers and laundromats and notaries and cell-phone stores, and while most everyone spoke Urdu, enough spoke Arabic, and a few had some English. He began to sit in the cell-phone store near Newkirk, and the men, all Pakistani, allowed him to pass the day there and even sleep under one of the desks at night, until they heard after a few weeks that just around the corner there was an apartment that might come available. They sold almost everything: faxes, translations, phone cards, Internet access, pagers, overnight delivery, post office boxes, couriers, paralegal services, real estate advice. Aziz made some dollars helping an old man sell books in front of the store, and then, one day, a man came in and said, "My brother needs someone at his store in Flatbush." So Aziz began working for the Haha Smoke Shop.

An apartment did come. Tahir Hussain, the cell-phone store owner, told him it was beautiful good luck, because the owner of the building was a doctor, and he had treated some Algerians who had come—completely legally and well on their way to asylum, because they were tortured—and the honorable doctor took pity on them and said, Here, rent this place, but they could not yet work, and would Aziz be willing to live with them and pay the rent.

This was clearly all false, but Aziz accepted it as true to their eyes.

They were Rachid and Waheb. It felt good to say exactly what he meant to say, even if they were not what they said or even what they appeared. Sitting with them in the apartment above the grocery store, listening to them speak Algiers Arabic, his mind got into a place where he could stop and rest from the climbing that it took just to think.

At the Canadian border, the agent assigned to Ghazi was a woman. Ghazi had gone to the restroom, thinking he might thank God for this, but unluckily, there was another man there and so Ghazi pressed his forehead to the tile floor only mentally and hoped it would count for something. There was not a woman Ghazi could not see into.

He spent a day talking to her, what she called the entry interview, at the crossing at Burlington. She was in a uniform, a dark navy jumpsuit, but she was shaped in such a way that he was constantly aware of her. Her hair was black-brown and hung in a braid down her back. She was at first shy with him. He was shy in return, waiting to see when he might say something that would move the curtain just an inch or so past formality. The time came when she asked him whether he was married, and he looked at her and said quietly, "If you are not, then I am not." She laughed and pushed her hair, where not a strand was out of place, back from her forehead. Then he dropped his head and gave off that he was shy again. But then, with his head still bowed, he looked upward and met her eyes, just the moment that was needed. He saw the shift in her instantly. She was susceptible to him.

Ghazi believed that all any woman wanted, as all men wanted, was to be considered, to be paid mind to. And it amazed him how this simple fact was unavailable to most men he knew. They seemed under the impression that contempt got in at a woman's heart and made her want something she could not have. *Ebaad tehla, ebaad teghla*. The farther you are, the dearer you become. But he had always found that when he was with a woman, when she was there before him, she was dearer than when she was not.

This Canadian woman was beyond that. This woman was

evoking in him the feeling that cannot be posed; when a woman senses it, it alone can be the decisive turn to make her want him or consider wanting him. He knew that this woman, this L. F. Martin, as the laminated card hanging from her neck identified her, was lonely.

When she had completed the paperwork that gave him a date for an asylum hearing, she told him it was a formality. All Algerians in Canada were granted "immediate and unconditional and indefinite residency because of the grave human-rights crisis that existed in their homeland." She also said that her shift was ending, and she wanted to help him by driving him to the train station so that he could get to Montreal, where there was a sizable Algerian community, not to mention a national welfare system that would make it possible for him to "get his bearings and recover from the trauma he had suffered."

They walked out to the parking lot, which was filled up with cars and buses and trucks, and looked at the long lines on either side of the border. It was snowing. She took out a broom and swept off the windshield and side windows of her truck, an old red pickup. He stood there, his back against a wall, watching her. She was conscious of this and at one point he almost looked away; his focus was too strong. But then she opened the passenger door and said, "Guess you don't know what to do with snow, do you?"

He looked at her and said, "I don't want to offend you, but I feel it's wrong for me to take this ride from you."

She said, "Hey, it's okay. Honest." So he got in the seat, a little ocean-sick at how she affected him.

When they were past the parking lot and out on the road, he said, without thinking, "I see your heart, and it is beautiful, and I want it." He stopped and looked out the window. "I want you in my hand." He had planned to say more, but she pulled to the side of the road, and when she turned the engine off, she turned to look at him, and she was, he thought, a kind woman who also happened to be unerringly beautiful, and he wanted to get his fill of her.

So he spent a week with her, nights and nights in which she could not stop and he could not stop. When she took him to the train station, he imagined he would come back for her and marry her. That was what he said to himself. "You will never be free" was what he told her. "Come with me." She stayed behind.

19

It was a walk-up above the Fair City Supermarket on Coney Island Avenue. Roaches strong from grocery leavings lined the underside of the stove, the sinks, the baseboards. His roommates Waheb and Rachid looked to be improvements over the Chinese and the sick Nigerian. Unfortunately, Waheb was stupid. So dumb, that while it was true Aziz could tell him the most intricate of his thoughts with all the words needed, Waheb was mostly incapable of understanding what it was, even halfway, that Aziz meant. As for Rachid, he was constantly on the phone to someone in Germany, and this someone spoke German, and Aziz had no German.

Then there were the shoes. Waheb and Rachid kept them in boxes stacked in a closet. They filled it top to bottom. He never saw them wear them. He did not ask about them. He had learned. If they had packed the closets with grenades, he would have been silent. After the first few weeks, he avoided them.

So when he was not working at the Haha Smoke Shop, Aziz sought out the old man he had helped sell books outside the cell-phone store. He felt comforted by him, in his so-washed djellaba and their easy talking about not much. Whether it would be better to get an orange from the man who sold them around the corner or from the one who came into the store, but not every day, with his basket. Whether Hussain's daughter would marry the man with the over-big gold watch. Whether Hussain's wife was against the gold-watch man. But Aziz could not explain to this man, who had lost his family to some strange scourge of hyper-justice in Yemen, how it was that Boston had become to him something close to home. Something he grieved he had lost.

Mourad had no interest in Heather as an object of lust, but when he realized she had no interest in him that way either, or any way, he was heartbroken. They were, after all, in the same bed, night after night. True, he always found her in the bed in a long nightgown and a longer bathrobe. He knew she pretended to be asleep, because when she was actually asleep, which he had noticed many times when he lay awake in the middle of the night, her breathing was slightly different.

But he let her pretend. It was maidenly in a way. It had been a long time since he realized she was not the spoiled child he had assumed. It was a long time since he had half expected to be required to fight her off. He had judged her objections about sleeping in the same bed to be a coquette's pose. They were not. And it was unexpectedly gratifying that she was naïve but he, Mourad, was not, about the dangers of surveillance. He felt protective of Heather.

Heather thought of moving back to Virginia, but that meant her mother. And her sister, Sweet Briar's field hockey champion and Bum Chum Tap Club president. *Work for the good, work for the right, holla holla holla*. Lying awake at night, she thought of how cops tailed her boss's client. They took letters from his mailbox, steamed them open, photocopied them, resealed them, and slipped them back in the mailbox. This client got a letter from his brother saying "You know what," and the cops said *You-know-what* was gunrunning. "You know what" was honestly a surprise birthday party. Her moving to Virginia, they'd call that *absconding*. If Kamal had tried to get Aziz in trouble, Aziz who'd never done anything against Kamal, there was no telling what Kamal might say about her. He knew she had a copy of the U-Stor-It key. He knew, before Aziz came, she had helped Rafik sell hash.

Mourad picked her up at work every so often, so that the fiction of their couplehood, in the event they were being followed, could look more real. When he did, he often brought a carnation. He thought this would be a good touch. When he gave it to her, he kissed her on the cheek. Mourad also suggested that they go to the movies, like couples do. He decided to leave the choice of movie up to her, because he had observed on television that it was often the woman of the couple who made the plans for things like dinner or guests or vacations or movies.

Heather actually liked the movie suggestion. It was good to get out of the apartment. It was good to stop watching television. It was good to be certain no one was listening to them. Who could see you in a movie theater? If only Ghazi were there, he would know what to do. But he wasn't. And that made her remember the whole mess, and she felt cornered, and she decided it was easier to just do what Mourad wanted.

Ghazi lived in the Montreal YMCA. It was thick with Algerians. He went cautiously, pretending he was Italian. Since they thought he had no Arabic, their talking at night was unthinking. There were, he could gather, a thousand ways to steal. There was the government dole, which was far better than anyone could ever hope to have in Algeria. There were the women, who, even if they were the lowest-paid of the lowest, made more than anyone in Algeria. They could be bedded and lived off, and during the day, when at work, there were other women and other things. There were also the ways to make money from spies, because Algerian spies were everywhere in Montreal. They had taken the trouble to come here! It astonished Ghazi. It seemed that one was listening to another who was listening to another who was listening to the first one. To find out what? This was not said. Were they talking in intrigues to make the dull of cold Canada seem less? He knew one thing. He wanted, badly, to return to the border agent. He felt, perhaps, this was the time he was in love.

He learned where to go to get the government check and decided it would be best to be himself, a man who had come over the border with his own real name. He showed the paperwork his beautiful agent had given him to a man taking his application for assistance, and true enough, he was given a check every two weeks and a thick manila envelope with information on affordable housing, food vouchers, and job training. He wondered if he could go to school to be a chef, a good one. He would figure it out. Maybe he did not even need to go back to Boston. But as soon as he thought that, he missed Aziz. Not the others.

The apartment the government subsidized was small, but it was close to where Ghazi liked to be most, a coffee shop that had newspapers from the world. He spent his days reading them. No one spoke to him. No one looked at him. If there was one thing he knew how to do, it was wait.

It had taken Aziz a long phone conversation to get his father to comprehend what had befallen them. Aziz had to count on his father's not knowing American ways, because Aziz had to leave much unsaid. He could not speak of Rafik's crimes. He could not speak of secret police grabbing Ghazi. Aziz also had to explain that Mourad was not able to call home and that his father could not reach Mourad in Boston anymore. Aziz could not say that Mourad was certain his phone was being tapped, because of course that would make his father and his mother fall down prostrate in tears and recriminations at why they had let their sons make dangerous journeys only to have them fall into treachery.

So he told them that work was hard to find in Boston. Mourad had been fired from his security job. That's why he didn't have a phone anymore. Aziz and Ghazi had lost their jobs at Del Fuegos. Aziz had heard of work in New York. Ghazi had heard of work in Canada. Rafik had gone to Rhode Island after his job at the moving company ended. They had to leave Boston; they had no money.

"No money?" his father exclaimed. "You were sending us so much money. Is it all gone?"

Yes, Aziz related. Since they had sent all their money home, they had no money saved.

To which his father would say, more than once and over several phone calls, "You left here for no jobs and no money to go to no jobs and no money!"

Aziz had to tell him, several times, "The economy is very bad. It is not good at all."

His father had no newspapers, no news, no nothing of how things in America were, so this was something his father could not directly contradict, even though it seemed highly improbable, well nigh impossible, from the perspective of a man who had lived in a country where the state of the economy had been a disaster for the last twenty years but was, according to government announcements, twenty years improving. His father also wondered, more than once, how it was that he, Aziz, could talk by phone to Mourad in Boston when the family in Algeria could not. Aziz told him the international calls were too expensive for Mourad to afford. "But we will call him," his father insisted. "We will find a way to talk to him." No, no, Aziz countered, we cannot let you go to that expense. He, Aziz, had a job in New York, and so he could afford to call home and relay all the news of Mourad. It was better this way. Did they believe this cavalcade of lies? Sometimes he didn't care if they didn't.

20

There were lemon tree orchards all around it, but the village was not much more than alleys of mutilated bushes, its parks untended, grass gone to seed. They were in the Mitidja, not far from Haouch Gros. The village's militia, a small band of farmers and herders, had killed Antar's father and taken his sisters to the prison in Berrouaghia. The younger sister was under torture: *kdoulha esslah*—guest treatment—they called it. Soon word reached Antar that Khalida, his other sister, had told the woman who brought her water in her cell, "They beat me so much that I have become like a small black olive."

Now there was nothing Antar did not believe was his right. There were those among Antar's men who took to depravity the way birds take to air. They had imaginations bloated with ways to inflict suffering, and they saw the permutated hell of their nighttimes as an underground heaven they had never hoped to enter. Then there were those who were sickened into a dullness they believed made their acts less vicious because they took no pleasure in them. And then there was Aziz, who died each death in crushing closeness, because to numb, he believed, was to lose the cunning and the propellant to escape.

From the day they met, Antar had not only believed that Aziz was Nazzar, he had also given Aziz his trust. He suspected Aziz was a messenger from God. Antar kept him by his side almost always. But over the months, Antar had begun to fear that somehow Aziz would be lost, that the government's hyenas would divine the necessity of Aziz and kill him. As killing was the routine of their nights and planning to kill the routine of their days, killing was the only thing Antar could imagine: as a remedy, a dread, a desire, or a respite. It was all there would be and all that had been, and he began to think it might be better to kill Aziz himself rather than suffering when others took away from him what he had to have most.

Antar was thinking of this after midday on his hammock. He wore the same nomad headdress he wore the day Aziz met him. His feet had new wounds—it had been six months—but the new wounds were, like the old ones, undressed and rank.

Below him, Aziz was bent into sleep on the ground. The day's windless heat amplified sound. An irregular fluttering had awakened Antar. He lay there for some time, listening. He turned to face the others, keeping his eyes closed. It sounded like water along a gutter. But that was impossible. He looked. The bearded one, Sellami, and four others were huddled over the noise.

"Brother," Antar said.

Aziz moved on the ground. Eventually he stood up. "I am here," he said.

"Go find what they are saying," he said, motioning to the men grouped by Sellami.

Everyone knew that Aziz was Antar's spy, but Aziz had learned the stance to take with Sellami and his men. He would explain Antar's curiosity. He would ask them what they wished Antar to think. He would then relay their words with any shading needed to make it acceptable to Antar. Antar required such mediation. A few bowed to him, but they were teenagers. Aziz sensed that Sellami, an old Marxist and now a careerist in killing, put up with him.

Sellami watched Aziz more closely than the rest. Aziz first noticed it the night they were in Had Chekala, close to Relizane, to take on government sympathizers from a local militia who had killed two FIS party members. Antar wanted to kill the family of the patriots; the patriots themselves were too hard to find. Families, in Antar's soldiering, were the hill to be taken, the bridge to be blown. That night, Antar had decided to gain access to this family through a village nursery. The babies were there at midnight, tended only by old women, because the young women, many of them pregnant, were too weak by this late part of Ramadan to watch their children. It was at a mountainside, in houses of ground and sod; it was more than four hours' walk to the first telephone. With them was a new addition: Ahmed Rahman, said to be an Afghan veteran. Ahmed had arrived malnourished, and that night he was light-headed—Antar's men were also fasting—and Ahmed began his work ahead of them. He had no respect for those who kept the fast or for the *djeddat* who had delayed feasting to keep watch over the babies. He cut their throats, the *djeddat*'s, one by one, so some saw their fate played more than one time.

When Sellami and Aziz found him, Ahmed was throwing babies against a wall and standing among and on the ones he had flung into pieces. Aziz pulled him out and took him to Antar. Sellami had argued with Aziz over it. And Antar looked at Aziz oddly when they returned. Aziz had to say he saw one *djedda* escaping to warn the rest of the family. Sellami didn't back him.

For days after, Aziz planted questions about Ahmed's loyalty. He is a spy, Aziz told Antar. How did he arrive here? Who knows him? See how he sleeps apart. See what I found in his pack. One night, Antar woke suddenly to see Ahmed stabbed dead near his hammock, and Aziz saying he had caught him, gun in hand, poised to assassinate Antar. Antar believed Aziz had saved his life. But Sellami kept asking questions, Aziz learned afterward. Had anyone seen Ahmed with the gun? Why had Nazzar been awakened but not Antar?

Now, on this dry afternoon many months later, Sellami looked up to see Aziz's sleepy face. Sellami smiled, shaking his head slightly, as if to say, Time for pantomime. Aziz was a wall. He stopped and crouched in the circle of men. They were looking at a copy of *Vogue*.

"From Boufarik?" Aziz asked, yawning.

"No. Three weeks ago. Blida."

"A long time to hide such booty," Aziz observed.

"The women are magnificent."

The pages were glistening.

"He heard something," Aziz said, yawning again.

One of them turned a page. There was the sound.

"In French," Aziz said, looking at the word *maillot* upside down.

"In French," Sellami said, a little apart from the rest.

"That girl, that one with the red scarf," said Riad.

Aziz nodded.

"This was hers," Sellami said.

"I killed her," said Rïad.

"You killed for a French *Vogue,* you sick fuck," Sellami said, laughing. The others joined in. Aziz motioned with his eyes toward Antar.

"Tell him we are reading a Hadith."

Aziz nodded.

"Antar cannot read, so Hadith or *Vogue,* it's all one to him," said another.

"And we laugh over a Hadith because?" Aziz asked.

"Because we know tonight we kill, and the ones the prophet predicted—we are coming for them."

"A prayer might be good around now," Aziz counseled.

They put the *Vogue* into a bag and turned to the east.

People seemed to leave parts of their houses uninhabited in Haouch Boughfi el-Khemisti. Many rooms were unfinished, as if money to build had run out, and there were hallways and inner courtyards given over to vines and ants. Aziz carried a sawed-off shotgun. Only he and Antar were so armed. The rest had knives. Their long beards and hair would have made them look like sleep-roused Bedouins, but many were wearing new leather jackets just stolen, and the fantastically white Adidas not yet worn until that night. Aziz declined these, and Antar, by his side, saw the white of Aziz's djellaba and drawstring pants. He was in the company of a holy man, and this dress, this humility, to Antar was another sign. To kill him, Antar thought once again, what would it bring? He threw off this thinking. His duty this night was to avenge his sisters.

They walked like soft kittens. Antar turned down a small alley bordered by low trees at the exit east of the village. There were a few groups of mules, loaded with carrots, lettuce, and coriander, ready for the morning to go to market. The air smelled of vegetables and dirt. The houses were identical. The agreed-upon sign was to be a basket of potatoes at the back entry of a house where an army colonel lived. One of his sons had come home only nights ago from his tour of duty. Now his son, Antar thought, will taste what his own sisters had tasted.

The houses were close together. There were thirty men with Antar that night, and the neighborhood had hundreds of families. Aziz guessed this would last until morning, and since it was early March there might be fog. As he always did, he considered whether this village could be gotten lost in, whether disappearing was possible, if he could make the fiction of his death convincing to Antar. For months Aziz had studied the reaction to those of their band who went missing. There had been five of them. In all cases, Antar made the search for their bodies a mission. Two were found. On the other three, word was sent and the families were found. Those families were killed.

But Antar thought Aziz was Nazzar. As long as he did, Aziz's family was safe. But Nazzar's family, by Aziz's escape, would be killed. This had been enough to keep Aziz from trying. Then came the woman and the shovel. Nazzar had wanted to join men who killed so. His family created him, so they made such killing. But such thinking made Aziz like Antar. Kill the families of patriots if you can't find the patriots. If Nazzar can't be killed, kill his mother and father. Widen the circle of guilt if the guilty are too clever to find or, in Nazzar's case, already dead.

Such thinking, such renouncing of killing Nazzar's parents, nonetheless left Aziz stuck with Antar and a killer, not of Nazzar's family but of many other families. So his thoughts rearranged. Escape *might* lead to Antar killing Nazzar's family. Perhaps Nazzar's parents had died years ago in a plane crash. Perhaps Nazzar had no brothers or sisters. Perhaps the family had moved some years ago to Tunisia, or Italy, or even Malaysia. Perhaps, if they were still in Algeria, there was a chance they would be smart enough to escape the *irhabiya* of Antar. It did happen. Didn't he believe he could escape them?

He thought of Soumeya. He hoped she could wait. When their fathers arranged the marriage, Aziz's tour of duty was soon to start. The plan was to marry in two years when he completed his service. Soumeya's father owned great orchards in the Mitidja, but he had only daughters—six of them—and he needed men, greatly, to run what he could no longer run alone. But it was far from Arzew, and Aziz was not sure. So before his father said yes, he showed Aziz her picture. The day he left for training, his father gave him the photograph to keep. In the desert, it stayed in his boot, wrapped in paper and foil. When he was certain he was alone, which was almost never, he took it out and studied her.

She had eyes like an open window. He saw in them that she did not like this photograph being taken, and that she was not afraid of her defiance. She looked like a girl who had worked in orchards all her life, though why he thought this he could not tell. She was not smiling, but her lips were not pouting. They, like her brow, were relaxed. She looked not so much impatient as unconvinced—of what, that her life was about to begin? That anyone her father chose would matter? She seemed to be saying to Aziz, You may think I will be your wife, but I will do so only for the world to see. Inside I will be a brown nut, and it is that nut you will have to woo to open, because I can very well keep it shut from you for lifetimes.

21

For the first time in her life, Heather was thinner. It was something that just happened, no effort. Mourad said one day, "Your clothes don't fit you." She was wearing a pair of blue jeans. The roll of her that had lifted over the top of them was gone, and she could stick both her hands under the waistband down to the tops of her thighs. The shirt where the buttons were straining as long as she could remember was so loose she felt cold.

She couldn't sit around leafing through magazines. She couldn't stand watching television. She didn't want to go to lunch with her friends at work because she didn't want to talk about anything, so she ate at her desk, and eating usually turned out to be a Coke. She went in early so she could be hard at work, deaf to chitchat, when everyone else arrived. After a while, she even started staying late, though Mourad wasn't wild about that development. She looked for ways to make things run more smoothly. She anticipated what her boss wanted. Sometimes, she made his travel arrangements so thoughtfully that he teased her about being a mind reader.

Then one day a bigger guy at the law firm than her boss went to her boss and said he needed Heather to be his executive assistant. It was more pay. The guy had a corner office, and she even had her own office outside his. The main thing was she didn't have to see or talk to any of the other secretaries anymore.

So when Mourad said her clothes didn't fit, she went shopping. Mourad came along. He didn't even bother to say what he had been saying for months now: *That's what couples do*. They went to a mall in the suburbs.

It had become a relief to be with Mourad, actually. She looked forward to their talks after work. At least with him there was nothing to hide. They knew exactly who the other was and why they did everything the way they did it. They were in agreement, by now, on everything that was important to accomplish in their relating. Mourad was solicitous of Heather on the street and near windows. He made a point to hold her hand anytime they were outside. In cars, they were particularly affectionate.

When she picked out clothes in a department store, Mourad helped. "Beautiful," he said, about an orchid dress. "Try this one," he said, carrying a filmy skirt no one at her law firm would wear. She tried them. In the mirror, she looked at herself in lavender. Rafik would have called the dress corny, a word Heather was sorry she taught him. Everything that had any sweetness in it, Rafik made it corny. Lahouari, whom she missed terribly, was corny. So were the proverbs she put on the wall. And the cards she left on Rafik's pillow.

So she bought the orchid dress. Mourad was happy. The proud look stayed on his face as they took a transparent escalator to another floor of the mall and made their way past store windows with tiers of tiny silver cameras, spotlighted emerald and diamond rings, and a giant stuffed panda in a toy-store palm-tree glade. Even though he had been to malls before, they were still a spangle circus to him. She could feel him trying to look casual. Other people were rushing and rattled. They were busy and get-me-out-of-here. But Mourad was excited; he wanted to linger.

"Let's buy lunch," he said, as if suggesting a waltz on a star.

It was new, made over for her, the most ordinary thing.

Lahouari had been the first to acquaint her with these kinds of makeovers. To him the dead-ended everyday—that she had stopped seeing—was a pinwheel of delight. An elevator made him smile. Bubble wrap threw his head back in a yelp. A bookstore in Cambridge hushed him. She knew his family was smart: a novelist in Europe was an aunt or something, and his mother was a doctor. But by the time Lahouari came along, the troubles in Algeria—terrible violence that he described to her—were too great and everything had gone too wrong for him to go to college or taste what the rest of his family saw as their due. And now, he was crammed in a tiny Everett apartment. Lahouari, even there, would see something she couldn't.

She looked at Mourad. He was watching a boy in a starched white apron toss broccoli in a wok. She could smell French fries. Someone walked by with a gyro. There were all kinds of choices.

Only the rotisserie chicken place had a long line. They were just past it when she saw him: Kamal, sitting like a lord in the mall's food court, chewing on a straw in a milkshake.

He looked right at them.

He didn't recognize Heather; he had never met Mourad. He glanced and turned his head. He was alone. She felt her stomach fall. "Mourad, Mourad," she said. He stopped and looked where she was looking.

"It's Kamal," she said. "It's Kamal! With the milkshake."

"Where?"

"Straight. Straight. Then the pillar right."

"The blue coat—"

"No. Next to the lady in yellow."

"The Burger King milkshake."

"That's him."

"Did he see you?"

"No."

"I have an idea."

. . .

"Kamal. How are you?" Mourad acted like a forgotten friend. In the distance he could see Heather on the escalator, off to find the bus home.

"Thanks to God I am well. And you?"

Kamal, skinny, was wearing black pants and a silver earring. He had his ponytail.

"I can't complain," Mourad answered. He was wider than this bony one, his arms thick.

"Who are you," Kamal began, "if I may ask?"

They were speaking the most polite Arabic.

"My name is Mourad Arkoun. May I?" Mourad pulled back a chair.

"Of course." Kamal tried to place Mourad Arkoun.

"You have caused many problems in my family," Mourad said. His tone was flat, pleasant. He felt almost cheerful.

"What do you want?" Kamal said. He put on the air of someone who was too busy to chat.

"You know, of course, my brother Aziz."

Kamal showed nothing. "What of it?"

"You fucked him. To get out of your own shit."

"You have me mixed up with someone else." Kamal picked at a fingernail.

"Hank Bridges?" Mourad smiled as he said the name.

"He is crazy." Kamal's eyes were looking around the food court. "He is gone from here," he added. Mourad could see him realizing it was not an easy place to leave. Tables and people were bunched and blocking the way.

"He must be gone or you would not be sitting here," Mourad said, reaching into Kamal's pocket, taking money and credit cards. "With—let's see—one, two, three . . . many different credit cards with many different names."

Kamal was now uneasy. "Bridges killed someone," he said. He spoke too fast. "They found it out. They moved him to California. Bridges is gone."

"When?"

"Last month," Kamal said. He scratched the back of his neck. His hair felt dirty.

"So now you will help me to find Rafik." Mourad moved his hand as if to pull Kamal's collar.

"I have no—" Kamal began.

Mourad was close enough to fix Kamal's chair with his boot. He leaned into his face.

"He is here. He is with me."

"Where is that?"

"In East Boston. Thirty-four Dorfman, apartment eight. But he is not well. I have just this morning seen him in the worst fever."

"You will take me there."

"He may not be home. I do not control Rafik."

The bus from the mall took forever. She looked for anyone following her. She thought one woman was too stylish to be on the bus, but the lady got out at Newton, so that made sense. Heather had to take another bus from downtown to East Boston, and so by the time she turned the key at Brooks Street, it was dark and almost suppertime. She heard voices as the door gave. She waited. A scuffling and then the door pulled back so quickly she fell forward with her packages careening on the stoop and into the hallway. Someone was picking her up. It was Mourad. He kissed her and pulled her against his chest kind of abruptly.

"Oh, Mourad!" she said. "I am so glad to see you. I was so worried."

"Are you all right?" he said into her ear.

"I am now." She tried to pull herself back a little, but Mourad wouldn't let her. "I'm okay, really," she said.

"Heather, Rafik is here," he whispered. Then he let her pull away enough to see into the living room. Rafik was sitting on the sofa, smoking. He was tapping his foot. He wasn't looking at them. It hit her that he didn't care one way or another about her. He just wanted to get out of the apartment.

Without turning her head she walked past him into the bedroom and closed the door. Of course he saw her. Not a hello, not a word. She'd done the same, though. Four years they were together. Nine months since she'd seen him. She felt nothing. Not mad, not sad, not anything.

That was good, wasn't it? Better than freaking out. Tearing up money that night in Reach, throwing it at girls. Mean, she was so mean to Aziz that night. He had almost no English then. Rafik. She had been crazy for him. How could she have loved him?

She sat on the bed. A snapshot of her dad was on the dresser. She had not wanted to be like her sister. Who would want to be like her, people who let life happen to them? Rafik upset her mother, which delighted her father. Rafik treated her, at least in the beginning, like a storybook princess. Rafik, who was handsome.

But it had been Mourad who had gotten to her. In the last months, sometimes it was like something was scraping her chest, as if someone had taken an emery board to her inside and tugged it across, not quite down to her backbone but somewhere in between where it sat and her heart, not particularly painfully stabbing, just a sawing motion of sensation. She felt this whenever she thought Mourad was losing interest in her. It would begin in daytime at work, maybe because he had forgotten to do something they had been in the habit of doing—packing her lunch, for example. But say he hadn't made the lunch. Then she would worry that his curiosity and need were lifting. Or around the end part of the day—and, let's just say, after not packing the lunch—he didn't call to say, Well, how is the plan for dinner? If she got home and he still wasn't there, and there had been no call and no packed lunch, then she would feel it in her chest, a rubbing. He could do that.

He was probably the ugliest man she had ever dated. No, that wasn't true. But he had an enormous nose, really not even within the range of being normal. And he had no chin. His cock was not fat and not long, as Rafik's had been. He was shorter than Rafik. And he had had an unlucky bout with acne and had those craters that she feared she would get but, thank God, never did.

There were a few things that were better. Mourad had a deep voice. Rafik had such a squeaky voice, it could never go low, only when he had a bad cold, and then he didn't want her around. So. Mourad did have the better voice. And he had large hands. This was a great thing. Rafik's were small slender hands that were smooth. Mourad had calloused fingertips, and when he took her face in his hands, she felt the roughness and the strength and, for all she intended not to, all these many months, she loved him.

She thought, for about the hundredth time, about the way he took his time when they got into bed, not rushing at her but thinking about her. Sometimes he would play with the last curls in her hair and then move them between his fingers, and then he would take his hand and move under the mass of her hair with his fingertips on the back of her neck and then her scalp, and then his hand would be lifting up her heavy hair and taking all of her head in his grasp. Then he would stop and he might say something, and since it was dark, and his voice was low, this was another time Mourad affected her. He might say, "You know, I thought about the way your hair cannot stay up when you put the pins in it. The way it falls down in parts, and you try to pin it back up. I thought about that at work today, and I even asked Tom if his wife had hair that could not stay up. And he said his wife did too, and we talked about how amazing it was that hair so soft could be so hard to control." And then he would say, "It's a beautiful thing about you, Heather."

In the old days, she would have taken his cock in her mouth right there because that was about as good as it was ever going to get, and it would all be embarrassment and missed chances from there out, someone taking her nipple in his mouth in a way that made her feel like a nursing bottle, or someone sticking a finger up her to check if she was wet, and even if she wasn't, it was like they had to make sure you had a pussy. And on the whole it was much easier when you knew they didn't have the slightest idea who you were, and didn't have any need to know; it was just a big relief to everyone if you took care of the business that was pressing.

She didn't do that with Mourad. She had let him take her hair and settle it over his chest. He had put her head in the crook of him, some way, and made her hair drape onto him. He had a wide, wide chest. It looked almost malformed when he was standing up, because he had short legs. But lying down, and when he held her, it was nothing short of heaven. And when she had been overweight, at least when all this mess started, which turned out to be not a mess but the best thing for her, if not for Aziz and Ghazi, Mourad had taken in all that she was and loved what was spectacular and made do with what was not anything special and pretended—as she did with his nose and his chin and the too-short legs and the cratered skin and the not very imposing dick—that she was his finest flower. Sometimes, she didn't know how it began, but sitting on the bed with Rafik and him out in the living room, she knew. It began where she was least lovable. Mourad began there, with his unsought attention, with his unbelievable poetry of physical approach, and he had made her a woman who would forever be aware that such things and ways existed in the world.

After a while, Mourad opened the bedroom door. When he smelled that combination of nail polish remover and Coca-Cola that was her smell, he was overtaken with relief that she was still, in the most immediate way possible, his. He told her Hank Bridges had been transferred out of Boston for misconduct, which meant everyone could come home. Rafik and Kamal were on the defensive, fearful that Mourad would turn them in. He did little to clear away their fright. He hoped they might leave Boston because of it. "Rafik was always criminal, even in school," Mourad said. "But he was small scams. I thought America changed him."

It would be horrible if Mourad ever found out about the U-Stor-It. She'd never set foot in it, but she promised herself she would find the key while Mourad was at work and throw it away. Mourad looked at her as if he were angry. It was like he had learned her so well, he knew her plan.

"He seemed—dangerous—to me tonight," Mourad said. He was quiet a moment. "But Rafik is a snivel. A dandelion of a person." He muttered those words in Arabic without realizing it.

Heather waited for the translation. His face relaxed. He took both her hands and kissed them. Whatever he'd said didn't matter.

After they made love, she fell fast asleep. He saw her scrunched down into the covers, with her head off the pillow. She always ended up the night like that, as if she were trying to fit herself to the foot of the bed. Sometimes he tried to pull her up. Rest your head on the pillow, he would say. That night he lay down beside her and let her sleep.

22

The heat baked Atlantic Avenue. Aziz had gone there, a good way from Newkirk and Coney Island, to find a man just back from Montreal. This man had no phone, but he knew an Algerian named Ghazi in Montreal. Waheb swore this. A chance at Ghazi's phone number dangled before Aziz like a high tree blossom. It had been months since he had told a single human being a completely truthful sentence. Loneliness was choking him.

On the street, people were easily insulted. He made the mistake of not stopping quickly enough when a boy came around a corner, just tapped this boy really, and the boy turned out to be someone who screamed obscenities, ceaselessly, until Aziz fled into a dry cleaner. There, a woman told him, "No clothes, no stay," and poked her finger in the air at a poster of a cross-armed police officer. As he tried to move quickly out the door, he ran into a man with an armload of wedding gowns in plastic sheeting, who threatened, seemingly out of nowhere, to charge him two thousand dollars because Aziz had tripped him, splaying the bustles and chiffon where someone had tossed half a hamburger on the sidewalk. In his first days in America, Aziz would have emptied his pockets to make amends. He gave the guy the finger.

He had pretty much decided that no matter what this man just back from Montreal said, he was going to go back to Boston. There were all kinds of ways to disguise yourself. He could sneak into Brooks Street wearing a wig. There was a wig store not far from the Haha Smoke Shop. Or he could dress up as a nun. Or a cop. It was October. They had Halloween costumes for sale on the street.

He looked at the piece of paper with the name and address of the Montreal guy. He craned to see a street sign. It was nowhere. There was a street, but no sign. He walked up to the next block, but again no sign. How did people know where to go? It was ridiculous. It angered him out of proportion to the harm. Everything was impossibly impossible. He decided. Fuck this Montreal guy. He spotted a pay phone. He would dial Mourad's work number.

Ghazi looked at Dhakir. He was prancing around for the old man, a chimp in a tutu before a mountain. The old man's face was badly disfigured. Ghazi couldn't tell if it was a birth defect, a cancer removed, a gun blast, or government guest treatment. The father's lip looked as if it had been unfinished. Was that a hare lip? Ghazi had never gotten that straight. Or was it a cleft palate? He'd also heard that sometimes they managed to imitate these problems and then say, Well, this man was born this way. To have such power, what was it like? What was it like after you did that to a man and went home to your woman? Did you cradle her in your arms? Did you fuck her good, or tell yourself you did, because God knows you didn't ask her. Or did you jack off in the shower and spare her the trouble? Looking at Dhakir, playing the Muslim bridegroom for this mangled old duke of the revolution, pained him. Because the old man believed—or pretended to believe, or willed himself to believe, or playacted that he believed—that Dhakir was what he advertised, the new owner of an Indonesian and Malaysian import-export business that had just taken the bold step of opening a retail establishment in Montreal's hip new corridor where the college kids were spending money on nothings.

Whereas Ghazi suspected the trinket shop was under surveillance, by whom, or why, he didn't know but could guess. A brother had sold it to Dhakir. A serious brother, as Dhakir put it, who hailed from Algiers by way of Paris. Now he was gone—"to Jordan," Dhakir said, but in point of fact he was now in the custody of Philippe Ste.-Marie Renier, the judge investigating the Paris subway bombings, a prosecutor jurist who was said to go into the Algerian slums of Lyon with ski mask and Glock to shoot vagabonds for sport.

So here was this old man, with his *hijab* meek daughter on his peach leather sofa in a sublet on the outer edge of Montreal where all there was were gas stations and parking lots. Outside the apartment this same daughter wore hair highlighted with blue, eyes kohl and topaz, her tight tits in a lamé bustier or a Wonderbra with emerald sequins. It was in the sequins that Ghazi first met her. He was at a club with Dhakir. She was dancing. Around four in the morning, within an hour of first seeing her, Dhakir took her outside and fucked her in an alley. From then on, the con was on, the girl claiming pregnancy to Dhakir, Dhakir pretending respectability to her father, the old man in a shed where not a chink of light got. It sickened Ghazi. But only a little more than Montreal sickened him.

He had gone backward: to thieving. When he was seven he took a note from his father's wallet and hid it in the Qur'an. He waited. His father didn't notice the missing money. No one, for all the piety professed, actually read the holy book. For months and months, Ghazi waited. He checked the book as often as he could, which was almost every day. After a year, he took the money, told his mother he got a job helping a man load a truck, and bought himself a soccer ball. For a time, he was king, but he soon discovered he had no talent for soccer, and the boys who came to him for his soccer ball thought less of him with every game. Dhakir, on the other hand, was a primeval triumph. He had tremendous speed. He threw himself into the chase for the ball, forever falling and diving and bleeding and bruising. In their neighborhood, Dhakir had thighs like torpedoes and, even at seven, a cock like an angry elephant. When they went diving naked into the ocean near Aziz's father's hotel, no one could take their eyes off Dhakir's man of a dick.

He was not the smartest. That fell to Ghazi, who, as it turned out, was the only one from their street to get to university. Dhakir, a few years older, went to a trade school in Sardinia but was expelled and, instead of coming home, disappeared. Ghazi had heard he was in Morocco, but that was wrong. Dhakir said he had been in London, playing soccer and working in a washing machine factory, hoping that he might yet push his way into fame, even though his speed was now just above average, his thighs subwarrior class, and only his cock still in the range of the extraordinary.

Now, Ghazi sat in this living room a disgruntled witness to a charade, the father sizing him up as a suitor for one of his other two daughters, back in a bedroom with their mother. Since the father believed that Ghazi was Dhakir's real and actual brother, he was considered family, and the plans for the wedding were part of his duties. The *hijab* temptress was sent back to join her blank-eyed sisters and exhausted mother, who had kept the family under roof and at table by taking two jobs, one behind the counter at a computer store and the other as a maid at a downtown hotel. It shamed her husband but it had to be endured, as he, with his grotesque deformity and ruined knees, was unemployable.

The conversation had veered from weddings.

"The constitution forbids an Islamic state," the father said. "We are a secular nation. And now, since they cannot have *sharia* by democracy, they will have it by killing."

"I hear it is calming," offered Dhakir.

"The generals are saving Algeria," the father said.

"The killings, they are less," Dhakir said.

"When I fought the French before you were born, I did not fight to have Algerians killing Algerians," the father said.

"Maybe it is working, as they say it is much better," Dhakir said.

Ghazi nodded, but as neither was looking at him, he stopped. What would happen, he wondered, when those following Dhakir came to this place and found this old man, proud of his long battle for freedom, with a wolf in his tabernacle? Maybe they would never come. Sometimes, they just watched.

"His brother. Not his mother, his brother," Aziz said slowly into the receiver. A motorcycle on Atlantic Avenue ka-powed. A sweaty passerby pushed into him.

"Are you for real?" said the woman who had answered Mourad's work number.

"Is he on duty?" A small girl stepped on Aziz's foot. Now someone was leaning on a car horn.

"Sir, even if you were his mother, I couldn't give out that type of information."

"Just tell him I am on the phone. His brother from Algeria."

"He's not from Africa. He's Arab. See, I know that. Who *is* this?"

"Aziz Arkoun. His brother. I am standing at a pay phone, and—"

"A pay phone in Africa?"

"In Brooklyn, New York, United States of America."

"There's no need to raise your voice, sir."

"I'm at a pay phone! I can barely hear you!"

"I don't like your tone."

"Please. My thanks to you would be great."

"Don't *'please'* and *'thank you'* me. This conversation has ended. Any questions, write a letter. Commonwealth Security Services, Logan Airport Command Station, five hundred Terminal E, East Boston, Mass., zero two one two eight."

She hung up.

Aziz slammed down the receiver and accidentally kicked the man who had been waiting behind him for the phone.

"You got a problem?" The man was easily twice Aziz's size.

"You stand on my ass!" Aziz shouted.

"Fuck you, motherfucker."

Aziz kicked him, hard this time, and ran.

This was not good.

He was insane to be this angry.

He looked over his shoulder. No man was running for him. He saw a drugstore and slowed to walk through the automatic door.

He put fingers over his nose and palms over his mouth. He was breathing hard next to a long wall of cosmetics. He could not believe it—a security guard was eyeing him already. Aziz made a quick turn down an aisle of aspirin, cough syrup; he was almost at the cough drops but no, the guard had headed him off.

"Excuse me, sir."

Fuck. Fuck. What to do?

"Sir!"

Aziz was running back toward the aspirin. I took nothing, he said to himself. I did nothing.

A voice on a loudspeaker came on. "Security needed at the front. Security report to aisle five at the front of the store."

Where was aisle five? Had he come from aisle five? He did not want to go to aisle five. He was confused, his blood thwacking inside him, when the guard was on him. Standing right in front him.

"Sir, you dropped this." The guard gave him the piece of paper with the address of the guy from Montreal. "Take it easy," he added. "I'm needed at the front. Catch you later."

23

One of them had found the basket of potatoes. There was no moon that night, so it took the rest of them a while to reach where the scout had located it. As they got close, it was plain the colonel had a dog; it had slept through one man nosing around outside his wall but barked like one scalded at the approach of thirty. The sound was ten horns in each of their ears.

"It barks at beetles, this dog. They will not wake for this," Antar counseled, in a whisper loud enough to be heard. But no one seemed to hear him. Several were already retreating into passageways between houses. The men's movements brought more barking dogs from other houses. These nearby dogs barked back at the barkers until, slowly at first, kerosene lamps got lit, and then the entire neighborhood in that moon-gone night was twilight.

They heard the first gunshot, from someone—the colonel's targeted son, another son, perhaps the colonel himself—perched on the wall. One of their own fell. Then another gun, this from another wall, aimed. Aziz and Antar, the only two of their own with guns, began shooting at the two on the walls, but the gunmen jumped down behind the wall, and all Aziz and Antar had done was lose ten precious bullets. Aziz looked for Antar's eye, and in a glance saw Antar was afraid.

Men with knives and hoes and shovels and flashlights were coming into the alley. Their sons were coming too. Uncles and grandfathers and son-in-laws and nephews joined. Unseeing, Aziz collided into one of Antar's men. The man ran. Behind him, Aziz saw Sellami slice through a man's throat, and then another man came for Sellami. That man, too, was cut down and fell. In a dim blur, Sellami seemed to pirouette toward a rake. Up ahead, Riad was better at killing than these sleepy good men; Aziz saw him take one man's hoe and crush another man's head.

Aziz crouched. Antar was trying to poke his knife into a man's throat, but the man kept saying, "No, no," and ran away. Someone had jumped on another leather-jacketed one's back and was straddling his head, hacking at the man's eyes and forehead with a knife too dull to kill but sharp enough to get one ear halfway off. Aziz fired his shotgun over a wall. Nothing happened; the scenery of carnage was untouched, the participants neither paused nor turned nor exclaimed. The one Aziz had just run into continued streaking down the alley. Antar was firing his rifle at a pack of villagers running toward him. Some fell, but most kept coming. Aziz realized too late that he too was about to be overtaken by this mob.

He heard huffing. He could smell the metal of their hoes and shovels, and for a moment he was confused by the zagging beams of flashlights. One said, as if in pleasant conversation, "They are there." Then they were gone. He saw them jogging away along the alley. He had been invisible to them. Then he knew. He was dressed as they were. They had the same drawstring pants and lank djellabas as he. Antar's men, in their alabaster sneakers and bat-black jackets, were who they wanted. The defenders had mistaken Aziz for one of their own. In this chaos, this was his chance.

He looked for Antar one last time. All he saw was a man aiming his knife for the legs of the man on his shoulders, while another was stabbing him in the chest. Brown blood on all of them made a glint in the low light. Antar was missing. Had they mowed him down? Aziz looked for signs of him, but there were none. He began to walk quickly, and in his excitement he fell against a broken tree. As it gave way from his weight, he dropped his gun and fitted himself into a passageway, compressing himself into its meanderings until it opened out onto a road.

The night heaved past him in gulping breaths. On his right and left he saw the mud houses, the mules, a few women and girls at windows with candles. The air sped into his eyes. He tripped, fell partway, twisted into running again. Then there were houses but no lights in them. His feet slapped, slapped, slapped on the dirt, down a street, into a courtyard, over dirt again, until the one brief braying of a horse was louder than the cries of pain and shoutings of killing. He stopped. He turned. Left. Right. He even looked up. The back of his throat was raw. He was alone.

He dropped to the ground and gasped. When his breath was back he could smell the smoke. Behind him, the sky was orange. Antar was setting the village on fire.

There would be no way to know who lived and who died. This thought brought him to his feet. He was jubilant. This village was two, maybe three hectares total. If he kept running, he would reach the lemon orchards. Soumeya and her family would be there.

If not there exactly, there would be farmers who knew of her father. He would find them.

He was lying asleep behind a juniper outside the village. He looked up. Sellami was standing there. The black SUV was behind him, motor running. Aziz didn't have time to readjust his expression. His insides hurt and blood thrummed in his head.

"Thank God you're alive!" Sellami was wearing shorts and a black T-shirt.

"Brother," Aziz mumbled.

"Are you hurt?"

"No . . . I am well." But as he got up, he felt pain on his right side. His arms were badly slashed and covered with dirt and leaves.

"There is a doctor. I will take you." He helped Aziz into the passenger seat.

Sellami pulled away fast and the road turned into cloud. He had his long hair in a ponytail and he didn't look like himself. Aziz slumped into the front seat, his head light with despair. He had been dumb. He had not noticed he was hurt; he had not thought he would fall asleep. He had told himself he would take only five minutes to rest near the juniper bushes. Everything had depended on running and not stopping. He cursed his weakness and began shivering; Sellami had the windows up and the air-conditioning high. A cell phone rang. Sellami switched something on the dashboard. He had a wire hanging from his ear. A tiny plastic arm reached across his cheek.

"I have him. . . .

"You tell Tahar he has fucked us."

"Yes, he is hurt. Of course he is hurt. . . .

"He is not dead. . . .

"We wore what they said. . . .

"If Tahar said that, he was wrong. . . .

"No, no, it was Antar who was wearing the *barnous*. . . .

"And all who had Adidas and leather, they fall on them. . . .

"You have fucked us. . . .

"No one can kill him. . . .

"I am not coming. . . .

"They are in Ben Aknoun. . . .

"You tell Tahar he has fucked us. If he continues to fuck us, he will find himself with problems."

He leaned over and pushed a button on the dashboard too hard. Its red covering fell off and bounced on the black carpeted floor. Everything was immaculate inside the Expedition. The windshield was glossy.

"Nazzar, listen."

"Yes," Aziz said.

"You sound weak."

"I am fine."

"What happened last night is: everyone except you, me, and Antar was killed."

Aziz sat up more.

"And right now I am driving you to Algiers to get you some help. When we get there, this is what we do. We are going to Ramdane Benane's house."

It was Benane for whom Aziz had been searching on his last day in camp, serving tea for the officers. And that night, one of Antar's men had turned to him and said, *Vite, mon frère, Benane attende.*

He shifted an ache in his arm. No one had mentioned Benane since. At the time Aziz saw nothing strange in *irhabiya* telling him, a seeming army deserter, that Colonel Benane was the next terrorist target. But Sellami was driving him to Benane's. Benane, quite alive. If the voice in his ear that first night near the desert had meant they were going to kill Benane, it had not happened. It occurred to him now that the words also could have meant, *Benane has been waiting for you*. Waiting for you to join this undercover mishmash with these Islamist, Salafist, jihadist freaks. But how did months of killing government sympathizers help the government cause?

Wait. Hadn't Sellami on the phone just now said *Ben Aknoun*?

If only his brain would work. It stopped just as it got started. Ben Aknoun was military intelligence. It was where the DRS shock troops came from. It was where Islamist jihadists were tortured. Aziz had interpreted Sellami's telephone talk just now in the SUV about Ben Aknoun to mean that other terrorists, allies of Antar's, could not help Sellami with the wounded Aziz. They were being held in Ben Aknoun. Comrades were out of commission. No help could come from them. But what if Sellami meant it another way? What if Sellami's comrades were not the ones being tortured but the torturers?

You tell Tahar he has fucked us. Sellami said that on the phone too, more than once. Aziz felt near to understanding something, but when he got close it fumed into gas.

He was back in the sand when they were holding his feet.

How many know of Ben Aknoun? That was what Aziz had asked them. *Perhaps these ones were they,* he remembered thinking.

These ones, Antar's ones: Tahar's men? No. No. It could not be. Antar's men were the men Tahar wanted to kill. Aziz strained to remember his own words. *What if I belong to Tahar?* Maybe he had said it a little differently. *What if I came from Tahar?* He had assumed they took him to mean he had come from being tortured at the hands of Tahar. Some of the men holding his ankles that night were confused. Some wanted to let him go. Some said no.

"There is an underground entrance," Sellami was saying. Aziz shook himself. "And it will be dark by the time we get there. A doctor will be waiting for us."

It had to have been Sellami who said those words that night. *Vite, mon frère, Benane attende.*

"Will Benane be there?" Aziz asked.

"I do not know yet."

Aziz feared he could not hold his thoughts; they seemed to be so fired as to be visible in air. He longed, improvidently, to tell Sellami he was not Nazzar. The temptation to believe Sellami was a good man pulled at him. Rescue, Aziz thought, the rescue of being understood by Sellami, I could have it, if I just give up trying to understand, if I accept that there are no right sides, no wrong sides, no sides on any sides. What reality could any one person know? Stop thinking, he told himself, that you, the one small you who sees only from your own eyes, can know it.

Then he remembered the woman. She was one of many, but the first for him. Sellami had been the one with the shovel who finished her. An act of compassion. But the way he did it. He pulled her head from its roots into dirt. *All merciful.* Those words from her. Aziz felt the familiar sickness. He tried to swallow. Nothing gave. It was not an image; it was not anything he could push out of his mental pictures. He had trouble looking at her then, and he had no real face for her or any of the others now. But he had watched. He had done nothing.

He sometimes did as they did, but only when there was no other option. When his not participating would have looked suspicious. When they would have killed him if he had not. In his mind he could see his own pickpocket face, hear his sisters singing a mocking song. Stop doing that with your eyes, his father was saying. The roundel of his sisters teased him. *Squinting, squinting, Aziz is always squinting.*

"Shit, you need to puke," Sellami said. He braked and lowered the window automatically from the driver's side. Aziz pushed his head out but thought better of it and began crawling, as best he could, out the window.

"Nazzar, fuck," Sellami said, trying to hold onto the wheel and Aziz's drawstring waistband. "You're delirious." The Expedition bucked into a halt. With the jolt Aziz flew out the window; Sellami was left holding his pants. Sellami found him passed out a few yards behind the rear bumper.

Aziz awoke in Benane's garage. It was a place of scrubbed concrete, orderliness, new aluminum ladders on new nails on just-cut lumber. It smelled of sawdust and gasoline and grass. There was a lawn mower large enough to sit on. Three brilliant bicycles stood in a line. The garage could fit six cars. Two were there, both white Mercedes-Benzes.

Aziz tried to open the Expedition's door, but he couldn't get out. Then Sellami clicked the locks and Aziz pushed onto the floor, banging his elbow on the running board. Sellami hit a button on his cell phone. "Send them. We're here."

Two orderlies in white came through a door at the far end of the garage. They had a stretcher.

"I have talked to Tahar," Sellami said.

He and Ramdane Benane were sitting in a gallery that abutted a pond. The doctor was working on Aziz in another part of Benane's house.

"And?" Benane said.

"He says it was a mistake."

"A mistake."

"Killing twenty on our payroll: that is his concept for mistake."

"They *were* criminals," Benane reminded him.

"Tahar's people are welcome to kill the criminals I travel with and you hired, but Tahar's people were trying—and eagerly—to kill *me.*"

"But they did not."

"There were guns. I had a knife."

"I am sorry for this. Really. I am."

"We will never get that close to Antar again."

"I know."

"That took two years."

"I know."

"We had every single sadist in North Africa in this group. It is not going to come easy to assemble it again."

"We should have just had you kill him."

"As I had said."

"Zahaf would not have it."

"You have to admit, he is unrealistic," Sellami said, sitting down on a taupe armchair. "Would you bring me something exquisitely alcoholic?" he said into an intercom box on a side table. A green light went on.

"You cannot have someone like Antar killed to the script Zahaf wants. People do not *want* to kill Antar. The sick fuck is a *hero*. Zahaf? We could get some villagers to kill Zahaf."

Benane sat down and put his head in his hands. "I have lost the ability to talk to him."

"That is what happens. How many whores did he bring in this weekend? Ten, twenty? What was it?"

"He is without conscience."

"Just like Antar."

"No."

"Keep telling yourself that."

A man came into the room with a cart of liquor and bar glasses. He brought Benane a glass of red wine.

"I want Pernod," Sellami said.

"None is here."

Sellami looked at the cart. "Vodka, then. Ice."

They sat drinking in silence.

"You are convinced Antar survived it," Benane said.

"I saw him kill many men. After he killed them, he ran to a truck, got in, and drove away. I saw it myself."

"Headed?"

"North. After, he could have turned east, then south, then west. There is no way to know. We were *it*. *We* knew where he was. And I am here and Nazzar is here and the rest are food for flies."

"He cannot go to his family," Benane said.

"Are they in Châteauneuf?"

"No, they are still in Berrouaghia."

"There is another problem," Sellami said. "He was obsessed with Nazzar."

"So?"

"He will try to find him."

"Maybe that is not a problem." Benane said each word slowly.

Sellami sat there thinking.

"Maybe we send Nazzar home," Benane said.

"So that Antar would follow him there?"

"You seem to think he might."

"Antar might kill Nazzar's family. He might think Nazzar abandoned him. He has done it before to other families because of other men, men he loved less than Nazzar."

"Would that be a tragedy?" Benane asked.

"Not if we were there before Antar."

"That is my idea."

Sellami sat back in his chair. "Do Nazzar's parents know he is alive?" he asked.

"His mother. His father is dead. Just his mother," Benane answered.

"Brothers? Sisters?"

"None."

"Unusual. So what does this mother know?"

"Nothing, naturally."

"The unit reported him missing."

"He was declared a deserter. There is a warrant for his arrest."

"We should fix that."

"Not a good idea to fix. It would be poorly timed. They have a good way of knowing this kind of thing."

"Okay."

"Talk to Nazzar. The doctor says he is stitched up and there are no internal injuries to speak of. I think it would be better to move quickly rather than slowly."

"Antar was wounded. He will not be moving yet."

"When has that ever stopped him? Most of the time he walks around smelling like days-old chicken. I do not think he has any toes anymore. There is also this: Zahaf will not know where Antar died; in a village burnt to the ground there is no way to know. So we will, if we are quick, deliver Antar according to script."

The sling on his arm was not helpful. The stitches were no doubt a good thing. The bandaging around his waist felt strong, comforting even. The doctor had been excellent. He spoke French, looked German. Aziz answered his questions—Does this hurt? Can you move this?—and nothing more was said between them. The doctor gave him pills for pain, but Aziz kept them under his tongue and took them out when he left.

He was in a room at the back of the house. Its Palladian doors opened onto gardens and an incomprehensibly green swath of grass. He had never, except in movies, seen such a thing. Outdoor lighting powered upward into the trees, great tall canopies that moved gently in a low wind. Blooming vines and groupings of tender plants wound around the periphery. The grounds were so big, he could not see to the end or the side of them. This was how Benane lived. This was what he could not give up, or perhaps what he told himself he didn't need but his wife did, or his children. There was nothing Algerian here. It was a European estate, a French château without plated gold or ornate rickrack. It was stately, as he imagined Benane himself was.

What idiocy to think Benane would have ever come to his army unit. He had imagined finding Benane while bringing officers tea. Imagined that Benane would look in his eye and intuit him as one of his kind. Aziz had not known enough about anything to know even one thing. He had thought Benane would swoop down and save him from the appalling insensibility of his unit, a place where men disappeared without comment, where it seemed that everyone beside you was not what they seemed, or watched you to find out your thoughts before you had any. He would trade for such uncertainties now. Child games, those questions whispered by his fellow soldiers.

Did you vote for the FIS?

Too young to have voted.

Your father?

My father never voted. ("What is the point? It will be what it will be," Aziz's father always said.)

One or two soldiers didn't believe that answer. To them, his father was an Andalusian butterfly under glass.

He had believed that Benane served under General Zahaf but was a better man than Zahaf. Evidence of Benane's being better was scant. What was plentiful were rumors of Zahaf's malevolence. He lived not in Algiers, or even Algeria, but in Lyon, where he controlled networks of mercenaries and, it was even said, retired Israeli intelligence officers. Did they not know how to track Arabs? What better way would there be? Aziz discounted these tales. He convinced himself of Benane's honor and conceded that Zahaf was corrupt but no sorcerer.

He had no basis for this. The miracle, the blue light shining that he had not really seen until now, was that he had convinced Sellami he was Nazzar. It was fantastical. And yet it was so. A baby had deceived a panther. It was not like his deception of Antar. Somehow tricking a madman was easy. But he had not even known the role he was to play with Sellami, and yet by some grace he had played it.

The best way to be an undercover operative, it seemed, was to know nothing about the undercover operation.

There was a knock at the door.

"Nazzar," Sellami said, as he walked in.

Aziz turned and saw he had a drink. Behind him he could hear the wheels of a cart. A dark man, maybe Mauritanian, pushed it into the room.

"What would you like?" Sellami started pulling bottles from the cart. "Gin? Campari? Cognac?"

Aziz froze. He was too weak to drink and keep his footing.

"I need food."

"What would you like?"

"There is lamb," the dark man said evenly. "Lamb chops that can be made directly. I will bring rice as well."

"He needs oranges, bring him some oranges."

Aziz nodded yes to all of it.

The man left. The cart stood there.

Sellami poured himself more of what he was drinking. "Sure?" he asked.

Aziz waved him off.

"Broke your arm."

"It would seem so."

"How many stitches?"

"I did not count."

"I talked to Benane."

Aziz waited. He could not trust himself to speak. The turn from here was hard to see.

"Tahar got the wrong message. His men thought they were to kill the ones who were not wearing a *barnous*. That they *were* to kill the ones in the leather jackets. Wearing Adidas."

Aziz let out a stream of air between his lips. "Not good," he said.

"Not good," Sellami repeated. He took another swig.

"I told Benane you were flawless," Sellami added.

Aziz shook his head.

"No," Sellami said. "You were. It was almost a year, and you never fucked up. *They* fucked up."

They were quiet. Aziz willed the man with the lamb to come quickly. He could not think his way into this conversation. It called for closeness. They had spent months killing together, engaged in an elaborate delusion about which Sellami no doubt had countless questions to ask and reminiscences to share. There was still much Aziz did not grasp. His left hand, on the unbroken arm, quivered. He tried to lean it on the chair.

Sellami pushed a button, Aziz did not see where. "Get the food here. Bring kebab, anything," Sellami said. "Fuck the chops."

"I am fine."

"You are shaking."

"It is nothing."

"I always crack up when the game is over. Always. Or I used to," Sellami said. He took another swallow of vodka. "I mean you are there, you are doing it, you start to believe you are what you play. And when it ends, when you are you, it can be too much. And Nazzar, you have never done it before."

Aziz was relieved to hear this. He was a novice. Allowances would be made.

"You must want to talk to your parents."

"My parents?" Aziz's relief evaporated.

"I am sorry. I meant your mother."

Aziz tried to construe what this meant, and as he did the dark man appeared carrying a tray of platters, and behind him was another person, a boy. He had bowls of water and towels. They were to wash their hands. But the boy knelt and washed Aziz's hands for him, perhaps because of his sling. Sellami rubbed his hands in the water and the boy handed him a towel. The food was spread on a series of tables the boy brought in from the hallway and covered in white tablecloths.

When he was done eating, Sellami was on another drink. Aziz decided it was important to join him.

"I want whiskey."

"Good. That helps. It will turn off your nerves."

"I am better now."

"Can you believe Antar? There he is in the *barnous,* and he starts firing, and no one goes after him. Who did they think he was? Me?"

"It was dark."

"I wondered, though, why you did not wear the leather jacket. Or the Adidas. By the time I noticed, we were in the alley. All I could think was you were planning to put a jacket on later, but that was risky."

Aziz told himself to go slowly. He took a sip of his whiskey.

"Ice would be good."

"Sure."

Aziz went for a leisurely tone as he shook the cubes in his glass, to which Sellami had added more whiskey. He was going to yawn for added effect but couldn't pull it off. He was drawn tight. "Antar believed I was—different." Another sip. "From God." He put his glass down. "It would not have been like me to take the stolen jacket and shoes. It would have been against his thinking of me."

"Kill, yes. Steal, no."

"Something like that."

"The fuck is insane."

"He is."

Their killing went unmentioned. It was for them to kill in the service of killing one who killed others. They helped Antar kill. They killed for Antar. To create the illusion that they were with Antar. But why not just kill Antar? What had the killing and waiting been for? Was this something he could ask Sellami? Maybe he was wondering the same thing. Aziz could feel the speed of his own bloodstream; it was almost as if it were motorized. The muscles around his left eye had been twitching since the ride in the Expedition. He rubbed his eye with his free hand. Sellami refilled Aziz's glass. He must remember not to drink all of it.

Sellami leaned his elbows on his knees. His face was closer.

"There were times you were so good, I thought you had gone over."

Aziz had to drink another sip. He tried to keep it small, but when he put the glass down it was empty. He looked out into the garden and found himself saying, "We sleep in lice and Benane gets this."

The moment he said it, he realized he should not have. There was silence. He kept staring into the garden. More silence. He would not be the one to say the first next thing. There was no rescue he could imagine from his stupidity.

"Our day will come," Sellami finally said. "There is plenty for us coming."

Aziz let out a breath without thinking. It had been okay. He shook his head and tried to clear his throat. "I am tired," he said, hoping to end this talk. He needed Sellami gone.

Sellami said nothing. He went to the cart again. Aziz heard him pouring the vodka, getting the ice.

"You worry me," he said to Aziz.

"I am tired," Aziz said again.

"Did you kill Ahmed?"

Aziz paused. "No."

"Antar thought you did."

"He thought many things."

"There were others too."

"Others?"

"You killed."

"We all did."

"Ahmed—he was one of us," Sellami said.

Aziz could not risk another sentence. He sat there, iron.

"You tried to make certain things . . . right," Sellami continued. "Fix things."

"You did not?"

"Those babies."

"What about them?"

"He was standing on them," Sellami whispered.

Sellami was drunk. And he was crying. Noiselessly, but his face was completely wet. His eyes were bloodshot.

"Fuck, it is hot," Sellami said. He got up and threw open one of the Palladian doors. An alarm sounded. Sellami was taking his shirt off. He didn't seem to hear the ringing or notice that stadium lights had flooded the garden. It occurred to Aziz that he was not crying but sweating. Then Sellami poured what was left of the vodka and ice in his drink on his head. He ran out onto the grass and disappeared behind the last stand of visible trees.

The house had come to life. Uniformed men were driving golf carts across the grass. There was commotion in the hall, and phones ringing. The dark man came into the room, looked at Aziz immobile on his chair as he had left him hours before, and closed the doors to the garden. The alarm stopped. "Are you all right, Officer Nazzar?" he said quickly. Aziz nodded. Off he went. Two boys came in and began taking away the cart, the platters, the tables. The dark man came in and drew the curtains on all the windows and doors overlooking the garden.

Aziz had a powerful need to lie down. There was no bed in this room though. He was about to ask where he was to sleep when a tall man entered the room. The dark man said, "Officer Nazzar, this is Colonel Benane."

Aziz tried to get up, but Benane said, "Sit."

The dark man left, closing the door behind him.

"This is most unfortunate," Benane said, sitting in a chair across the room from Aziz. He was stiff.

"Sellami?"

"He does this," Benane said dryly.

"The pressure."

"What amazes me is that you have not joined him in a romp through the grounds."

Aziz held up his cast and sling.

"Once, Sellami came back and he had two broken legs and an incision in his abdominal cavity he had endured during a makeshift operation," Benane said. "He not only drank a liter of vodka, he managed to drag himself across a highway into a lake. He nearly drowned."

"I am sorry to hear it."

"You went through much together."

"We did."

"Well. We have things to discuss."

"Certainly."

"You have nothing to fear; they will find Sellami. He cannot get very far."

"Of course."

"You are a man of composure, I see. But even you, I believe, need recuperation. It is time you go home to your mother. I have made the arrangements. You will be driven to her house tomorrow morning. The good woman has suffered unduly. When she got the news tonight you were alive, she had to be sedated. Luckily, Dr. Andrews, who was here earlier, was able to make it out to her home."

Aziz stopped breathing.

"No doubt you miss her. It has been difficult."

Aziz stayed still. He could not bring himself to nod. This woman, she would know he was not Nazzar. This woman, she would be his undoing.

"Perhaps not. Sellami told me you are a man without feeling."

The sound of a dog scratching outside came into the silence. A woman's voice said, "No." The mechanical gearing of a golf cart came close and then fell away.

"I am a man of feeling, Colonel Benane," Aziz finally said. "I felt when I killed mothers—in your service. I felt when I killed girls—in your service. And I will no doubt have with me those mothers and those girls when I see my own mother tomorrow morning." It was foolhardy to talk to this man this way, but Aziz was more tired than he ever thought was possible. He closed his eyes.

When he opened them a few moments later, Benane was no longer in his chair. Aziz looked around the room for him in consternation. He was off to get henchmen, *klashes;* perhaps he was readying the place where Aziz would be given over for *kdoulou esslah*. Aziz wanted the chambers of Ben Aknoun; it was his due. But no, Benane was on his knees. He was at Aziz's knees, and this time the man was weeping. His sobbing had been too long coming. Aziz could not understand most of what he was saying. Benane continued for a short time only, but he was still overcome when he pulled himself off the floor and walked hurriedly out the door. The last noise Aziz heard was sniffling, then a cough, in the hallway.

24

Aziz dialed Brooks Street. "The number you have dialed, six one seven, two nine one, seven eight six four, has been disconnected. Please check the number and try again." He had dialed at different times for days now. It was always the same. Mourad had changed the number, not left it off the hook by mistake.

Aziz decided to write his brother at work. This meant getting the address again. He had no memory of what the dispatcher on the pay phone had given him. Now he worried she would answer, recognize his voice, and refuse to tell him what she had told before.

He weighed what he should say. It all felt risky. Then it came to him. He asked the old man selling books to make the call for him. The sound of his ancient voice—surely that would inspire respect. Yet all the old Yemeni had was Arabic. But he could read. As long as the sentences were short.

Aziz wrote the English words using Arabic letters, because the old man could not read the Roman alphabet. He sat with him outside the cell-phone store for several mornings while the old man peddled his books.

E-X-C-U-S-E

That was an excellent word in Arabic.

M-E

Also good.

I N-E-E-D

The old man learned this in one day.

T-H-E A-D-D-R-E-S-S

He could not say it. There were no *th* sounds. He could not write it either. Aziz switched *the* to *an*.

A-N A-D-D-R-E-S-S

Problem solved.

F-O-R Y-O-U-R F-I-R-M

Company, after many tries, was rejected.

T-O S-E-N-D

Send was a disaster. To *mail* worked.

T-A-X I-N-F-O-R-M-A-T-I-O-N

What was he thinking? *Info* was good enough.

After a week, the Yemeni in the well-washed djellaba had it. He held forth at the cell-phone store for the men working. They agreed to pass honest comments and suggestions. Most felt that *info* was too informal, yet no one could get him to say the *tion* until Aziz saw that spelling it *shun* was completely readable in Arabic.

With *information* conquered, the old man was ready. "It is my boyhood again," he told Aziz. "Like memorizing sura from the Qur'an."

There was one other comment. It was about procedure, not pronunciation. The store owner persuaded Aziz that his original plan of taking the phone from the old man immediately after he said *information*—so Aziz could write down the address—was mistaken.

"We have here a machine that can put a rubber ear on the phone receiver. This rubber ear is connected to a tape recorder. The address will be recorded. You will have an actual tape of this address."

There would be no charge to use the machine. Everyone at the cell-phone store wanted Aziz to reach his brother. Not wanting to offend, Aziz still had to insist the rubber ear, which was more like a rubber cup on a wire, go through a trial run. He was annoying everyone, he felt, but he would not accept it until a series of calls was made that was clearly recorded.

The door, someone was pounding it. Lahouari rolled over. He waited; the noise went on. He looked at his clock radio. It was 6 a.m. He pulled on boxers and a sweatshirt. His brothers were at work. It was morning chilly. He was going to put on socks but then he heard someone yelling at the door. Maybe it was that crazy girl his brother Ali had slept with last weekend. She had done this already once this week. What was her name? Kathy.

He opened the door, which always took forever with all the locks and burglar stops. "Kathy," he said, when the last one gave way, "you—"

There in the dark were a crowd of men. Some had on coats and red ties. Others had windbreakers. They all had short hair. One of the ones in a windbreaker had a holster with a black gun in it. Handcuffs dangled from another's waist.

"Lahouari Khaled," said one of the red ties.

Who were they? Police, but what kind?

"May we come in?"

Lahouari stepped backward numbly.

"Your passport, Mr. Khaled?"

"It is back, in kitchen. I get."

"Officer Melhaney and Special Agent Brown will accompany you," said the red tie in charge.

What would the others do? They could barely fit in the living room. Maybe they would open drawers. Or take letters. He glanced nervously at the mail.

He went back to the kitchen and got his passport with its long-expired visa. Others had told him to get a fake one, but he wouldn't. Overstaying the visa, everyone did this, but fake papers? That was too much. Now he wished he had. He gave the passport to the one in a tie, who handed it to the one in a windbreaker.

"This visa expired two years ago, Mr. Khaled."

"I am sorry for that one." Lahouari was fully awake, fully afraid. "I am sorry. Please."

"Step back into the living room, Mr. Khaled."

He inched back there, red tie and windbreaker close by his elbows.

"Please have a seat," another red tie said. It was their apartment now.

He sat down, and three of them, two ties and a windbreaker, sat down too. The rest stood straight and watched.

He looked down at his hands. They were stained from the auto shop, the nails cracked. His bare legs were bony. He couldn't even look at these confident men and their well-laundered prosperity.

"You are in violation of eighteen U.S.C. nine eleven, ten zero one, fifteen forty-six, and sixteen twenty-one; eight U.S.C. thirteen twenty-five. Fraud and Misuse of Visas, False Personation, Unlawful Entry, Failure to Depart, Failure to Report, Working Without a Permit. To name a few sections of the statute that come immediately to mind." This was delivered by a windbreaker. He was angry.

"These are serious violations, Mr. Khaled, each of which carries a prison sentence of fifteen years. Given the nature of your case, the government would seek jail without bond pending final adjudication. Deportation, after serving your sentence, is virtually a certainty." A planned pause stretched.

"However, Agent Pelton and the Immigration and Naturalization Service might be willing to overlook these violations, Mr. Khaled, if you were able to assist us," said a red tie, not the one in charge. "We have reason to believe there is a terrorist cell operating here in Boston," he continued. "Information I'm not at liberty to disclose indicates this is an Algerian cell. It has ties to operatives in Germany, Pakistan, Great Britain, Yemen, and Afghanistan." Another red tie said, "Do you know the GSCP?"

Lahouari had not heard of such a thing. Was it a United States police? He shook his head.

"The Salafist Group for Preaching and Combat."

Lahouari knew it. Salafists, yes, everyone knew of them. The other words, he wasn't sure. They called them Afghans. Or *khandjiya*. Algerians who came home from Kandahar and were crazy.

"I read about those ones."

"We would like you, when you are at the mosque, to help identify for us those individuals."

"I do not go."

"You don't go to the mosque?"

"No. I work every day. There is no mosque for me."

Two red ties looked at each other as if this were a revelation they weren't ready for or didn't believe.

"But I help. I help you much."

"Hey." Ghazi hoped Kamal was awake.

"Yeah."

"Your package didn't arrive," Ghazi said.

"It didn't?" Kamal sounded sleepy.

"I swear, I didn't receive it."

"Nine forty-four, right?"

"Yeah."

"Apartment two?"

"Two. I swear, I didn't receive it."

"Why didn't it arrive?"

"How should I know? Do you have the receipt?"

"Receipt?"

"Call them, the number there," Ghazi said.

"Hold on, I will look."

"You cannot throw it away."

"Fuck you. I thought it would get there, like the others. Why keep the receipt? Problems, every time, every day, problems. Nothing has materialized and—"

"Nothing came today?" Ghazi could not believe it. Kamal had been expecting a FedEx of stolen Belgian passports for a week.

"Nothing came today. Nothing. At twelve noon I opened it, and there was nothing. Hold on."

Ghazi waited.

"I don't have a number at all," Kamal said. "The paper they gave, that paper, I threw it away."

"Fuck."

"Fuck you."

"That paper is everything."

"It will get to you."

"Priority Mail?"

"Yeah."

"Are you sure you sent it Priority Mail?"

"Of course! What did I tell you?"

"Dhakir told me it would arrive today."

"He lied. It will get there tomorrow."

They were a ring, a credit card ring. It was Ghazi's idea to involve Rafik and then Kamal. Dhakir liked it. There was a waiter in a restaurant in Montreal, no one knew who he was, except someone who knew someone who knew Dhakir. These waiters, they had readers, little electronic boxes; they fit in pockets. A customer at a table gives a card. The waiter takes a leak, the little box reads the card. There were other waiters in Boston.

It was a deplorable situation.

Fake papers. Fake shipments. Everything Hank Bridges had accused Ghazi of doing, now Ghazi was doing it. He began by telling himself he was setting up Rafik and Kamal. That was three months ago.

Ghazi had no excuse.

Go to Boston, he told himself, turn in Rafik and Kamal, take your vengeance. Finish this.

So, with a pristine passport in the name of Manuel Marquez,

Ghazi went back to Boston, not by bus but on American Airlines. He went home in too-small Gucci jeans and too-long cowboy boots. He had been led to believe his coat was cashmere. Whatever its makeup, it was black and warm and he felt, in his depressive state, almost good about it. He took a taxi to 6A Brooks and arrived around dinnertime. He still had a key. The lights were on, the shades down.

25

So what do we have?" April Baron-Evans, FBI special-agent-in-charge of the Boston field office, was heading the meeting.

"Khaled was right about this what's-his-name," said one of the red ties that had been at Lahouari's apartment. "Oh, here it is. Kamal."

"Point of order, if I may," said a state trooper named Malcolm. "Can we agree to use both names for these individuals? Khaled. Khaled Mohammed? Khaled Abdul? Kamal *Something*? For those of us not privy to all JTTF three-oh-twos."

One question into the meeting, April said to herself, and who-shares-what-with-who was started. You were in the Joint Terrorism Task Force, you read the 302s. And everyone here was JTTF.

"We all know the guidelines for dissemination of three-oh-two reports," said the associate U.S. attorney, who was the Massachusetts Anti-Terrorism Task Force coordinator. "Malcolm, for all practical purposes you get all the three-oh-twos. The foreign intelligence component to this investigation is just starting. And when it goes full throttle, I assure you I will be holding extremely detailed declassified briefings, with written materials, for all concerned."

"To answer your question, Malcolm," said the red tie, "Khaled is the last name of our CS. His first name is Lahouari."

"Can you spell that please?" This from another FBI agent new to the task force from Detroit.

"Okay, it's L-A-H-O-U-A-R-I."

"This confidential source," said a Boston police officer. "Remind me again. Is he someone we learned about from the so-called Charlie Stone?"

"Negative," the red tie said. "Charlie Stone was unable to gain access to Kamal Gamal. He was on the periphery of the cell but was never able to penetrate. Khaled—excuse me, *Lahouari* Khaled—came to immigration's attention because of a hotline tip. He was living in a studio apartment in Revere that had at least eight occupants. Landlord called him in, along with quite a few others."

"Gentlemen, I think it's important, for these meetings to be a success, that we all read—and I mean *read*—the reports in your packets," said the associate U.S. attorney. "For some of you, this is your first exposure to names of a Muslim or Arabic type. It is not easy, I assure you. But familiarizing yourself with these names can be done."

April motioned to the red tie who had started the meeting. "Richard," she said. "Please continue."

"Just to summarize. Lahouari Khaled was not cooperative. He gave excuses regarding the mosque issue. But he did give us the name of an individual he indicated was involved in credit card fraud and—this is the important part—identity fraud. That individual is Kamal Gamal. Kamal Gamal is an Algerian national who came legally to this country in 1994 as an asylum seeker. He was granted asylum in 1996. His application and the INS finding in the case are in your packet. I won't go into too much detail now, but we believe Gamal is not Algerian. We believe he obtained an Algerian passport through fraudulent means during the Gulf War. He may be an Iraqi, he may be a Saudi. The chaos in Kuwait during and after the war was such that identities changed hands like quarters in a Coke machine.

"Last year, Kamal Gamal was picked up in a botched Treasury operation. Secret Service, as we all now know, had a problem with an agent in their fraud division they've since reassigned to a desk job in Sacramento."

Nods around the table. "Hank Bridges."

"Amazing situation."

"How media didn't get wind of it, I'll never know."

"All charges against Kamal Gamal had to be dropped," he continued. "Kamal Gamal, naturally, disappeared. We had been unable to locate him, despite a lot of help from Boston PD, until now."

"This means an expansion of surveillance," April said. "And that means developing evidence to send headquarters so we can get the kind of FISA warrant that includes everything we need. Right now we have pen register and trap-and-trace orders in place. But we need roving wiretaps, confidential searches, mail covers, and access to airport, hotel, storage facility, and car rental records."

"After the millennium bombing plot," said the associate U.S. attorney, "which was foiled at the Canadian border thanks to Customs—and which was an Algerian operation that the Seattle task force and Washington handled—Justice and the FISA court have been more willing to provide assistance to field offices. This is not an invitation for sloppiness. I say this only because I know this field office in particular has experienced some frustrations and disappointments in this regard in the past. I've been liaising with the FISA people at main Justice, and I think there's been real progress."

The Boston cop was lost. April could see it in his face. A smart detective. His specialty had been the mob. And racketeering and terrorist conspiracy were not all that different in principle.

She stopped the cop on the way out. His name was Tom Baker. "Detective," she said, holding out her hand. "Don't let these blowhards fool you."

"I appreciate that," he said. "Give me RICO, I'll give you chapter and verse. But FISA. Jesus."

"Foreign Intelligence Surveillance Act. Just a bunch of backflips and somersaults we do to convince headquarters, main Justice, and a federal judge that we can sneak into a terrorist's house when he's not around. And a few other things. You have time for lunch?"

"I was just heading to the cafeteria."

The key didn't work. They had changed the locks. Ghazi paused. Maybe Mourad and Heather didn't live there anymore. It certainly would have made sense to give up the shithole. He put his ear to the door. Nothing. But the lights were on. He had to know about Aziz. He knocked.

The taxi honked. The driver wanted out or in. Ghazi put up two fingers. When he turned around he saw that someone had lifted up a blind from the living room window, then let it fall back fast.

He heard running inside. The first lock opened. Then the second. Then the long steel rod on the floor.

Heather swung open the door.

"Ghazi!" She threw herself onto him.

He didn't recognize her. Maybe she was a friend of Heather's.

"Excuse me, excuse me," Ghazi said, pushing her away. She wouldn't let go. She was, he realized in dismay, crying.

"Hey, hey. Calm now. Calm." He put his arm around her shoulder. "Maybe we go inside a little."

He gave the cabdriver, who was bringing suitcases out of the trunk, a hundred-dollar bill. He went inside.

Rafik was fed up. At the U-Stor-It, Kamal was useless. He was on his cell phone to his new girlfriend the whole time. Rafik was so pissed off he almost took the revolver out of his waistband and fired a warning shot. Instead, he took the phone out of Kamal's hand and started yelling. "Look, you stale dank pussybitch, this is work; we are working, enough!" It was no girlfriend on the line, however. It was Dhakir.

"Rafik, are you stoned?"

Rafik dropped his chin. "Dhakir?"

"I told you, none of that. None of that."

"I am not stoned."

"What are you doing?"

"We are taking care of the stuff."

"Yeah."

"Listen, Dhakir, I thought you were this piece of ass he likes. That is all."

"Kamal was listening to me."

"Right."

"This is not play."

"No. Not play. No."

"These are serious things."

"I am with you."

"If you don't fear *me*—" Dhakir stopped. "What about hellfire? How will that be for you? It burns, I tell you, it burns."

"It burns."

Rafik rolled his eyes. Kamal rolled his eyes back.

"Make your ablutions."

"Yes."

"Good. Peace be upon you."

"Peace upon you."

Rafik looked at Kamal. "He is fucked up."

Kamal shrugged. "It happens."

12 October 2000

Mourad Arkoun
Security Services
c/o Boston Logan Airport
Boston, Mass. 02128

Dear Brother,

I hope this letter finds you well, and that Heather is also well. I am writing to you because I have tried to call and no one will let me speak to you. The number at home is not working. I am afraid to write to you there. I need to know if it is safe to come to Boston again. I want you to call me and let me know. Please understand that it is best to call me at 212-888-4343. This is a cellular store near to where I am living. The owner is helpful to me. His name is Hussain, Tahir Hussain. He will come and get me.

How is Ghazi? I am hoping you heard from him. Is he still in Canada? Maybe he got a chef job up there. I am working at Haha Smoke Shop.

I want very much to come home. I love you.

Aziz

"I do not like this," Rafik said. He was standing inside the U-Stor-It. Kamal was by the truck.

"Why not?" Kamal asked.

"I do not."

"You wanted it."

"Not this way."

"Rafik. You are in it."

"I can get out."

Kamal stopped. He put the box he was carrying down. "You sorry bastard, you will be eating your mother's shit."

Rafik laughed. "That may scare your little Brazilian whore—" he started.

"It is not—" Kamal began.

"—but not me!" Rafik finished.

They were screaming over each other.

"Not you what?" Rafik yelled.

"They will have no mercy. Not me, they."

"Who is they?"

Kamal picked up the box again. "You make me insane," he said.

"I make you tell what's going on," Rafik said.

"I have told you."

"What?"

"Much larger numbers on the cards," Kamal said. "Bigger shipments. More cigarettes. They are moving the cigarettes faster. There are more trucks."

"So open that box."

"If they see this is open on the other side, you know that cannot be. You know that."

"I know I do not give a fuck if we lose whatever it is we stood to make if this box stays right here in Boston."

"It is ten thousand dollars!"

Rafik was taking a knife out of his boot.

"Rafik, this is crazy."

"Really? I'll tell you what is crazy. Me not knowing enough. That is what is crazy."

"Please."

"And all this Allah talk from goat dick up there in Montreal. He was a fuck in Arzew, and he is a fuck times two now."

He moved toward the box Kamal had put in the truck. Kamal blocked his way.

"You want it like that?" Rafik said. "Fine."

He turned around and slashed at a box that was sitting in the storage unit. Kamal rushed toward him. It was too late. Tumbling out of the box were dozens of plastic bags filled with something white. Rafik had cut open a box of Pampers. Nestled inside were fire extinguishers.

"Heather?"

Ghazi didn't know how to make his face look. She was easily half gone. She looked so much older. The breasts—small. That face like cream. But with the pounds missing she looked less inviting. At least the coppery blond hair was there. She had it in a ponytail down her back. He wanted to touch it to make sure it was her.

"Where is everyone?" he asked instead.

She said, "Hold on," and took his coat and disappeared down the back hall. He looked around. The place was clean. He had never seen it so clean. No sleeping bags on the floor. The Three were obviously elsewhere. Rafik's Tour de France posters were gone. No Madonna on the wall either. It smelled good too, like Heather was baking apples.

"Sit down," she said, her face still wet from crying. She wiped off her chin with the sleeve of her shirt. "I have a six-pack in the fridge."

"Good. Good. Thank you."

He was feeling formal. Very formal. He sat on the sofa. His Guccis were too tight. He looked at the boots. Way too long. Suddenly, he couldn't sit there like that. "Heather," he yelled, "I'll be right in, I gotta wash up."

"Sure," she said. Her voice was the same. The kind of whiny thing she always had.

"I put your stuff in the guest room."

Guest room. Fuck. Where was everyone? Did Heather live here alone?

The room was done up in yellow. He looked at a framed poster over the bed.

One Day at a Time

Help me believe in what I could be
and all that I am.
Show me the stairway I have to climb.
Lord, for my sake teach me to take
one day at a time.

This was written over ferns, daisies, and a misty green lake. What went on here? Had Heather gone holy? He closed the door, opened his suitcase, and pulled out old jeans. He left the boots in the closet.

When he padded into the living room, Heather was sitting on the sofa, drinking a glass of wine. He couldn't believe it. Heather never drank. So maybe she hadn't gone the way of angels. His beer was there. Sam Adams, his favorite.

"I kept that in there. Waiting for you. I never would let it not be there." She was crying again.

He took a long swallow. Then two others. The bottle was empty.

"I'll get another," she said, getting up.

He caught her wrist as she went by. He looked up at her, really looked. She looked gorgeous with wet eyes. Did he look as diffcrent to her as she did to him?

She read his thoughts. "I know I look different."

"Come here."

He tugged some on her wrist and took her other hand. She was a swan. She had been a walrus.

"Sit here, like this." He made a place for her under his arm, then picked up her wineglass and gave it to her. "Your head goes here." He pulled her head to his chest. "We're going to get drunk. We're going to sit on this couch and get absolutely fucked up. One thing."

He waited. She was taking a sip of wine.

"Yeah."

"Do you remember the first word you taught me?"

"I don't know. Hello?"

"Think about it. That night. Rafik was at the club with Aziz. And you answered the door and it was me."

She lifted her head. "Fox bitch. It was two words."

He needed something to feel it was her. They started laughing. She drank some more of her wine.

26

Aziz rode a bicycle out of the garage. The open door, the empty driveway—he had the search for the vodka-soaked Sellami to thank. After following one macadam path and then on to another driveway, Aziz saw a trail through trees, away from the stadium lights, toward the road in front of Benane's house. He heard sprinklers and the rustle of palms. He was calm, almost nourished. For the first time in a long time, he understood what had happened to him. It occurred to him that he should be more wary. He was still trapped. There were walls and guards and most likely dogs. All he could feel was free.

At the end of the trail there was a small house. Was it for the dark man? The boy? He got off the bicycle and walked it on the soft dirt. There were no lights, just cicadas, and their loud came faster as he realized he couldn't see where to go next. The windows were open; a curtain flapped against a screen. He passed a seesaw and a baby pool. Finally by a clothesline he saw a rutted driveway grown over with roses.

The disappearing driveway had been invaded by olive trees. He weaved between and around on the bicycle, coming into clearings and then back into foliage. After a while, he thought he saw a stone wall in the distance. Closer, he saw it was at least ten feet and had concertina wire coiled at the top. He sat there, looking at it twinkling in the dark. How badly, he calculated, would it injure? Painful, yes, but not fatal. Then he remembered he had the pill the doctor had given him. He reached in his pocket. It was there. He had bandaging from the doctor around his arm and his ribs. He could stop the bleeding, what bleeding there was, with some of it. That left the bicycle.

He needed it for speed from here into the center of Algiers. Then he'd head for the marina. There was always someone going to Arzew. But walking would be too slow. They would see he was gone soon. They'd be driving and they would have him before he had a chance. Then he remembered the dark man's house. Could there be something left outside he could use to hoist the bike? He pedaled back.

He was blessed, because there was a ladder. It leaned casually against a plane tree. He took clothesline and tied the first rung to the bike. He walked it slowly near the house; once clear of it, he rode, the ladder bumping along behind him.

At the wall, he fidgeted out of the sling. He would have to use his broken arm; there was no other way. Then he stood the bike vertically against the stone, took the clothesline in his teeth, and climbed the ladder. To get over, he had to use both arms to hoist himself. He lost his footing for a moment and then pulled. He heard a snapping. He had to go fast or the pain would make him lose heart. The concertina wire ripped through his pants and into his ankles. When he jumped to the ground, some of it came with him, tangled around his foot. He pulled the bicycle with the line, and it came for a bit. But he had forgotten to slip the rope under the wire. He could feel it fraying in his hand. He heard the bicycle's wheels and handlebars clatter on the other side of the wall.

. . .

He did not recover from the loss of the bicycle until he smelled the sea. High from the painkiller, his arm like a rubber bat, his sliced ankle nimble, he had been running or walking for close to an hour. The brackish scent edged away; then he caught it again. The air softened. At the top of a hill of steep streets, he saw ships anchored in the Mediterranean and, closer in, wooden boats in the dust-blue harbor. A few lights broke the dark; the city was asleep. The newest yellow of dawn was opening on the horizon.

He stopped, out of breath. He knew it then. They would not find him. They would, just about now, be at Nazzar's mother's house, somewhere in Belcourt, far from here. Even if she had a photograph of her son on the wall, they would not realize Aziz was not Nazzar. Only Benane and Sellami would remember Aziz's face, and there was little chance they would be at the mother's house. Underlings would go. He had left one in sobs, the other, drunk and lost. He started smiling and wanted to laugh as he started running again below the arched colonnades.

By the time the sandpaper roofs of the Casbah were picking up the wider light, he had found his father's friend Nasim and his fishing boat, *el Karam*. Nasim was tinkering with the motor, his beard rumpled with gray. A younger man Aziz did not recognize on the boat yelled, and Nasim looked up.

They fell together in an embrace, and the man came running to join them. Nasim was overjoyed; Aziz, hopping and clapping. *Alhamdu-lillah* was said over and over. Suddenly Nasim's friend pulled them apart: A fisherman nearby was staring; a group of men on a pier were pointing. Aziz motioned Nasim and his friend belowdeck and explained the boat must leave, immediately; he could not say why but would say why in Arzew. Without asking more, Nasim returned to the motor, which he started after a few tries.

Aziz expected the harbor to be empty. Few would be on Arzew's short beaches. He pictured the rusted umbrellas along the esplanade. His father's inn needed paint when he left two years ago, and its sign on the beach, LA MEHARIA HOTEL, had collapsed into a storm. It was as if Arzew were returning to ruin. Soon it would be like the Roman stones from a temple they had played in as children. It amazed him that Arzew had ever hosted pirates; it seemed too meager for any romance. As long as he could remember, each year brought less of less than less.

He climbed on deck. Through the wind, he heard Nasim on the boat radio. He was shouting, but Aziz couldn't make out what he said. They were closer than he realized. He must have slept for hours. There were the rocky cliffs, so forbidden when he sailed as a boy. Starboard he could see the outlines of tankers, only three today. Other fishing boats were plentiful. That surprised him. It was wonderful to see. Nasim would probably be checking his trawl lines after he took Aziz ashore. The refinery was operating, the smoke not too bad. But then, past the old slaughterhouse, as the crescent of the bay came into view, he saw them. Not just his family—his parents; his brothers Latif, Bilal, and Mourad; his sisters Anissa and Hazar; their husbands Ghaleb and Issam; his father's sisters Dalal and Ghadah; his mother's sisters Hala and Hassibah; all their husbands; all their children—it was more than his family; at least a hundred or more had come. They were standing on the beach near his father's hotel, some with infants in their arms, and a few he saw had brought chairs for the older ones. But when one of them caught sight of *el Karam,* they told another and another. They began to wave.

He had no thinking; all he wanted was to be there: now, now, now. And the waving continued.

"I told them, in Algiers, I had found you," Nasim said. "I did not tell them to do this."

Aziz stood on the prow. He waved.

27

Aziz planned to wait one week for Mourad's call. He spent his days at the cell-phone store. The owner made sure everyone knew Mourad's name, and if Aziz was in the bathroom, or out of sight for any reason, they were to keep Mourad on the phone and find him. At night he slept on the floor on some pillows. He kept two of the store's phones at each ear. One night the phone rang. It was a woman speaking Farsi. He tried to talk Arabic and French and English to her, but she only answered with sounds he did not recognize. He had no hint at even one word's meaning, but he could hear she was frantic. It was rapid talk, and her voice sounded like the highest piano keys being hit out of order by a child.

He had schooled himself not to be upset if Mourad did not call. It was important to follow a plan, not slide into the anger he felt that day on Atlantic Avenue. Mistakes got made and problems multiplied with that kind of attitude. So on the seventh day of his vigil, with no call from Mourad received, Aziz quit his job at the Haha Smoke Shop. His boss was mad so he didn't pay him for the last week. Aziz tried to get him to rehire him on the spot, but the man was too smart for that. The loss of this money was bad. He needed it for his bus ticket to Boston. He needed it for when he got there, because he suspected Mourad and Heather had moved. They might have even decided to go to Canada to find Ghazi. Heather could have gone to Virginia to her father. He couldn't picture her leaving Lahouari behind, but after a year he had to be ready for anything.

So he asked the old man if he could sell beside him for a few days. He needed something to sell, though. He tried selling shoplifted chewing gum, but he could never fit enough in his pockets to make more than a few dollars a day. Plus, he was terrible at it; twice he got caught. So, before dawn, he crept to street corners and with two quarters emptied newspaper boxes of ten or twelve copies. He sold them at half price. Then he had another idea. He borrowed a giant coffee percolator from the mosque down the street and sold an extra-thick brew in paper cups he decorated with Arabic sayings. *Min ratl hakya tafham wiqya.* From a pound of talk, an ounce of understanding. *Al ketheb bem'hallu ebada.* Lying in its proper place is equal to worship. *Kun namla wa takul sukr.* Work like an ant and you'll eat sugar. The cheap papers and the strong coffee were good, but the cups—people liked those the most.

Heather watched the October morning on Brooks Street. A neighbor was trying to clean the pressed aluminum awnings every house had, just scrubbing as hard as he could these ugly stripes the color of old blue washcloths and pistachio ice cream. Gina's Auto Body across the way had a new chain-link fence topped by concertina wire, but for all that trouble, there was only a totaled Toyota Tercel in the lot. The remote parking for the airport at the end of the street was empty except for way too much litter. Someone had left a brown television on the sidewalk.

Mourad had been gone for over a month now, though he did call. He was not good on the phone. He was uncomfortable. It was expensive. He could not find Aziz. That was all there was to say. He was going to try again tomorrow. He had quit his job to find his brother. Heather wondered where he was living, but he wouldn't say. He still had his cell phone, but he talked about getting rid of that too.

It felt like betrayal how she wanted Ghazi. And it didn't help that Mourad called less and less. She couldn't even count the times she replayed how Ghazi took her wrist that first night or the times when she reconsidered the hints, none too clear, that he wanted her.

She stood up from the window, when she heard his bedroom door open and the bathroom door close, and got a toothbrush she had hidden in a drawer so she could brush her teeth in the kitchen sink. She brushed fast, but then she heard the shower, so she had plenty of time. She made coffee. She put frozen breakfast buns in the oven. Ghazi was still in the bathroom, so she took a look at her hair and saw it looked wild: perfect. She licked her finger and erased yesterday's mascara that had clouded under her eye overnight. Finally she heard the bathroom door. Then his door. The apartment smelled wonderfully of molasses.

She had two mugs on the table when he came into the kitchen. "Coffee?" she said. His hair was still wet and his goatee trimmed. He looked down, really blue. He nodded without looking at her. She poured and pushed a mug toward him. "How'd you sleep?" she asked.

"Not good." She brightened, hoping she was the cause of his sleeplessness, but then he added, "I don't sleep good anymore. Not ever."

He took the coffee into the living room and turned on the TV.

Disappointment scoured her out. She poured her own coffee so sloppily it splashed onto her hand. Good, she told herself, good, wake up. Wake up. She could hear him skipping from channel to channel with the remote. When she got out of the shower, he was still doing it.

Her hair was just about dry when the phone rang. She was not dressed entirely, so she yelled to Ghazi to pick it up.

When she came into the living room, the television was off. Ghazi was speaking Arabic on the phone. She sat on a chair and tried to tell what he was saying. Couldn't. Then he said "Mourad" and almost yelled the next few words: "You call your father!"

"No!" Mourad shouted back.

"Why not?"

"He cannot know I cannot find him."

"Mourad, I am sure Aziz is talking to your father, and if you tell your father you now have a phone again, that is the answer. He will tell Aziz; Aziz will come here. Simple."

"What if he is not talking to our father?"

"He is."

"How do you know?"

"Trust me."

"You do not know, then."

"Why wouldn't he? He talked to your father—shit—all the time."

"What if he is not able to call?"

"Mourad, you are not making sense."

"Is Heather there?"

"Of course she's here."

"Give the phone to her."

"Mourad."

"I want to talk to her."

Heather was standing a few steps away. "Hey," Ghazi said angrily. "Talk to this jerk."

He got up and went out the front door. Heather sat down on the sofa.

"Baby," she said to Mourad. "Where are you?"

"I am in New Jersey."

"New Jersey? Mourad, please, please come home."

"I have learned many things. I believe Aziz may be here."

"How?"

"It is not something I can talk about right now."

"But you never can! Mourad, I'm worried. I'm so worried. You can't find Aziz this way. New York is too big, and New Jersey—it's too much. Please."

"I cannot call home."

"You just did. What are you talking about?"

"I mean Algeria. I cannot call there. My parents, for Aziz to be missing; it will be too much for them. He was missing before; this time it will be too much."

"Missing before? You're not making sense."

"What did you do last night?"

"Watched television."

"And was Ghazi there then?"

"No."

"You swear?"

"Yes, I swear!"

"You are different, I feel it."

"Come home."

"To what?"

He hung up on her.

She stood there with the phone in her hand for a few moments. Then she put it down gently as if with ladylike behavior her inner feelings might be better hidden. She felt positively see-through.

The old man was wearing a new djellaba. Aziz instantly missed the old one. "Thanks to you," the old Yemeni said, "I have sold many books these weeks. I bought new clothes." Everything was crisp, the djellaba a frost blue, the cotton drawstring pants pale saffron.

"Stay away from the coffee then." Aziz smiled. "You must keep this one new as a lamb."

"I have been thinking," the old man said. "We have lines for this coffee in these cups you make. Let us buy another coffeemaker. I will help you to make the cups the night before. There are many Yemeni sayings you have not used yet."

They were crouched together on the sidewalk. Aziz was setting up the cups on trays, the old man choosing which books to display prominently. "I fear the journey you make for your brother," he said.

Aziz looked at him, surprised. "You have not said this before." Then he grinned a little and cocked his head. "You want money, that's what you want. You see money when you see me!"

They both laughed.

"You are a buried treasure," the old man said. "What is on the surface—plain. Below—boxes of silver."

The flirting, brief, was over. Heather was okay with that. At least Ghazi's mood seemed to be improving. He had a supply of cash. He bought cases of beer, cases of wine. He bought veal and shrimp, the best. He picked out a new sofa for the living room. He hired some guy who replastered the kitchen ceiling and they drop-kicked the blue bucket out the front door. He bought her a hat he saw in a window. He bought himself a new pair of boots. He cooked for them. He baked pies and cakes. No more frozen, he told her. He was good at Italian—lasagna, manicotti—and better at Mexican. He was experimenting with Cajun. She tried to help out; he wouldn't let her.

"Montreal was good to you," she said, after dinner one night.

"Some ways," he said, getting up to do the dishes.

"What was it like?" She moved to get up too, but he gave her a look and she sat back down.

"Terrible," he said. On went his apron.

"Jobs, though."

"No jobs."

"But—"

"Let me put it this way. Do you know I saw up there one I went to school with—infants' school. What do you call it here?"

"Elementary school."

"In a coffee shop. Right there—*boom!*—we go into business together."

"What kind of business?"

"Imports. A store of things from Indonesia, some African. Jewelry, mostly. Also exports. To the home country and to Pakistan; we try to get something going in France soon."

"Maybe Mourad could get involved."

"Not Mourad."

"You are mad at Mourad."

"No."

"Yes. I feel it."

"To be honest with you, I am not. Get me a beer," he said. "Please."

"Ghazi," she began.

"Hey. You don't have to say anything."

"But I want to. I need to."

He shrugged. "It's up to you. But if you think I see anything wrong with you and Mourad, don't think that. Seriously. Don't think that."

She poured some open wine from the fridge.

"I can see how this happened, from his place. You? Maybe harder to accept. Listen, things have been not good here. I know that."

"He convinced me they were watching us."

"Who was watching?"

"Hank Bridges."

"He is crazy."

"He said we had to pretend to be a couple or they would know we had lied."

Ghazi smiled at her sideways. "That is good, very good. I did not think Mourad capable of this one."

"It wasn't like that."

"Hey, whatever it was, or is, you have done nothing anyone could say anything against."

"I thought I was in love with him. But then, when we found Kamal, and then Rafik, and we realized there was no Hank Bridges anymore, he changed. He had to find Aziz. It wasn't anything I could reason with him about. He had ideas that scared me. Like going to New York and walking around asking people where Algerians lived. At first I went along with it. But when I said it was a bad idea, he got angry. Really angry. And one day, I came home from work, and he was gone and a note on the table said something about he'd be back in a few days. That was last month."

"It is his brother."

"Do you have a brother?"

"I have one."

"Would you do something like that for him?"

"It's not the same."

"So you wouldn't."

"My brother, it is a long story. It's not like Aziz and Mourad."

"What were they like, in Arzew?"

"Who?"

"Their family. Aziz as a kid. Mourad too."

"I wanted to be in that family."

"You did?"

"There is great love in that family. Their father is not hard. His mother, she"—Ghazi shook his head—"she is best friend with my mother. She is—how do you say in English that she is—oh, large inside?"

"Bighearted."

"Something like that."

"Their father, he has a hotel. On the sea. It is small, not expensive. Not cheap, but good for people who like something sweet. There was music, because his father pays people to come in, maybe just a small drum, or a flute—*gasba* we call it—a *gasba* flute. There was a flute player there when I was young. Do you know the clementine mandarin? It first grew in the garden of an orphanage near Oran. It is seedless, so perfect. He had these clementine trees. And the hotel, and their house on the side of the hotel, it smelled like them."

"Why didn't they go into the business? With their dad. Run the hotel with him."

"Not enough guests anymore."

"But why?"

"Algeria is fucked. The people at the top who run things are living well, and the rest—nothing."

"It's better here," she said.

"For citizen, maybe. But outside the house, you feel the cold."

They went to bed after midnight. She was tired. She was a little anxious, too. How would it be with Mourad and Ghazi and *her*? When she and Rafik had been together and then Aziz, and then the Three, and then Mourad and Ghazi—somehow that was fine. Maybe the Three could come back. But Lahouari and his brothers sleeping on the floor—it didn't fit anymore. Ghazi with his money wouldn't sleep there again either. He would probably get his own place.

It was just as she was drifting asleep that he knocked. He must have been having trouble with the light switch in his bedroom, which was kind of tricky and sometimes wouldn't go off. Or maybe Mourad was calling on Ghazi's cell phone.

"I'm coming," she said. He opened the door before she could turn on the light or get out of bed.

"It's cold in here," he said. It wasn't really. It was a nice fall night, a mild cool.

She thought she heard him leave. Before she could think much, he came back with a blanket from his bed and shook it onto hers. He situated it at the foot of the bed, at the side she was not at, and then as he was bringing it up to her so that it would cover her, he stopped. He put an arm behind her, and lifted her just below her shoulders. He was about to bring the pillow under her head but instead he slowly brought her to his chest. His heart was beating fast. He was trembling.

He pulled her out of the bed and against the wall. When he took her head in his hands she knew her breathing changed. He put one hand through her hair and then pulled her head back with it, achingly slowly. He kissed her hard. Then he did something she didn't want him to do. He opened the curtains. Pushed them back so streetlamps lit the room. He dropped his sweatpants, lifted up her nightgown, and moved into her, looking, looking so intently, in her eyes while he did. Each time that he went deeper, their looking and her one gasp, and her head against the wall were like something she had waited for too long, and she felt the quick of her heart pleading for him.

28

What did he want to see in her eyes? A sign. Of what? Something unquestionable. He could feel she wanted him, and he knew he wanted her. In the past, those two things made the intoxicant, a thing so precisely without meaning as to give meaning to each touch, each time he put one finger against a woman's neck or felt the butter-silk of skin or found in his hand a thing that surprised and could not be expected about her. But now, he was thinking, what was it he wanted when he said he wanted her? To feel his cock in the warm of her? To see how she would behave in their fucking?

Not enough. Not close. Maybe, when you could bring most people into your arms, you eventually stood at this crossing. He could see in her eyes that she, so wonderfully, was not even close to where he was. She ached for him. He recalled feeling that. Maybe the problem was he knew what it was to want, and be denied, and then get what he wanted over and over and over.

He didn't want to come. He didn't want to make her come. He

wanted nothing. No, that was not honest. He wanted sensations that had no names.

He kissed her in an exploratory way and almost started talking to her. He would not say her name, that was too easy. He thought of the things he had said in the past, to other women, and meant. "I have wanted this for so long." "You make me crazy." "What are you thinking?" "Am I anything to you?" "I cannot have enough of you." He could not bring himself to say any of them. He wanted to go into his room and sleep, but that would upset her. There was only one thing to do and that was finish. He thought of her breasts, the way they were before she became so thin. That fullness that was only Heather's. He could not come with the new Heather in mind. In mind? She was there; he was in her. What was wrong with him? He wanted the old Heather. He fucked that memory; he came then.

He pulled up his sweatpants and held on to her. Then he whispered, "Lie down with me." Black old birds, the usual questions, were arriving. Why couldn't he fall in love? What was it that cut him off from that nectar of being alive? Once again, he put his hands through the sand of his past and pulled, hoping this time to find something that might explain it. There was nothing. It wasn't that his fiancée had fucked his brother. He didn't love her before that. He didn't love her when he told her he loved her. He didn't love her when he told himself he loved her. It looked like he had been wronged, but he had been relieved. It had given him room. Excuse enough to leave.

As he held Heather, it was plain to him that he could only respond to an assembled woman, one cobbled together from the old Heather's fullness and the new Heather's wanting him. Together, she was desirable, but even then, this compiled Heather of his mind, she failed him.

Aziz took Bonanza Bus Lines. They had the best price between New York and Boston, thirty-three dollars one way. The old man tried to stop him from going. At first it was touching, then a sharp nettle. Maybe the old Yemeni was more selfish and canny than Aziz had wanted to see. But what stopped the old fool from making the coffee himself? The cups were easy too. Aziz had shown him how. "They come to see you, your young face," the old man kept saying. His eyes were wet when Aziz said his last goodbye, and he pressed one of his used books into Aziz's hands for the ride. It was *Manteq at-Tayr* by the Persian poet Farid ud-Din Attar.

The original was in medieval Farsi. This was the Arabic translation, so when Aziz got on the bus he tried to read it. It was about a hoopoe. This bird was supposed to lead all the other birds to a king of birds they had never seen. Even though all the birds had gotten together and said they needed a king, when they saw how difficult a trip it would be, they started making excuses. The nightingale said he loved his mate so much he couldn't leave. The parrot said she wanted immortality, not a king. The peacock said he wanted paradise, not a king. On it went. Everyone had an excuse.

Reading on the bus gave him a headache, so he stopped after a while. He wished he could fall asleep. His impatience irritated him. Fifty-two days in the hold, and he was unsettled on a five-hour bus ride? He decided to skip around the book, just read a line here and there.

Here the Self rages like an unquenched fire,
And nothing satisfies the heart's desire—
Encompass all the earth, you will not find
One happy heart or one contented mind.

Everyone said that. He had read it before. He closed the book and opened to another page.

The hoopoe answered him: "You do not know
The nature of this sea you love: below
Its surface linger sharks; tempests appear,
Then sudden calms—its course is never clear,
But turbid, varying, in constant stress;
Its water's taste is salty bitterness.

"You do not know the nature of this sea you love." It was like his army tour. He had loved an idea of Benane, as rescuer, that carried only little resemblances to the real Benane. Benane's crying on his knees at Aziz's feet; that was what was left of the rumors that Benane had a conscience. Benane cried and did what he did, long before Aziz and long after; he cried some more and did what he did some more.

All things are possible, and you may meet
Despair, forgiveness, certainty, deceit.
The Self ignores the secrets of the Way,
The mysteries no mortal speech can say;
Assurance whispers in the heart's dark core,
Not in the muddied Self. . . .

He had been unfair to the old man. It pained him, thinking of the old Yemeni's tears. What was left of the whispers in his own heart's dark core? He had stopped hearing them. Not because of his muddied self; he had a single-minded self, one that saw clarity where there was silt and storm. The one clear thing was running. Running from his unit, running from Antar, running from Sellami and Benane, running from his family, running from ship's police, running from Algeria, running from the Egyptian, running from Rafik, running from women, running from trusting Ghazi, running from Hank Bridges, running from the stranger he kicked, running from the helpful security guard, and running now from the old man who had loved him. He had seen each only as threat. He had made each strange rich creature into one person with only one quality. He had made a world where there was only one person beside himself: a person to run from.

He looked out the window into an afternoon of sun. They were on a highway with leafy trees behind concrete walls. High in the bus, all he could see distinctly were the tops of cars. From his vantage, the faces of oncoming drivers were interrupted by bursts of reflected light. He looked back inside the bus. He had taken a seat in the last row, to stop anyone he could not see from approaching, a carryover from his nights at Antar's side. Light was faint behind the bus's smoke windows, and it took him a minute to realize that every seat was taken. He could see backs of heads and some shoulders. Every so often, a head would turn to someone or something to the left or right, and if he craned to his side or strained higher, he could see the unmistakable face of someone he had never seen before, someone too, he understood with full force, like no one else on board.

Everyone was talking at once. A judge had granted the FISA warrant. "Gentlemen," April said. She did not smile, even though she was feeling good. She had learned women don't smile in the bureau. You smile, you're pegged as weak. "We are all aware of the good news, so I won't repeat the obvious. In keeping with last meeting's breakthrough in information-sharing, let's go around the table, five-minute time limits. Detective Baker, why don't you start?"

Baker was uptight; he was trying too hard.

"Kamal Gamal is known to Boston PD," Baker said. "Picked up on rape charges in 1998. The complainant was a woman he met in a nightclub. She skipped and the case was dropped. Then in 1999, another rape case, this time involving a girlfriend. She was the Brazilian individual from whom Kamal Gamal stole the social and green card numbers for the card fraud that attracted Treasury's interest. She was all set to testify but left for Brazil two days before trial. Ugly cases, both of them. Mutilation, pretty unusual stuff. The officer who worked the first case told me naturally he had suspicions that foul play was involved with the disappearance of the victim, but with no body and no relatives to speak of, it didn't go anywhere. He did, however, get a warrant to search Gamal's apartment.

"Forensics for a homicide, looking for typical biological evidence. Instead of finding blood or tissue residue in the drains of the sinks and the shower, lab finds trace amounts of powdered aluminum, carbon tetrachloride, and tetrachloroethylene."

"Tetra-what?" someone asked.

"Hold on," Baker said. "This is a homicide. Everyone's looking for biological, so these items never got mentioned in the final lab report. I found out about them by talking to the original lab technician, who still had her notes. She indicated to me that carbon tetrachloride is basically fire extinguisher fluid, and tetrachloroethylene is dry-cleaning fluid. Powdered aluminum, it turns out, you can get in artists' supply stores—they sell it as bronzing powder paint—"

"So let me get this straight," April interrupted. "Kamal Gamal, cabdriver rapist, dry-cleans his shorts in his shower, refills his own fire extinguishers, and is looking to be Picasso."

Laughter all around. "That's one way of looking at it," Baker said. "I was thinking the FBI lab might be able to come up with another interpretation. The original samples are gone, but we've still got the technician's notes and report."

"That's enough for us to work with," said an FBI agent across the table.

"I apologize for speaking out of turn," said another agent, "but those are the ingredients for carbon-tet explosive."

Two other FBI agents nodded.

"It's a solvent," one of them said. "Kind of like paint stripper. And it will blow up, just like paint stripper. But there is the question of why not just buy a solvent that's out there on a hardware store shelf."

"Isn't there supposed to be an ATF person on this task force?" Baker asked.

"Part-time, not full-time," someone said. "Plus, our esteemed colleagues at the Bureau of Alcohol, Tobacco and Firearms can be proprietary. Stretch a simple question into a deposition with a hundred objections."

"I'd like to hear their thinking on this," April said, ignoring a few head shakes. "Let's send the information we're sending to FBI to their lab too." She looked down the table. "Mark?" Mark Blake was her least favorite FBI agent. He was also her deputy.

"The trap-and-trace and pen-register orders have yielded a substantial cache of phone numbers," Mark said. "We—"

The state trooper interrupted. “Trap and trace, pen register—those are devices that pick up incoming and outcoming phone numbers?”

“*Outgoing* phone numbers,” Mark corrected. “On Kamal Gamal’s phones, cell and land line.”

“Anything of interest, Mark?” April asked. “Patterns? Repeats?”

“At this time, no.”

“Headquarters has software—” she started.

“I know your affection for database analysis,” Mark said. “But as this is my third counterterrorism case, I can assure you that these entries are riddled with errors, not to mention the errors that riddle the phone company records regarding the ownership of these phone numbers. When you add to that the problems with transliterating Arabic names to English, the variants are essentially endless. There is no other way except the human eye. And this human eye is not ready to make even a preliminary report.”

Kamal and Ghazi were trying to sort out some social security numbers. They had bank statements and credit reports spread out on Kamal’s coffee table.

“Dhakir is crazy,” Ghazi was saying.

“Where did he get this one from?” asked Kamal, pointing to a Niagara Falls address.

“None from Niagara Falls. That one Dhakir uses there—not for us.”

“Problems,” Kamal said.

“This one, this Niagara Falls friend of Dhakir’s, he thinks he’s Mr. Khandji.”

Kamal’s eyebrows rose.

“Jihad,” Ghazi said. “On my cock.”

“No.”

“I swear to God. Dhakir is fucked up.”

“Is he with a group?” Kamal was checking off numbers on a piece of paper.

“What group would take Dhakir?” Ghazi asked.

Kamal laughed.

"What the hell is wrong with him?" Ghazi shook his head.

"Did I tell you what happened with Rafik?"

"No," Ghazi said.

"So we are loading the shit, and I am on the phone with Dhakir, and Rafik grabs the phone."

"Uh-huh."

"And then Dhakir starts in on the hellfire," Kamal said.

"You see what I mean."

"I hear Dhakir's brother, he is crazy. They put him someplace in Oran."

"Mustapha?" Ghazi thought that was his name.

"Was he the one, they called him *bad boy*?"

"The cats. Always with cats," Ghazi recalled.

"Mustapha. I forgot his name."

"I need to get out of this crap," Ghazi said. He started on another page, marking off numbers.

"I tell you," Kamal said. "I am thinking of Paris."

"So, Rafik," Ghazi asked. "He is all right?"

"Yesterday, he comes back from New York, he has these suits with him."

"Fuck. Risks, risks, risks."

"It is the risks he likes, not the suits," Kamal said.

"To be honest with you," Ghazi said, "with Rafik, it is the suits."

"He goes out all night."

"Kamal, listen," Ghazi said. "Once I am at Brooks Street, about two years ago, and I come home, no one there, no one expected. And he is there. He has nail polish on his feet. On his toenails."

"Fuck."

"On my mother's head."

"Rafik. Gay? No."

"Maybe that," Ghazi said. "Maybe something else."

"Rafik."

"See, I tell you, you don't know someone."

"I told Dhakir the other day"—Kamal recounted—" 'Look, I will buy the satellite phone, but I want nothing to do with it.' "

"Did you?" Ghazi put down his pen.

"Did I what?"

"Buy the phone?" Ghazi asked.

"I told him I could not find any."

"Good."

The Depression, Ghazi called it. The Depression came to visit. The Depression cooked dinner. The Depression goes on vacation, then I call home. His plans were one hour long or two days, maximum. One day he was moving to Australia. Another day he was thinking about Seattle. He called Realtors and made appointments; he didn't show. The only place he felt a little okay was the movies. He took in two, sometimes three a day. Al Pacino was his favorite actor. Even when Pacino was in a bad movie, Ghazi loved it. And since it was Pacino, he could watch it twice, three times, even five times. *Sea of Love,* that was the one that started it. It wasn't that sex with her against the wall, though he'd tried to imitate it more than a few times. It was how Pacino looked lost but acted sure.

When he wasn't watching Pacino, he was in the public library. He'd learned from the homeless you could stay there for hours, and as long as you had a book open and your eyes mostly open and didn't smell like rat piss, they couldn't make you leave. He went there after dinner. He wasn't trying to avoid Heather, but that night with her was a factor. She seemed to understand it had been a one-time situation. He was the uneasy one.

To shut Dhakir up, he tried to read the Qur'an at the library. Naturally, they didn't have it in Arabic, so it wasn't really the Qur'an. It got to him, he had to admit, when he checked out the *fatihah*. He'd repeated it whenever anything scary happened as a kid. *You only do we worship, and You only do we beseech for help.* Shit, he'd said it in the hold. And more than once. *In the Name of Allah, the All-Merciful, the Ever-Merciful*. Jumping in, making that last long cold swim he needed to make. *Guide us in the straight path.* Or when his dad beat the crap out of him. *The All-Merciful, the Ever-Merciful.* Or his brother, when he made it like Ghazi stole stuff, when he didn't. *Other than that of the ones against whom You are angered, nor the erring.* Of course, he was stealing stuff, but he never got caught for the stuff he stole. *The Possessor of the Day of Doom.* He always got the punishment for his brother's thefts. Shithead was a master snitch. Shithead stole, pinned it on Ghazi, and guess who got the fatherly ass-kicking.

We believe in the unseen, he read in the next sura. That was good. But he couldn't keep his mind on most of it. *Deceive and believe;* so many times he read those words. *Righteousness, pious, all-embracing, ever-knowing, beholding, therefrom, inordinance, errancy*—where did they get these words? And once in a while, there was something like *in their hearts is a sickness.*

But why did Allah need so much worshiping? He had it all, was it all, knew it all. Never made sense to him as a kid and still didn't. So he read by starting an *ayat,* and if it didn't interest him by, say, the fifth word, he went to the next one. One great *ayat* was:

> *Thereafter your hearts hardened even after that; so they were as stones, or (even) strictly harder. And surely there are stones, from which rivers erupt forth, and surely there are (some) that cleave, so that water goes out of them, and surely there are (still others) that crash down in the apprehension of Allah. And really Allah is in no way heedless of whatsoever you do.*

You had to know Dhakir never read that.

> *Did He not find you an orphan and give you refuge? Did He not find you lost and guide you? Did he not find you poor and make you self-sufficient?*

That, Ghazi had to say, was good.

. . .

Aziz could not believe he was walking down Brooks Street. He felt liberated, so awake. A few things had changed—new chain-link fence at the body shop across the street, a nice-looking motorcycle bolted to a porch railing, and a new doorbell and new peephole on their old door, which had been repainted blue.

The doorbell lit up when he pressed it. He heard a chime like tolling from old bells.

The door opened and there was Heather, a smaller Heather, but very much Heather. "Ghazi!" she screamed. "Ghazi! It's Aziz!"

Aziz was a tambourine. "Heather! You are here! I am so happy to see you!"

There was Ghazi. He picked Aziz off his feet.

29

Aziz's unit never missed him. So he learned when he sailed into Arzew's harbor on the boat of his father's old friend. The procession of family on the beach came to the marina; they greeted him as honored son. His brothers—Latif and Bilal, even Mourad—carried him on their shoulders to their father's hotel. His weeping mother held on to his hand on the walk along the shore, and his sisters, Hazar and Anissa, singsonged, "Our pigeon has flown home!"

Aziz should have felt relief. His time with Antar and Sellami—nine months—was equal to the time left on his two-year tour of duty. To his parents, he had come home on schedule. No one had knocked on their door and told them their son was a deserter. No one had visited with rehearsed respect to report him dead.

Aziz felt crabbed. His arm was partly to blame. Arzew's one doctor said it had fractured in three places, and near his wrist the bone had broken in two. His father set up a hotel bed on the peeling veranda to save him from sleeping on a couch. "The harbor air will do you good," his mother told him, smiling. Rest, they said, you need rest.

He became a sleepwalker. One morning they found him under the kitchen table. One night he climbed a neighbor's roof and slept by their chimney. He crawled under his parents' bed, but not entirely. His foot tripped his mother when she rose at dawn. Soon they were afraid he would walk to the bluff and teeter to the rocks below. His mother wanted his brothers to fasten him to his bed, but please, she begged, not with ropes. So they looped him to the mattress with cleaning rags and much-mended scarves, all of which came in with the tide by morning. They found Aziz under a wet sheet in the sun.

They had no choice; he had to sleep on the sagging couch with doors locked, windows boarded. Even then they could hear him pace the room, come up against doors, test windows, overturn a stool. Many nights he scraped back and forth, pushing a chair like a baby carriage on the uneven floor.

His mother made his favorites: *lahm lhalou, chorba, berkukes, chlada fakya*. They made him queasy. "Just chicken," he told her. "Plain good chicken is all I want." This hurt her, he knew it, but apologies came hard to him. Paying mind to her feelings was a draining slog, her dear understanding a burden.

"You will be better soon," she said, smoothing his hand.

Go to the market, he wanted to say. Go to the hotel. Go out. "Let me sleep," he said instead. She kissed his forehead.

His brothers caused the least distress. One night, Aziz was on the couch, his broken arm propped on two pillows. His two older brothers were talking, joking. Then one of them was imitating Mourad's walk like stilts. Mourad, pretending to read, was offended. Their mother had just cleaned up the kitchen and gone into her room to lie down when the phone rang.

"You have the wrong number," Aziz could hear his father say in the kitchen. "I am sorry. . . .

"I am sorry," he said again. "There is no one by the name of Nazzar in this house.

"Who is this?" his father said. "I want to know who this is." His voice was raised. "I am telling you, you are mistaken."

The calls continued. Sometimes it was a voice claiming to be Nazzar who wanted to talk to Aziz. So Benane and Sellami had figured him out. They were on their way to kill him. Sometimes it was an unnamed voice wanting to talk to Nazzar. Perhaps Antar had figured Aziz out and *he* was on his way. Aziz went back and forth, then round again. Perhaps it was only Antar. Perhaps it was only Benane. Or only Sellami.

Aziz told his family he knew no Nazzar. He looked unconcerned. He looked bewildered. He looked impatient. He looked resentful.

"It is you this person wants," Mourad insisted. "You must know him."

"It is aggravating," his father said.

"Just answer the phone, Aziz, and tell whoever to stop," his mother pleaded.

"Take the phone off the hook," Aziz said. They did for a few days, but within an hour of putting it back on, the phone rang. It was evening, after dinner, and everyone was there, his sisters and their husbands and granddaughter Asa. His two older brothers were playing dominoes. Mourad looked at Aziz after the first ring and said, "You are hunted."

His oldest brother, Latif, went to the kitchen, picked up the phone, and in the next instant slammed it down without talking.

Then they told him. How no letters from him had scared them. "You wrote every week; then this silence." How when they called the army, all they would say was Aziz was stationed near Biskra. "Again and again your father called, always the same thing." How others from his unit had come home on leave, and one of them said Aziz had inexplicably disappeared. "It was the friend of the pharmacist's son. We asked him what was said about your absence in the unit, but he recalled nothing. He was not even sure it was you that was missing when we showed him your picture." How when they called the army and told them that, they said they would look into it. "This will take first priority, I assure you." That was the lie they told. "We will be reporting back to you at regular intervals." But they never called back, and after a while they would not take his father's calls. "They were rude. They said a son not writing letters home was not a national emergency." How they begged Ghazi's father, in military intelligence, to see what he could find out, and he told them there was no record of Aziz going for basic training at all. "You saw him go with your own eyes!" Aziz's father exclaimed.

While they talked, his mother kept pulling at the hem of her sleeve; her fretting was starting to take out the stitching. His oldest brother kept interjecting, "Let him talk." His next oldest brother tapped a domino on a domino. Mourad was sullen. His older sister, Hazar, was rocking a fussing Asa in her arms. Her husband had his hands on his hips. His other sister, Anissa, was trying to get their mother to sit down. Her husband, who worked for Algeria's nationalized energy firm Sonatrach, which everyone believed gave him special knowledge of inner workings of all mysteries, was waiting like a marabout to be consulted.

"What happened?" His father was gentle when everyone quieted. He had seated himself next to Aziz on the piebald couch.

"What happened doesn't matter," said the oldest, Latif, trying to be too level headed for hysterics.

"It is obvious to me," said the Sonatrach sage.

"You!" said his wife. "You have said nothing before now."

"Does no one in this dewdrop family pay mind to anything outside their corner of Arzew Harbor?" Aziz's brother-in-law demanded. "You are petals dancing on moonbeams while Algeria staggers and burns. These Salafists are slaughtering our children, and you, you are nothing but flute players for French tourists. And here, your own son, haunted and broken, has come to you from what was no doubt the most secret, most honorable mission, only to be hounded by these jihadist madmen and harried by his hopelessly naïve family."

"Was this so?" asked his father. "This mission Ghaleb describes?"

Ghaleb preened. "He cannot answer you, you old fool."

"It would explain what has happened," his father said. He looked unaffected by Ghaleb's scorn. Aziz's mother had stopped picking at her sleeve. To everyone's surprise, she said with composure, "If this mission was as you say, why have they not come to protect my son? Why are *irhabiya* calling our house without fear?"

"Because Ghaleb is wrong," Aziz said. He glanced at his brother-in-law. Ghaleb looked like a man getting a manicure in Paris, or a haircut in Rome. He was neat and pampered into a plumed self-regard. He always looked like that. The rest of them were forever pulling at threads or caked with sand or napping.

"I was in my unit," Aziz said wearily. "After we got outside Biskra, it was hard to write. I did try—maybe, from the desert, letters got lost. Since when do we count on anyone in the government to know one name from the next? One day from another? To ever give one simple answer to one simple question? This is Algeria. It is permanently confused on all levels. That one—the friend of the pharmacist—who knows if he knew what he was saying? People came and went in our unit.

"Sometimes I thought if I had just walked away, no one would have known I'd been there at all. These calls are what every soldier gets. Ask in town. I spoke to one just yesterday who came to visit me on this couch—every other night someone pretending to be *irhabi* calls and says things like, 'I know where you are.' It's been days of these calls, yet no one has shadowed our doorstep. No one has stabbed me in the night. It is bluffing. Probably teenagers down at the docks making calls on stolen cell phones."

He turned to Ghaleb.

"You see cinema where there is only normal life."

He had not convinced himself. He began to feel better anyway. His arm would take much time to heal, yet it was not too early to make plans. All of them included Soumeya. Their first meeting could not come now, with him in a cast from his thumb to his shoulder. He wanted to court her, show her that just because it was arranged, his wanting her was not slight. But he imagined her as practical, wholly inured to larks. What he gave would have to be true. He decided he would write a letter to her each day but not send it. On their first meeting, he would present her with a bundle of these unsent letters, records of his thinking about her.

The letters made his days into occasions. He worked on them when he woke and just before he slept. No one knew of them at first. Then one morning his father was up early and saw him writing. Because of the boarded windows, Aziz had a candle lit. He felt like a Tibhirine monk.

"Who are you writing to?" His father sparked up to see him busy. He walked to the door to unlock it and let in the light.

Aziz had wanted to discuss what the news was from Soumeya's family. This was a perfect time before the others were awake. He blew out the candle, and the charred smell of the wick came into the room.

"Father, I am pleased to tell you I am writing to Soumeya."

The candle smoke twirled between them. His father's expression was strangled; his knee must be bothering him. It had always ached in the morning.

"I have written to her every day this week." Aziz pulled out a stack of envelopes from between the cushions. "My idea is to save them. To offer them as a gift to her when we meet. This way she will see how often I think of her. What I want for our lives together."

"Aziz."

"You think this is too much."

"Well. Let me explain."

"I am sure you told me she can read."

"Yes. But—I—"

"There will be nothing to embarrass her," Aziz said. "I write things her father could read."

"Her father—"

"Needs to see I am strong enough for the orchards. I will be! I swear to you. This will be off soon," he said, knocking on his cast.

His father said nothing. Aziz tried to settle down. He was like a

Ping-Pong ball: scramming over there, bopping over here. Soumeya would despise such a jackanapes. He remembered her photograph, the intelligent defiance. Just then, he saw.

"She has changed her mind," Aziz whispered, almost to himself. A spreading of his thoughts began an unanchored commotion of searching.

"She did not change her mind." That was his father. Aziz could just hear his words. Somehow his father was facing him, taking both his hands in his. Aziz pulled away.

"Her father changed his mind," Aziz said.

"Her father is heartbroken. He—I—"

Aziz's mother had walked in from the hall. "What a day this is," she sang into the room. Then she saw them. She looked to her husband for an explanation.

"Soumeya," he said, to her questioning look.

"Who did she marry?" Aziz asked. He was furious his mother had appeared. Now his father would try to temper it so she would not be upset. He was forever diluting things to protect her.

"Yassirah," his father said to his mother. He sounded like she might know what to do. Her? The worrier? And he never called her by her given name. It was usually pet names: turtle soul, inch child.

"Hmaam," his mother said, using Aziz's boyhood name and kneeling on the floor beside the couch. "Pigeon," she said again. "Look at me. Look." He wouldn't.

"Please, my son," his father said.

"Soumeya is dead." His mother said it.

Aziz looked at her uncomprehending. "Dead?"

"Dead," his father said.

"Dead," Aziz said. He looked closely at his mother. "Dead."

"Not now," she was saying to his father.

"Yassirah, we must tell him," he said back.

Now Hazar was walking through the open front door, Asa a papoose on her back. "Such a day!" Hazar trilled.

"Take Asa out of this house," Aziz's mother said. She was as fierce as Aziz had ever seen her. "Do you hear me? Now. Take her."

Aziz felt drained out, childlike. In the background Hazar and his mother were saying something quickly, and Hazar's footsteps melted into Asa's crying. A siren was screaming, but he knew it wasn't. Little babblings made hoarse accusations in his ear, or was it behind his eyes? His neck hurt. His arm was sore. He looked at his mother trustingly.

"Soumeya was murdered," she said.

"Irhabi." His father spoke the word so softly Aziz could only just hear him.

"Irhabiya." She corrected her husband.

His father nodded. "Many of them."

"Many violated her."

"They were animals."

"It knows no bounds what they did."

"They had a shovel."

Aziz remembered taking off his uniform to cover her.

He had washed her face, the face he had not recognized, with water from his canteen. With moistened lemon leaves he smoothed her to her shoulders. He went to a prone figure and took his possessions. Among them was a flask of olive oil. He rubbed her feet and softened the soles. He took the remnants of her dress, and a long shawl, and began to wrap her form in them, circling underneath and across her again with his eyes shut, going only by touch.

One of Antar's men who had gone ahead had fixed on Aziz. Keep going, Aziz silently ordered this straggler. Keep going. But still this man looked.

Let me bury her. This man still looked. Another had turned to stare.

Aziz picked up the shovel and hurried to catch up.

30

It was four years to the day since Aziz had rowed Arzew's night-black harbor to the tanker that took him. Soumeya was with him in the old *fluka* his oldest brother and he prayed across the water. The memory of her broken contour, the slime of men on her thigh, the lap of blood he tried to close—they were any woman until his mother's words made them Soumeya's. And the hold, it was her hold. He was running from reminders of what he had done, but they congregated around him, warring with the unnamed others he had slaughtered to occupy his enforced alone. What he remembered, he now resaw with the puncture and tint of unwelcome detail. An infirm throat under his knife was a Tamazight *baba* with eyes whimpered shut. A boy's skin like an egg's membrane flocked his thumbs. He smelled talc on an elbow torn from a girl.

What did it say that it had taken Soumeya to see vivid? It did not unveil him as monster, for he had known that months and months past. He thought it was an old story that remorse comes harder when we harm those we know, with names and parts to play in our ambitions and needs. It was comparatively little—in the tangible despicable of his memories—that he carried no instinct for brotherly love. Yet it wrenched him. Try as he might to scoff at the idea, and as deep as his self-loathing reached, still he searched for his own root causes. And one of them was his genius for extenuating circumstances, those razor-dire calculations he had judged necessary to ensure his survival: Antar had signaled distrust, a cohort eyed him funny, he had not openly killed for days, he had refrained from the heinous for too long. His innate talent was for explanations. He saw them in the hold for what they were, footnotes he had doctored to palliate his history. Unasked-for love—what he felt for Soumeya—clarified. It indicted.

He had not torn the arm. He had let it be torn. Yet he didn't have the nobility to be his own prosecutor. Some men dreamed of such a life story, of stowing home, confessing to family, surrendering to police, saying, I have killed the defenseless, stood by while innocents were maimed. The police could believe, lock him in a cell. They could think he was deranged, bid him back to the street. They could send him to Benane, to be condemned to die. But after all these years, he had to face what frippery this was—the drama of wishing his own death or just punishment. After all, had he not stolen from the ship's kitchen, not to be discovered but truly to eat? Hadn't he fought off drowning? Hadn't he tricked Linda Ricco to save his scorched feet? Hadn't he feared Ghazi's motives? And run from Hank Bridges?

The bright dust of being alive could not be shook out of him.

"There is nothing for me here." Ghazi was outside the library on his cell phone with Dhakir.

"Have you been reading the Qur'an?"

"Living this way—it is no way to live."

"Go make your prayers. When we get off the phone, I swear you will feel better."

"Uh-huh."

"You don't listen when I say come back to Montreal. There are many brothers here."

"I am tired of them. The same. Always the same."

"They will show you the way."

"Let me ask you something."

"They ask for you. I see them. Where is Ghazi? Ghazi, Ghazi."

"Answer this question: Muslim killing Muslim. Explain that."

"I know someone at the embassy."

"Uh-uh."

"He can get you a visa over there."

"No. No caves for me. Look, send the package FedEx. No more Priority Mail."

"You don't believe me."

"Dhakir, I believe you. Just the package by tomorrow morning. That is all."

"There will be one in North America. I will be that one."

"One of what?"

"The group. I will be near the top of it. But here, in Montreal."

"Uh-huh."

"You will see."

"Just send this one FedEx."

This was the anniversary of the day he left Arzew. Aziz harbored some joy because of it. But it was hard to get others to understand his small happiness. Maybe it was meant to be a private one. After all he had known and felt, he could not find words to explain how he had found it. It was not the Persian poet's lines, or the old Yemeni, or the turning faces on the Bonanza bus, though he continued to see them like hallowed portraits from a dignified museum. It was not anything as ridiculous as forgiving himself, or anything as false as the word Americans had for the end of grieving. They called it something like closing. How could grieving close? Grieving lived inside him whether it showed itself or not, and he had no powers to summon it or banish it. This new joy came from allowing that there were distinctions, that running from all—or loving all, he had to see that too—was little improvement over renouncing the subtlety of discernment because it led to excuses. Some explanations were footnotes. But some were a lens that focused.

Mourad, for instance, had lived too long in Aziz's mind as the unfeeling one. Algeria had been permanent unfathomable confusion; America was prettiness walled off from his touch. Women were only signposts pointing to Soumeya, Rafik only hijinks to be overlooked. Kamal was vengeful evil; Aziz would have to admit him to some larger understanding, as impossible as that seemed.

Only Ghazi had pushed through in fuller contradictions. He was a man Aziz could say he knew well and loved easily. Ghazi's remoteness, now that they were reunited, disappointed, but it also was familiar. Two nights ago, Ghazi had been happy, pouring sparkling wine on Aziz's head, dancing Heather through the hall in mock tango. It reminded Aziz of the night Ghazi had first arrived, because they were spilling thoughts and stories, eager for Ghazi's. This time, when Ghazi's stories of Montreal didn't come, Aziz remembered how long it took for Djamila, the one intended for Ghazi, to surface.

Now, looking for Mourad's Escort to come down Brooks Street, Aziz was smoking many cigarettes, maniacally greeting strangers on the sidewalk, offering to carry groceries for the infant- and toddler-burdened Sikh woman who lived two houses down, only to spill them on her front stairs in his distracted glee. But then, just as he had finished picking up the detergent and formula and canned peaches, the Escort appeared at the end of the block.

The brand-new car Mourad had babied, waxing it by hand in the street, was dented, its left front bumper skimming the ground. Apart from the half moons the wipers made on the windshield, it was covered in dust, and when it got closer Aziz saw sticky coatings of smashed bugs on the hood. His brother had sounded ecstatic on the phone—he had been somewhere in New Jersey called Union City—now, getting out of the car, he looked weakened.

"Mourad!" Aziz screeched. "Mourad!" He jumped up and down.

Now Mourad was smiling wide; such smiling exaggerated his

flaw of no chin. His eyes had disappeared; Mourad's magnificently giant nose was all anyone could see.

"Aasslamma!"

"Hmaam! Hmaam! Wa Allah!"

So this November 17 was the day his youngest brother, Mourad, came back to Brooks Street. Instead of its being an anniversary of running, it was now also one of returning.

April walked into the conference room. One wall was covered with faces, names, dotted lines: red lines, blue lines, green lines. Kamal and Rafik were together in a box. The box was shaded yellow. Below the box were their two land-line phone numbers and their four cell-phone numbers. The phone numbers were connected to an orange-shaded box with a red line. That box contained Dhakir. Below his box were his six land lines, three pagers, and eleven cell phones. Some of the phone numbers were in faint gray. Those were numbers he no longer used. Dhakir's red lines also ran to Ghazi's box, which was multicolored, with four names inside it. Mourad and Heather were shaded green. Ghazi and Aziz were shaded the same yellow as Kamal and Rafik. In a separate green-shaded box were the Three. Red lines went from them to the Ghazi box.

Then there were the purple boxes. They connected to Dhakir's box and one another with a fishnet of lines: red, blue, green, and dotted. One purple box was in London. Another was in Paris. Another was in Munich. Another was in Peshawar. A large one, containing seven faces, was in Algiers. Two purple boxes connected to Kamal. One was in Riyadh; one was in Basra.

Toward the bottom, there was a Brooklyn box: half yellow with Aziz in gray halftones, because he was no longer living there, and half blue with Waheb and Rachid. Red lines went from their phone number to Munich.

On another wall were a series of lab reports. April began taking notes. It was the second time she had tried to do it. Yesterday, she had gotten through only the first four. It would be so much easier to trust what the analysts told her, but she had done that on a case once, only to have a Congressional staffer who *studied* the lab reports prove that the lab had not only fucked up but that she and the prosecutor she was working with had missed that a fingerprint was *not* on a crucial car door. The case had to be dismissed, though luckily there were no public hearings. She had learned then, and many other times, that if you took something far enough apart, *nobody* did *anything*. It was like quarks. She had read something, it was a physics theory, about a cat being in a box in ninety-nine scenarios but not in the hundredth. So the cat *existed* and *didn't exist*.

FOLLOWING SPECIMENS RECEIVED ON OCT. 1, 2000 FROM U-STOR-IT STORAGE UNIT #532 AT 23400 PAUL REVERE HIGHWAY, EVERETT, MASSACHUSETTS 02149

Q1–Q21: LATENT FINGERPRINT LIFTS, ENTRANCE, WALLS, CONTAINERS, DRUMS, "PAMPERS" BAGS, SUITCASES

Q22–Q39: SWABS OF ALL CORNERS, ENTRANCE

Q40: AMBER SUBSTANCE FOUND IN THE LEFT FRONT

Q41–Q60: WHITE-COLORED POWDER TAKEN FROM ALUMINUM CONTAINERS (Q41A–Q60A)

Q61–Q72: CLEAR LIQUID TAKEN FROM COMMERCIAL DRUMS (Q61A–Q72A)

(Q73–Q81): "PAMPERS" BAG CONTAINING OFF-WHITE COLORED POWDER (Q73A–Q81A)

Q82–Q95: SUITCASES, PORTIONS OF SUITCASES

Q83A: ONE "FENDI" PURSE, BLACK AND BROWN FROM Q83

Q96: ONE KEY

Q97–Q109: ONE DOZEN CARDBOARD BOXES, VARYING DIMENSIONS

Q97A: ONE CARTON MARLBORO LIGHTS CIGARETTES FROM Q97

Q102A: MAN' S ARMANI SUIT, 38R FROM Q102

Q103A: MAN'S VERSACE SUIT, 40L FROM Q103

Q108A: ONE "BATMAN" ACTION FIGURE TOY FROM Q108

Q110–Q124: TWO DOZEN PANASONIC CALLER ID 900 MHZ TELEPHONES

SPECIMENS RECEIVED 11/24/2000

FINGERPRINT CARDS

PALM PRINTS

HAIR SAMPLES

FBI LAB WASHINGTON DC REPORT OF EXAMINATION
OCTOBER 12, 2000
CHEMISTRY UNIT, DANIEL M. HICKEY EXAMINER
ANALYSIS OF SPECIMENS RECEIVED 9/30/2000 FROM U-STOR-IT STORAGE UNIT #532, 23400 PAUL REVERE HIGHWAY, EVERETT, MASS. 02149

ITEMS Q22–Q39 CONTAIN ETHYLENE GLYCOL (ANTI-FREEZE).
ITEM Q40 IS RDX. RDX IS CLASSIFIED AS A HIGH EXPLOSIVE.
ITEMS Q41–Q50 ARE HMTD. HMTD IS CLASSIFIED AS A HIGH EXPLOSIVE.
ITEMS Q51–Q55 ARE SODIUM HYPOCHLORITE (BLEACH).
ITEMS Q56–Q60 ARE UREA.
Q61–Q72 CONTAIN EGDN. EGDN IS CLASSIFIED AS A HIGH EXPLOSIVE.
ITEMS Q73–Q81 ARE DIACETYLMORPHINE (HEROIN).

FBI LAB IN WASHINGTON EXAMINATION REPORT
EXPLOSIVES UNIT, GREGORY A. CARL EXAMINER

ON OCTOBER 28, 2000, A SERIES OF EXPLOSIVES TESTS WERE CONDUCTED IN SOCORRO, NEW MEXICO. THE PURPOSE OF THE TEST WAS TO DETERMINE WHETHER OR NOT A MODIFIED 12-VOLT FLASHING LAMP WOULD INITIATE AND SUBSEQUENTLY DETONATE A QUANTITY OF HMTD AND RDX TAKEN FROM SAMPLES Q41–Q50 AND ITEM Q40. THE ITEMS USED IN THESE TESTS WERE PHOTOGRAPHED BEFORE THE TEST. BASED UPON THE RESULTS OF THIS TEST, IT HAS BEEN CONCLUDED THAT WITH A MODIFIED 12-VOLT FLASHING BULB, HMTD AND RDX CAN BE ASSEMBLED TO FUNCTION AS A "HOMEMADE" ELECTRICAL BRIDGE WIRE DETONATOR. THIS DETONATOR COULD THEN BE UTILIZED TO INITIATE OTHER LESS SENSITIVE HIGH EXPLOSIVES SUCH AS EGDN.

NOV. 25, 2000
SECRET
IT-UBL/AL QAEDA
FOLLOWING SPECIMENS WERE RECEIVED ON NOV. 21, 2000 SUBMITTED TO FBI LAB WASHINGTON, SAMPLES TAKEN FROM 34-35 DORFMAN STREET, APT 8, EAST BOSTON, MASS. 02128, RESIDENCE OF KAMAL GAMAL

IMPROVISED TIMING DEVICES (4), NOKIA MOBILE TELEPHONE, WALLET, DARK GREEN BAG, CIGARETTE LIGHTER, NIKES, BLUE BACKPACK, MAROON CLOTH BAG, BLUE PLASTIC BAG, BLACK GARMENT BAG WITH 2 ARTICLES OF CLOTHING, BROWN LEATHER BAG, GRAY HAT, BLACK TRAVEL BAG, AIR

CANADA TIMETABLE, FRENCH MASSACHUSETTS TRAVEL GUIDE, FRENCH-ENGLISH DICTIONARY, AIRLINE TICKET FOLDER ENTITLED "VACANCES AIR TRANSAT," BLUE HAT, "NAUTICA" BLUE HAT, RED HAT, PLASTIC "GAP" BAG, WHITE T-SHIRT, BLACK T-SHIRT, BLACK GLOVES, TWO PAIRS OF SHOES, PLASTIC "OGILVY" BAG, WHITE SHIRT, YELLOW JACKET, BLUE FLEECE JACKET, BLACK SWEATER, YELLOW SWEATER, BLUE PANTS, GREEN SWEATER, DARK BLUE PANTS, OLIVE DRAB PANTS, BLACK PANTS WITH BLUE STRIPE, BLUE BLAZER, BROWN COAT.

SPECIMENS RECEIVED ON 11/22/2000 FROM 6A BROOKS STREET, EAST BOSTON, MASS. 02128

B1: KEY FOUND UNDER MATTRESS OF ABDELAZIZ ARKOUN
B2–B3: 2 KEYLESS REMOTES FROM KITCHEN
B4: PASSPORT OF ABDELAZIZ ARKOUN
B5–B6: 2 DRIVER'S LICENSES
B7: CASIO ALARM CLOCK
B8–B10: SONY CAMCODER AND TAPE, NOKIA AC ADAPTER
B11: SILVER BELL WITH "1999" ETCHED INTO SIDE
B12: PEN
B13: JAR CONTAINING WHITE SUBSTANCE
B14: VAPORUB CONTAINER
B15: HELMUT LANG PERFUME
B16: OWNER'S MANUAL FOR RENTAL VEHICLE
B17–20: MAPS
B21–26: BROCHURES
B27–38: 9 U.S. $100 BILLS, 1 U.S. $20, 1 US $10
B39: CASIO G-SHOCK WATCH
B40: ROYAL BANK VISA CARD IN THE NAME OF TAFFOUNNOUT BELGHAZI.

CHRIS ALLEN, TRACE EVIDENCE UNIT, FBI LAB, WASHINGTON
RESULTS OF EXAMINATION

B1 MATCHES Q96

She paused here. So the key under Abdelaziz Arkoun's mattress—she walked over to the part of the wall with that lab report—matched the key to unit #532 at the U-Stor-It in Everett—she walked to the part of the wall with that lab report. She looked at this Arkoun's mug shot, taken from his passport. He weighed only one hundred and forty pounds. Five-foot-seven. She was bigger than he was. He looked shifty. He was in a multicolored shaded box with lines going to Kamal Gamal and Dhakir Yahyouai. There was a Heather Montrose in this same box. What was a Heather doing with Abduls and Mohammeds? There weren't any Abduls or Mohammeds, to be truthful. Wait, was Abdel like Abdul? Abdelaziz. Abdelrafik. Maybe that was just another transliteration of Abdulaziz and Abdulrafik.

DAVID MILLER, FINGERPRINT UNIT, FBI LAB, WASHINGTON RESULTS OF EXAMINATION

—FINGERPRINTS OF ABDELAZIZ ARKOUN WERE FOUND ON Q22–Q39 OF U-STOR-IT UNIT #532 CORNERS, ENTRANCE

—FINGERPRINTS OF ABDELAZIZ ARKOUN WERE FOUND ON CONTAINERS Q61–Q69

—FINGERPRINTS OF TAFFOUNNOUT BELGHAZI WERE FOUND ON Q22–Q39 OF U-STOR-IT UNIT #532 CORNERS, ENTRANCE

—FINGERPRINTS OF TAFFOUNNOUT BELGHAZI WERE FOUND ON CONTAINERS Q61–Q69

This was significant. Abdelaziz Arkoun and Taffounnout Belghazi were the only ones whose prints were found on the corners and entrance to the U-Stor-It in Everett. They were the only ones whose prints were found on the containers with the most lethal explosive, EGDN.

It looked as if Kamal Gamal was the technical wizard; they had found four timing devices in his apartment. She went back to the wall with the boxes. Abdelrafik Ghezil lived with Kamal Gamal. That meant Abdelrafik Ghezil could also be the bomb man. Maybe both of them were. She looked for fingerprint results on the timing devices. Had someone forgotten to do that? She made a note on her pad to check with the lab.

Arkoun and Belghazi, they were the only two who had traveled. Wait, there were two Arkouns. She checked the charts again. It was Abdelaziz Arkoun—not Mourad Arkoun—who had lived in Brooklyn for a while. Belghazi in Montreal. And Abdelaziz Arkoun had the key to the storage unit with the explosives. And his prints, and Belghazi's, were on the containers with the most dangerous explosives.

. . .

Who talked about the big questions? The philosophy at university, it told him everything was words. Biology was monkeys and worms. Physics was uncertainty principles and relativity theories. His father told him to work for the government. His mother told him to get married. Work and make kids, so they can work and make kids. Ghazi remembered his favorite time to go swimming in Arzew was around eleven at night. He liked the pitch ocean, the white that came on the surface from stars or moon. He thought that might be enough to make a life from, salt water swallowed, ears bathed in sea, the mystery of ocean he swam. But it wasn't. Had to have sugar in his bowl. That's how he thought of the thieving. He always told himself he would eventually give up dessert. When he fell in love, that was when. Time came to marry Djamila, he was clean. But his brother conned him, just like when they were kids. Why did she do it? How could his brother get her to do it? That he never solved; nights and nights in mind, it never came clear.

He was ready long before their betrayal. He knew Rafik, Aziz, the Khaled brothers; they'd all stowed on ships and made it to America. He was smarter than any of them. America became the place he would come clean, stay clean, make it clean. The place to be apart from the ones who never tried. The place his brothers were too busy working for the government and marrying girls his father picked to even dream they could get near.

He didn't blame Hank Bridges. He blamed that knurl in his brain that he couldn't smooth out or cut through, his circling into thieving over and over and over and over and over. If he was smarter, why this mess? If he could get any woman to fuck him, why no love? Some men couldn't even get a woman to *talk* to them. He had nothing to offer, but how they talked to him, how they longed for him, how he wanted them to want him and they did.

There was a girl in the library. He knew what would happen. It always did.

Reasoning had not helped. Parts of him never fit under its tent. Believing, why not try it?

> *And the ones who have believed, and done deeds of righteousness—We will soon cause them to enter Gardens from beneath which Rivers run, eternally abiding therein forever.*

Not real gardens, just the idea of gardens. He could accept that.

Lahouari took a look at Mourad's bumper. Aziz had driven it over to the Old New England Body Shop, where Lahouari still worked. Aziz wanted to take the Escort home, fixed and hand-buffed, to surprise Mourad.

It was another bristling-with-sun day. Lahouari had trouble concentrating on the bumper. He kept jabbering about how he had arranged "a big revenge" against Kamal.

"Kamal—he has reasons. I do not judge," Aziz said.

"He will be in the shit," Lahouari said. He had wheeled under the Escort on a low trolley.

"Can you fix it today?" It was noon. Aziz needed time to vacuum, wash, polish.

"Perfect," Lahouari said.

"What?" Aziz got on his knees and looked under the Escort. Lahouari's hands were moving inside the bumper.

"This is good," Lahouari said. "I fix this quick."

"Your boss?"

"Is off today."

"I thank you for this, Lahouari. Many times, I thank you."

Lahouari slid out from under the car. "You can wash here with special things." Lahouari pointed to a sign that said DETAILING.

Aziz nodded. "Tonight—you, your brothers, come to Brooks Street."

"Heather is there?"

"She asks for you. You will not believe the changes in Heather."

"Rafik is—gone—and"—Lahouari stuttered—"a chance for me?"

Aziz remembered Heather in Mourad's arms yesterday, the way they enclosed each other. He remembered Ghazi's reaction: overpleased, overfriendly, later testy, picking at Mourad. He saw Mourad watching Heather's ways with Ghazi. He could tell Heather felt watched—by both of them. In these heavy branches, Lahouari was a twig.

"Cousin, tuck away your hope," Aziz said. "Heather, she loves you like a brother. In this country, that means . . . many things."

31

Linda Ricco, red-mad from hospital bills and collection agencies, kept turning a corner. This one. No, that was Webster. Was it Webster? She thought maybe it was Bridge. On this street there were only two houses that had windows. The rest plywood. She sat down on the steps at one of them and lit up a cigarette. No one around this place. Jesus. She should watch herself. She could have sworn she'd seen Heather's BMW around here.

She was on her way to pick up a friend from work when she first saw it. She was late, so she couldn't stop, couldn't check it out, couldn't write down the street. Last week, when she tried to find the car again, she couldn't. Spent an afternoon, a Sunday, going in circles. This weekday was no better. She decided to try around dinner next time.

They were in the biography section. The library was about to close. Five more minutes, Ghazi heard the loudspeaker voice say. She took her breast in her hand and offered it to his mouth. The lights were cascading off, aisle by aisle. Soon the dark would reach the aisle of shelves where they were kneeling. They would be locked in for the night.

He moved in and out of watching himself. Disgusted with himself and then so hungry for her. Revolted at the pointlessness, the repeating without end of it; starving for the closeness, driven to it recklessly. He turned her away and lifted her ass. She flinched when he entered, then he pulled her against his chest, so her neck, her jaw, and, when he turned her head, her lips, were available to him. He pushed her gently against the shelves so his other hand could go free around her. He kissed insistently. He was up her ass, with a hand inside her, his lips on her achingly fine face. Her heart and her trembling and her breathing were his. Closer was not possible. More of her could not be had. He began to tell her, silently, that he had to know her, had to know each thought she had ever felt or known. He went on like this until there was salt in his mouth. He was confused, not sure where he was. Then he realized she was crying. Her face was all tears, her chest wet with them. What was her name? What was her name. Megan. It was Megan.

"Megan."

"Please." She may have said it more than once. "Please, Marco, please." He had not given her his real name. He was hurting her. How long had she been trying to reach him? He sickened; it was a nausea not just in his stomach. He pulled out of her and to his surprise she turned into his arms. "I am sorry. I am sorry. I am sorry," he said. Her shoulders were narrow. All of her was. He was guilt and more guilt.

"It's okay. It's okay," she was saying.

Linda Ricco knocked. This had to be it. No answer. She looked at her watch. Six. There was a doorbell. It lit up when she pressed. Then she heard someone unlocking the locks. Like Fort Knox, she thought. She crossed herself. *Holy Mother,* she whispered. All of a sudden this felt scary.

A big guy, kind of homely, opened the door. Arab, that was for sure.

"English?" she said.

"I speak English," Ghazi said. His eyes were swollen; he looked like he'd been sleeping.

"I'm looking for Heather. Heather Montrose." He didn't seem to hear her. "I'm a friend of hers." Still nothing. She added, "We used to work together."

"Sure, Heather. Sure. She's at work."

So this was it. She tried to see around his bulk but couldn't.

"You want to come in or something?"

"Uh, is Rafik around?"

"No. If you are looking for Mourad and Aziz, try later, maybe an hour."

"Thanks," she said. "I'll try back then."

Ghazi found the mosque in Boston that Dhakir told him about. When he got inside for the noon prayer, he turned around and left. It was ludicrous. He caught a matinee of *Saving Private Ryan* instead. When the knife in the heart came, he wanted to be the heart.

"Listen. We will die," Dhakir was saying.

"That is it," Ghazi tried.

"We die, then up there we will account for our deeds. It doesn't matter, how long are we going to live? Sixty years?"

"That is it."

"Can I tell you something? They are afraid of Islam. They are afraid. That is why they are boiling. Do you know what the Americans are doing now? They are behind everything, everything in the home country."

"Ah-hah."

"They are the ones behind what happened. In Pakistan, they

were not happy about it because it was the military; they were not happy about that. And they were demonstrating their discontent by shouting Why, why, why? And when the others were about to rule Algeria, they asked the army to make a coup. And they were telling them what actions to take. They were behind everything."

"They were behind everything?"

"The CIA is everything. You have no idea what they are doing in the world. I swear, you cannot imagine. I tell you, everything you have seen is bullshit. There is nothing left. Nothing left. It is over. Didn't they say that it will arise from the Arab Maghreb?"

"Yeah."

"Know that it is coming from our area."

"It is coming from the home country?"

"God willing, it is coming from there. Oh, my friend, I swear, it is coming from there."

"If you die, you will die."

"I tell you something. Death is inevitable. Right? That is it. I am going to die anyway. Are you going to the hellfire? Then go. There you will find a fear that is greater than this one. There you will see the truth in front of you. You will see the Most Gracious God and the Angels and everything. That is the real fear, there you will find out the truth and your destiny."

"Ah-hah."

"How about the hellfire? Will you be able to live there?"

The Depression set up a coffee shop, opened a car dealership. It colonized Ghazi's brain. He couldn't go to the library anymore, not after Megan. So he pretty much slept on the couch. He didn't care if Heather or Mourad found him there in the morning. He thought about walking into traffic.

"So you can get me over there?" Ghazi said to Dhakir. He was talking on his cell phone on the front stoop at Brooks Street.

"Abu Belghazi, Mohammed—peace be upon him—may he strike me if I cannot."

Now it was Mohammed. Ghazi sighed. It was hard to kill yourself, at least in a way that would show your father and dick-kissing brothers you were a man. Still, this way his mother would have no shame. Cutting himself, hanging himself—the picture of that would be the last thing she would see on her deathbed. But if she could think he died fighting for something bigger than him? He would begin working on a letter to her. He would mail it once Dhakir got the visa.

"So when do you see the guy?" Ghazi tried to keep Dhakir on track. He kept saying he would talk to someone at the British embassy, who would get Ghazi's visa to Afghanistan.

"Please, from now on he is a woman."

Ghazi shook his head. Code again. "Okay. When is she coming?"

"Allah has not meant for me to know. But when I marry her, there will be fires between us, God willing."

He was lost. What was marrying supposed to be?

"Well, let me know."

When they hung up, he turned to the Qur'an.

> *And they say, "Our Lord, why have you prescribed fighting for us? If only you would defer us to a near term!" Say, "The enjoyment of the present life is little, and the Hereafter is most charitable for him who is pious, and you shall not be done an injustice even as a single date-plaiting.*

What was date-plaiting? His mother would probably know. She was a devout woman, in her way.

He began copying the verse into his letter.

There had been a long discussion about whether they should make arrests or wait for translations. None of them, except April's deputy, had Arabic. Then there was the need for foreign intelligence. Algeria had promised help three months ago and given none. French intelligence had given so much—twenty-three boxes of files—no one had read more than a small portion. British intelligence was helping but halfheartedly, in the opinion of some at the table. The thing April worried about was the intercepts the language specialist had not yet translated. He said he had incriminating exchanges between Dhakir Yahyouai and Taffounnout Belghazi, but five pages of notes were all he could give them right now.

Her deputy opposed arrests. The Boston cop supported them. She would make the final call, but not until the prosecutor gave her more hints and signs than he was giving her. Her tinker of a bell—yes or no—would ring up to headquarters, where it would be considered if not exactly heard by the section chief for counter-terrorism, the assistant director for national security, and the FBI director himself, in conjunction with the attorney general, the National Security Council, and the White House.

Aziz had a new plan. The coffee, the cups—they had worked in Brooklyn. Boston might like them too. He asked in Cambridge at the large magazine stand how they got their Arabic papers and could he get some too. They gave him a phone number. Maybe he could buy newspapers—not stolen from boxes—from the *Globe.* He asked Mourad if he would help.

"At least until you find another security job," Aziz said.

Mourad's old job at the airport was gone. But his boss said there might be an opening in January.

"I do not see the money in it," his brother said.

"I swear to you, each day I made twenty dollars, sometimes twenty-five dollars in Brooklyn. And I did not even have Arabic newspapers. You go seven days"—Aziz thought for a moment—"that is one hundred seventy-five! Times four: seven hundred a month!"

"You must buy the coffee, so you take that out of the seven hundred," Mourad said. "And a coffeemaker. And the cups. And you must sit in the cold, in December, outside."

"I want to do it," Aziz said.

Mourad smiled. "I will call the *Globe* for you," he said. "I will call this other distributor for Arabic ones. Today, maybe we drive around in my car you fixed for me. Find a good place for you to sell. You need permission, so the police do not arrest you. I will find out about that too."

"Oh, my brother," Aziz said. "Thanks to you, so much, thank you."

"Go get your coat," Mourad said.

Aziz ran to their bedroom. His coat was not in the closet. He went into the living room. Not there. "Mourad," he said, "have you seen my coat?"

Mourad put his head out the door to his and Heather's bedroom. "I will look."

"It is brown, short one."

Aziz could not find anything lately. His shoes, his keys, they were always where he thought they were not. A few weeks ago, he noticed his alarm clock by his bed, instead of across the room. If he kept it by his bed, he just turned it off in his sleep. It was always, always, across the room.

"Here it is." Mourad handed him his coat.

"My question is, why wait?" asked the Boston cop. April could feel everyone in the room not liking him much. But they agreed with him.

"For starters," her deputy, Mark Blake, said, "they don't have a bomb yet."

"What they have is everything but the box that says BOMB to put it in," said another agent.

"What's the damage with what they have, just ballpark?" That was a red tie.

"There's a lot of variables," began the Alcohol, Tobacco and Firearms agent.

"You told me this could blow a crater the size of Boston Common," said the state trooper.

The ATF agent tried again. "That's right, but that's assuming—"

"That's assuming they don't want to put this on airplanes," said FBI Agent Melhaney.

"Wasn't there someone CIA captured in Indonesia who wanted to blow a dozen aircraft in the sky at once? Gave it a test run and some Japanese businessman got killed." This was someone from the Naval Criminal Investigative Service. "Liquid explosive—in a plastic bottle. For baby oil, I think. Went through metal detectors easily."

"They could be filling shampoo bottles with EGDN and sending operatives to Logan as we speak."

"Let me remind everyone of a number of facts in this investigation. As opposed to conjectures." This was Mark again. "Number one: Walking into a storage unit, touching the walls of the storage unit, touching some drums in the storage unit, and having a key to the unit, while it may be enough for you, is not enough for me. This storage unit—how long has it been rented? Five years. We don't know what-all has been in this unit these five years. There's plenty in it even now that can't be linked to illegal activity, unless you want a Batman action figure my son has at home to be criminalized. These two, Abdelaziz Arkoun and Taffounnout Belghazi, who have prints on the EGDN containers—there is no residue on their clothes, in their drains—hell, we swabbed everything but their left ass cheeks. Nothing there."

"How do you explain the key that Arkoun has? No one else has a key."

"All that key means is that someone gave it to him and he went in. But when? Four years ago or four days ago? Maybe his other associates are wise enough to keep the key in their jocks."

"But no one else's prints but Arkoun's and Belghazi's are in there."

"Maybe Arkoun and Belghazi are too stupid to wear gloves. Maybe they don't wear them because, unlike Kamal Gamal, they're not planning to blow the cradle of liberty to kingdom come."

"Let's face it, there are only stolen goods in there," April said. "I mean, who has dozens of telephones, suitcases of designer suits?

Don't forget the heroin. And look at all the calls Arkoun and Belghazi made to Kamal Gamal. And to Dhakir Yahyouai."

"The phone number, registered to a Heather Montrose, at 6A Brooks Street, has called one of the numbers at Kamal Gamal's sixty-eight times in the last week," an FBI agent said.

"But there are—what?—four individuals who use that phone."

"Two of whom are Arkoun and Belghazi," Agent Melhaney said.

"What if Heather is banging Kamal?" Mark asked. "We don't know who's saying what to who."

"Yes, we do," said another agent. He pushed the notes of the translator toward the center of the table.

"That translator, I happen to know, is Jordanian. Do you know how many ways there are just to say *yes* in Arabic? There's *naam,* which is modern standard Arabic; that's the one they teach in schools, in every country. There's *eywah,* which is how an Egyptian says it. There's *wakha,* which is how a Moroccan says it. There's *eh,* which is how an Algerian in Algiers says it, and there's *wah,* which is how people in West Algeria, the city of Oran, say it. These fucks are from Arzew! They could say *suck my dick* when they mean *yes*!"

April had to laugh. Her deputy, who had delivered this primer, wasn't even smiling.

"I don't want to see thousands of innocents dead in Boston streets," an FBI agent said. "I don't want to know I knew what we know today and did nothing about it. If we wait, if we stand by, we are playing with the lives of every man, woman, and child in Boston."

"Gentlemen," said the prosecutor. Finally, April thought. "I certainly appreciate your well-placed concern for the lives of innocents. That's why we're all here, Mark included. But to put things in perspective if I may, every individual in this investigation is under twenty-four-hour surveillance. The chances that they could initiate any type of operation at this point are extremely small. I tend to agree with Mark that the absence of translations is troubling. Oh—and April, could you make a note about the nationality of our language specialist? We need to let headquarters know that we need Algerian translators, if at all possible.

"I think, though, that no harm would be done if we were to arrest these individuals—say, after we have more detailed notes from a translator, and that may turn out to be the one we have now, as long as he is informed of the dialect difficulties brought to our attention by Mark. Which brings me to my next question: Why isn't the language specialist here today?"

"He's got the flu," April said.

"I see. April, your thoughts on all this?"

"I'm inclined to wait," she said. "Headquarters may see it differently. But my recommendation will be that sending out the battering rams in forty-eight hours, while clearly doable, is not advisable."

32

The wind kept blowing the cups. That had not happened in Brooklyn. Aziz watched them scuttling into the street and disappearing under rush-hour cars. Cups bounced on windshields. Car tires flattened them. When the cars had passed and the street was empty, crushed cups lifted again in the wind. At least he had put a shoe on each pile of newspapers. They stayed, edges vibrating. He smiled at passersby, but it was not like the cell-phone store. His young face, that the old yemeni said brought Brooklyn business, had little draw in January Boston.

When Mourad came to pick him up in the Escort, Aziz had all of the coffee, all but one newspaper, and none of his cups inked in Arabic sayings. His brother helped him pour the cold coffee into a sewer grate. They sold the newspapers to a Starbucks for four dollars.

Rafik was at the U-Stor-It, supervising some Mexicans he had hired on the fly from the shelter. It was freezing. Some of these desperadoes didn't even have coats and gloves. They were unloading some shit Kamal and Dhakir wanted, and fast. Rafik was in the van with the heat cranked. He paid in beer, which is why they always came running when they saw him coming.

This was the greased crease to the high-hills villa. No more fat girls with rich dads. No more hash deals with club hounds. No more Tunisian two-bit embezzle. If people wanted to believe this jihad shit, so be it. They created opportunities for those smart enough to take them. You couldn't stop it, so you might as well make money off it. It's not like he was lighting the fuse. What was that billboard he saw? GUNS DON'T KILL, PEOPLE DO.

They were going to do this shit anyway. Dhakir had decided to be a mosque-head long before Rafik arrived on the scene. Dickbrain acted like he was the CEO of Jihad Ventures, Canadian Division. London calling, got to go. Board meeting in Jakarta. He *loved* talking in code. The wedding cakes are on time. The caterer is quite satisfied. The bride will have a beautiful reception. Her father will bring blessings to my house. If Dhakir thought his fat dick was going to impress anyone in Kandahar, he was crazy. That dick had ruined him. If he'd had a smaller one, maybe he wouldn't have gotten on this Allah train. If he'd been a little worse at soccer, he'd be thinking small, which was all he would ever be.

After this final delivery, Rafik was on his way to Italy. You could be a whole new person there.

Everyone on the task force had discouraged April from seeking a subpoena for Heather Montrose. They argued that Montrose had been at 6A Brooks for four years, harboring a terrorist cell, and she was—microcams don't lie—Mourad Arkoun's bedmate. There was evidence from a Somerville travel agent named Linda Ricco who had come forward in the past week that Montrose had been Abdelrafik Ghezil's girlfriend until a year ago, and it was well established that he was at the center of the conspiracy, though April's deputy, Mark, had doubts about Ghezil's motives. "If Ghezil's a religious fanatic, I'll wear a burka to the office," he said. But even Mark agreed that bringing in Montrose at this point would be a mistake. All they had her for was conspiracy to provide material support to terrorism; they would argue that paying the 6A Brooks phone bill, which she did, fell under the rubric of the statute. But once a federal judge saw her Richmond birth certificate, they would never get a sealed order to hold her without bond.

So April was advocating sending Linda Ricco, wearing a wire, to get Heather, once a close girlfriend, to talk. April needed a real live person. She was lost in the smog of reports. There still were no transcripts of the intercepts.

It was early Sunday. Aziz walked into the living room. A flashlight, still on, had fallen on the floor. Beside it was Ghazi, asleep, in briefs. Aziz went to turn off the flashlight and picked up a book lying beside Ghazi. It was opened to a page. He was surprised to see it was written in Arabic. It was the Qur'an. Ghazi had paper-clipped a passage:

> *And it is not for a believer to kill a believer, except it be by mistake, then (let him set) free a believing neck, and blood-money is to be handed (unimpaired) to his family, unless they donate it.*

Aziz felt his chest tighten. A believer doesn't kill a believer except to set free a believing neck. Kill this neck, but not that neck. Donated, blood-moneyed. Aziz could hear Antar on his hammock, reciting his favorite *ayat*:

> *Whosoever does not believe in Allah and His Messenger, then surely we have readied the Blaze.*

He wanted to kick Ghazi. He did push him, roughly, on the shoulder. It had no effect. Aziz took the flashlight, turned it off, and went to strike Ghazi's head with the palm of his hand but pulled back. Just then, Ghazi opened his eyes.

"Coffee?" Aziz said.

"Aziz." Ghazi started to sit up.

"Uncle, you have been reading," Aziz said, on his way to the kitchen. He could not look at Ghazi. He had no intention of making coffee. He took a step. He slammed an open cabinet door shut. He threw a fork in the sink.

"I do not want coffee," Ghazi said from the living room.

"Good. There is none," Aziz said.

Aziz returned to the living room, a menace. Ghazi was pulling on his pants.

"No prayers?" Aziz asked.

He waited. Ghazi looked up and met his eye.

"You read this," Aziz said, pointing to the Qur'an, "but no *salat*."

"Don't call it *this*."

"Just the *shahada* for you. Why pray five times a day when you can grab a key to the garden with one sentence?"

"I will go."

"To where?" Aziz raised his voice.

"Farther than you, ever."

"Afghanistan?"

"Maybe. Maybe Chechnya."

"You know nothing."

"You do not know me." Ghazi was pulling open the front door.

"Where are you going?"

"Mourad will be up."

"You fucked Heather," Aziz called after him. "Is that what started this?"

Aziz went to the door and looked down the street. There Ghazi was, moping down the sidewalk. He had to go after him. He pulled on a coat.

Aziz caught sight of him rounding the corner. He watched him pass the bus stop. Aziz saw a cab, but Ghazi didn't seem to notice it. Where was Ghazi going? "Ghazi!" He yelled from the bottom of his stomach. He must have heard him. He did. He stopped. Ghazi looked over his shoulder and turned around. He started walking to Aziz.

It had been a long time since April had been in the van with headphones, listening. She was glad Linda had a microspeaker in her ear. April had to fight the impulse to tell Linda every sentence. Linda was a bad liar. Hospital records showed she was deeply involved in insurance fraud, but she was stupid enough to think they believed her story about Heather Montrose and Abdelaziz Arkoun duping her. Sure they had, but Linda was a more than willing participant. She'd also insisted that all of them—Heather Montrose, Abdelaziz Arkoun, Abdelrafik Ghezil, Kamal Gamal—were terrorists back in 1996. When they asked how she knew they were terrorists, she said she saw explosives in their Everett apartment. What did they look like? Like bombs, she said. What kind of bombs? You know, she said, you're FBI.

Linda and Heather were set to meet for dinner. Linda wanted to go to a bar, but the noise was too great. The scenario was simple. Linda had come into some money, in the form of a third husband, and she wanted to take Heather to dinner at a quiet upscale place to renew their friendship. Linda said Heather loved the idea, it was all good, but April wondered. She had no conception of Heather. Heather was completely outside her experience. Heather wasn't—believable.

"Girl!" That was Heather. Sounded whiny.

"Miss Heather!" That was Linda.

"Look at you!"

"Look at *you*!"

"It is so good to see you!"

"Look, look at this rock on my hand!"

They had loaned Linda a diamond to make the new husband story credible.

"Let me see. Oh, Linda, it's gorgeous! Just beautiful."

Hostess was interrupting. Seating was happening. Waitress.

April had forgotten how much filler there was. She looked at the technician and Agent Melhaney. They were concentrating.

It wasn't until the second glass of wine, and the lateness of the entrée, which they had arranged with the kitchen beforehand, that things got interesting. It was Heather's doing, not Linda's.

"You know, Linda, I feel terrible about what happened."

"What do you mean!?"

"You know, the insurance thing. With Aziz."

Who was Aziz? Oh. She kind of remembered Linda said something about this. Not Abdelaziz. But Aziz. *Abdelaziz Arkoun,* she mouthed to Melhaney. He gave her a thumbs-up.

"That's all good now," Linda said, fairly unconvincingly. "My husband, he made the problem go away."

"Aziz knows I am seeing you tonight, and he wanted me to tell you he is sorry. He wanted to come. So did Mourad."

Mourad. Holy fuck, the Arkoun brothers wanted to come to this dinner! Melhaney looked at April and opened his eyes wide. That would have been a coup.

"Mourad?" Linda sounded genuinely puzzled.

"That's Aziz's younger brother. He—well, I'm with him now. We're together."

"What happened to Rafik?"

"Rafik is involved in some things. It just got to be too much."

"What things?"

Good girl, April thought.

"The main thing is, Aziz and Mourad, they wanted you to have this. It's not the full amount, but it's close. Mourad had a good job; he worked at the airport. And Ghazi has a good business. So."

Melhaney and the technician were looking at April. Ghazi? Ghazi? Did April know who someone named Ghazi could be?

Sound of ripping envelope. Riffling noise. Waiting. Waiting. "Heather. There's thousands of dollars in here. Cash money!"

Jesus Christ. Jesus Fucking Christ. April could not believe it. This was not just a dinner. This was going to lead to so much more. They wanted to make things right with Linda. This could mean

April might get the Arkoun brothers on tape in English. April could listen in on them! And they'd told her this was one of her wild gooses.

"It was wrong, what we did. I think—when I was with Rafik—I did things—well, that I wouldn't do now. And Aziz, well, Aziz is not that type of person. He and Rafik—they don't speak anymore."

They don't speak! That put Arkoun way out of this. April could see Melhaney trying to concoct a way in which Heather had been tipped to the wire. He had always been gunning for Abdelaziz Arkoun. Fingerprints were all Melhaney believed in.

"I never much liked Rafik," Linda said.

Wrong, April thought. Tell her you don't get why they broke up. Coax her. At the risk of changing the expression on Linda's face, April had to say something. *Linda, don't let your face change. It's me, April. Be cool here, Linda. Be cool.*

And then what happened was what always happened: Linda started talking to April.

"I'm cool."

"What?" Heather said.

"Nothing. I mean."

Don't talk to me, Linda.

"Yeah," said Linda. Always happens. Melhaney looked at April like *Maybe you should shut the fuck up.*

"I wonder where dinner is." That was Heather.

Get her to talk about the breakup.

"So, the breakup. I mean, you know, what happened and everything?"

"It feels like a long time ago."

"You were so in love."

Good, good.

"I was young."

"So good-looking. Rafik." Linda made a smacking sound.

"Looks aren't everything."

"Heather." Linda was doing her best conspiratorial whisper. "What was he into?"

"Linda, it's really—it's in the past—"

"Drugs?"

Oh, no. This was a question that could be answered either with nodding or head-shaking. Not recoverable on audiotape.

"I thought so." That was Linda. So Heather had nodded or shook her head. April had coached her not to elicit yes-or-no answers. Melhaney was putting his hand up. *Don't interrupt, April,* his hand was saying.

"Hash, right?"

Why did they always ask the yes-or-no questions? Why?

"I always wondered what he kept in that storage unit," Linda said.

April nearly lifted off her vinyl van seat. If she had told Linda once she had told her a million times, *Do not—do not—be the first to mention the storage unit.* She had not wanted the detective even to tell Linda about the storage unit. He was a hot dog. She regretted ever being nice to him.

"Everything," Heather said.

"Everything? In that storage he had out in Everett?"

"I don't think there was much in this world that didn't pass through there."

"Did you know the Benhadj family?"

Aziz had gotten Ghazi back to Brooks Street. Calmly, Aziz had done it. He was trying, nicely, to make Ghazi see. He had to go slow. The smartest one, it seemed, knew only what he read. He had lived, it turned out, little. His father was in military intelligence, and look at him. For a second he understood Ghazi's father. Maybe, knowing all he did, he found his son naïve, an overeducated jackass, or—what DRS prided itself on *not* being—an idealist.

They were both lying on the living room floor, staring at the ceiling. Most of the anger had trickled away. Aziz was smoking a cigarette. Ghazi was drinking a Coke.

"That one shaped like a peanut?" Ghazi said.

"Him. And some others I didn't know. Well, they went home for leave, and it came back to us: GIA had killed them. They beheaded them. They put one of their heads on a mule's body. And the mule's head—"

"—on Benhadj."

"Yes."

"I thought they made that up to make the GIA look bad."

"They did make it up. But it did happen."

"So—" Ghazi sat up.

"It happened to Benhadj. I saw it with my eyes."

Ghazi looked stunned. "God help him."

Aziz tried to look like what happened to Benhadj upset him. It was nothing to what he had seen. Benhadj was a soldier, at least. He was armed. Aziz put on a sad face. He sat up.

"So how was it made up?" Ghazi wanted to know. "You say you saw it."

"I saw him dead like that. I did not see him killed."

"But—"

"Even if I saw him killed, I could not say the motive. It could be some *irhabi,* angry at the people for forsaking jihad. It could be someone who knew that blaming the GIA makes fears higher and elections later."

"The home country—our government is sick. It—"

"*It* means a person," Aziz interrupted. "Another person. Many of them, maybe. But not a thing called 'the government.' "

"You know what I think?" Linda asked Heather.

Linda! April had to intervene again.

"I'm handling this," Linda said, affronted.

"Handling?" Heather sounded confused.

"I think Rafik is a terrorist," Linda declared.

Melhaney looked at April with disdain. They had told her this would happen. Heather would come home; say, Gee whiz, Mourad, Linda thinks Rafik is a terrorist; case down the tube.

"I think he has bombs in that storage unit," Linda said with satisfaction. "I think he's planning to blow up Boston."

"Because he's Muslim?" Heather asked. "That's—"

"He's Arab, isn't he?"

"Yeah. He's both. I mean, do you know the difference?"

"Arab, Muslim—however you slice it, trouble."

"The French taught us to torture," Aziz was telling Ghazi. "Now we do what our grandfathers died fighting to stop. The generals torture us for being terrorists. The terrorists kill us for not being terrorists. What are we?"

It was a simplification. But one Aziz thought Ghazi might get. It was true, in some ways.

"That is why Afghanistan for me," Ghazi said. "Not the home country. The CIA is behind all this."

"Says who?" Aziz felt himself getting mad again.

"Dhakir. Trust me, cousin. He knows people in London."

"Dhakir? Ghazi, think of who he is! With his overlong dick and his brain no bigger than a berry."

"But maybe the ones in London, they know."

"Who in London would tell Dhakir in Montreal about anything? Who?"

"It is complicated."

"And the Qur'an. What are you doing with the Qur'an?"

"Reading it."

"So you believe this garden with rivers under it?" Aziz asked, angry all over again. "You think, 'I go to Afghanistan, I kill *kafir* and get killed doing it—to the virgins in the garden I fly?' "

"It is an idea of a garden," Ghazi said. "The virgins are for people who cannot understand the idea of an idea."

"And you want what they want?"

"I don't know what I want." Ghazi said this flatly, as if it were self-evident. Ghazi's father was right, thought Aziz. Ghazi was an idiot. A gecko with wings.

"So Dhakir is the answer; the CIA is the problem; the Qur'an is the guided missile? Let me tell you something. The CIA has no one in Algeria. If they did, how would they tell who is who? I am Algerian, and *I* could not tell.

"The CIA lives in this place, Virginia, where Heather's father lives. You have seen pictures she has. Look on her dresser. It is green and velvet and everywhere forests and houses like French castles. No one from the CIA wants to sleep on dirt and eat sand to make a mule out of a man in a country no one in America ever heard of, except maybe when they mistake it for Nigeria.

"The sound of a man dying in Algeria is not even a whisper in the world. Arab man dies in Palestine, it is five orchestras, every instrument playing. Palestine boy huddled under his father, killed by a Jew, everywhere his picture goes. But where are the pictures of Muslim boys killed by Muslims in Blida? Where are the photographs of the Muslim *djeddat* killed by Muslim men in Médéa? Who makes this? It is not the Jew. It is not the CIA. It is us. *Us*."

"Don't try to tell me it hasn't crossed your mind," Linda said to Heather. Her tone was accusatory.

April wondered if they could extract Linda. Tricky; that's why they'd discouraged her from doing this. Once these things were launched, it was hard to put the bullet back in the gun.

"Linda, what's with you?" Heather said, but gently, placating. "I mean, why this all of a sudden, this *terrorism*?"

"I have my reasons." Argumentative.

Linda, you are jeopardizing this investigation, April said in Linda's ear, as sternly as she could.

Melhaney shook his head. The technician was making notations on a clipboard.

"Are you okay?" Heather asked. She probably could see Linda's face listening to April's words. Jesus.

"Take me there," Linda said, loud mouthed. "I'll show you!"

"Take you where?"

"The storage unit!" Linda actually shrieked this.

"It's in Everett!" Heather's voice raised now.

"There are bombs there," Linda said, a shrug in her voice. Take it or leave it was the tone.

"This is just . . . just crazy." Heather, stupefied.

"Prove me wrong. Just prove me wrong!" Linda raised her voice again.

"I don't have a key anymore, but I mean you can't think—just because—I mean, we're paying you back, and we're *sorry.*"

"For four years, you make my life a misery." Linda was gone. It was all about Linda now.

"It was wrong. Really, really wrong."

"You think I was stupid. You think: Little Puerto Rican, *she'll* never figure it out, oh, no, not her. You moved. You thought you are fooling me!"

Melhaney was pushing a note to April. It said, *What should we do?* April wrote back, *I'm notifying the task force and headquarters.* She hoped they had enough time. It was nine.

33

The hostess was getting Heather's coat. Linda was back at the table, paying for dinner. They hadn't even finished. It was upsetting. The people at the table next to theirs had been staring at them; Linda was practically shouting. The manager had to come and ask Linda to leave.

Here was her coat. Heather put her right arm in the sleeve. Terrorism? Rafik had talked about all kinds of things, when it was just the two of them alone, but terrorism? That was beyond illegal. They were normal people. They had a house, part of a house anyway; it definitely qualified as a two-bedroom apartment. They had jobs. Rafik had dabbled in hash and maybe some shoplifting, but that was a long way from something as out of this world as terrorism. Mourad was a security guard at the airport! Aziz—he was an angel.

Kamal was not. She was buttoning her coat. Violent, really violent. She had a really bad feeling about Kamal, always had. It was his idea to get the storage unit, wasn't it? No, Rafik had it before Kamal.

She could see Kamal as a terrorist. But Linda had never met Kamal. She pulled on her gloves and the hat Ghazi had bought her. What a disaster. The money meant nothing to Linda! Mourad had saved and saved, not for Linda, but he wanted, really wanted Heather to give it to her. Ghazi, he must have given up all of his nest egg. Aziz brought out some squished cereal box he'd been hiding all these years and there was three thousand dollars in it. He put all of it in the envelope. It broke her heart. She should have stayed home and helped Mourad write sayings on Aziz's cups. She'd told them maybe English sayings would work better. She'd left them some to copy before she left.

She opened the door of the restaurant. Two men were coming in.

"Heather Montrose?" It was Melhaney and the technician. They had handcuffs. The technician hadn't made an arrest in years. He was thrilled.

"Yes?"

"You're under arrest."

April was at One Center Plaza in a room with Mark.

"I fucked up," she said to him, covering the phone. They were on five calls at once.

Secretaries were dashing. The field office, the task force—New England law enforcement had mobilized. The director had been yanked out of homework with his boys; the attorney general was on his way to the White House.

"Can I put you on hold, sir?" she heard Mark say.

He got up and said something at the door. His pager went off. He looked at it for a while and then said, "Give me five." He closed the door.

He walked over to her phone and stood there. The lines on hold were blinking. "Can I—can I? Yes. Can I get back with you?" April said. "Thanks. Thanks." She said into the intercom, "Hold these for a sec."

"You did fuck up," Mark said, but nicely.

"I couldn't make sense of it."

"It takes time."

"It was Montrose being like me."

"I knew that."

"She—I had to hear her."

"That's what I want to know. What you heard."

"Nothing that would matter on the stand."

"But here. No stand."

"They've arrested her already."

"You know they have."

"She's a kid," April said. "Twenty-two, and not real smart, and a whiny voice, and my God what is she doing with these—"

"Your gut, though," Blake said.

"About her?" April said.

"No, not on her. She's easy," Blake said. "Heather's no Patty Hearst. But the Arkoun brothers."

"We all know what Kamal is."

"I'm not asking about Kamal. What's your gut about the others?"

"You have a feel for this. I don't have it. I—"

Someone was knocking on the door. "Five!" he shouted. "It's not our call anymore," he said, sitting down.

"My doing. All my doing."

"You did the right thing. I mean, you fucked up, but for the right reasons."

"They gave Linda back the money."

"Card fraud creates cash."

"But look how they live—it's just awful."

"Not greedy, I'll give them that. But what I'm saying is that wanting to get inside, to hear voices—that was right."

"But we don't have to *know* them. We can't, ever. We can just piece something here with something there and draw logical conclusions. It's flawed, of course it's flawed. But it's better than the alternative. Tribes. Posses. No one cares what the Arkoun brothers are *really* like in a lynching."

" 'Justice is the great interest of man on earth. It is the ligament which holds civilized beings and civilized nations together.' "

"Mark, you are a pompous sonofabitch. Even in a crisis."

"Hey, I'm just quoting from the walls of that brand-new federal courthouse they built us on the waterfront. Daniel Webster."

Aziz could tell Mourad was happy. Not about the cups—Mourad was down on them—but about Linda Ricco. Ghazi was too. It felt like the Heather tension between them was smaller, outweighed by this thing they'd made right. Ghazi had not hesitated—Mourad saw that—to contribute what had to be all the cash he had. When Aziz brought out the cereal box and Mourad dug into a pair of socks, Heather counted out nearly all that they owed. Maybe they were a hundred or two short.

They had been sitting at the kitchen table writing on the cups for over an hour. American sayings were a good idea, Aziz thought. Ghazi made fun of the overall concept, but he was coming up with sayings anyway. *Elli yestenna kheir melli yetmenna, welli yetmenna kheir melli yeqtaa layas.* Waiting is better than hoping, and hoping than despair. *Ki techbaa elkerch, tqul lerras ghenni.* When the stomach is full, it tells the head to sing.

Aziz wanted to use some Yemeni ones. Mourad disagreed. "It honors the one I knew in Brooklyn," Aziz countered. "There may be Yemenis in Boston."

"Let me see," Mourad said. He read, *"Lau kan al-kalaam min fedha fa al-samt min dhahab."* If speech is of silver, silence is golden.

"Go with that one." Mourad sighed. "Aziz, we have to find a better place. One that is inside, not cold. No wind."

"Tomorrow we look."

"Tonight is for writing," Ghazi said.

Aziz picked up one Ghazi had just written: *Maaza walu taret*.

"It's a goat even if it flies!"

Ghazi had a sly face. "What?"

"That is not good! We cannot say that."

"Why not?"

Mourad was laughing. "They used that one for me, back home," he said.

"I will not mock stubborn people," Aziz said. "Bad for business." But he was laughing. Ghazi raised his eyebrows. "Seriously, stick to the ones Heather gave us for a while," Aziz said.

"You are the boss."

"What about this?" Ghazi pointed to one on Heather's list.

"Where there's smoke there's fire," Mourad read.

Aziz looked up. He shook his head. "That's worse than the goat one."

"Here," Mourad said, "this one."

Ghazi looked. "Slow and steady wins the race." That made no sense to him.

"We just investigate and arrest them," Mark said. "We don't indict them, and we don't prosecute, and we aren't the judge or the jury." There was a lull in the phones.

"Please, I'm not just out of Quantico," April said.

"Let me ask you something."

"Go ahead," she said.

"Why do you think Belghazi's and Arkoun's are the only prints in there?"

"It's like you said. Either too innocent to be smart or too dumb to be smart about being guilty."

The phone rang. She picked up. It was her friend in main Justice, Melody Abraham. Everyone in Washington had signed off on the arrests. The official fax was on its way. Also a call from the director. "No doubt to chew me out," she said to Melody.

"Nope, not by my read," Melody said, and had to run. April hung up.

"You know what the Algerian intelligence abstracts say?" Mark said.

"Haven't seen them."

"They've been on the director's desk."

"So what do they say?"

"He's going there, you know, next week."

"Who?"

"Director."

"Oh."

"Meeting with their head of military intelligence. Farouk Aourak. Known more commonly as General Zahaf."

"Can't they just send the Cairo legat?"

"Uh, no. Not to Algeria."

"Touchy, huh."

"April," he said.

Don't lecture me, she wanted to say. I've lectured myself. Forgive me, Father, for I have sinned; it's been three minutes since my last confession.

"Algeria is—it's as old as the Balkans. Intractable. Such—I mean, you know that shit about Kamal, the mutilation?—Actually, both rapes."

Mark must be tired; he wasn't speaking in complete paragraphs for once.

"Algeria has a problem with these sickos," she said. "I know that. They've got ties to Al Qaeda. Lots of the Afghan vets were Algerian, went back home, viva Allah. Algeria. I understand Algeria."

"They have more civilians killed because of these jihad nuts than anywhere—*anywhere*."

"Except for Israel."

"No. You're wrong. *One hundred thousand civilians.* Same time frame, not even a thousand Israelis."

"Jesus, Mark, I'm an investigator, not a political science major."

Mourad kept looking at the clock. It was after eleven. Ghazi was looking too. They were passing around a map of Boston—Mourad thought a subway station would be better in winter for selling coffee than a sidewalk. He had circled three with a red marker for their search the next morning. Ghazi had circled a fourth.

Heather had gone to meet Linda at seven-thirty. Four hours—that was long. She had all that cash. Aziz wished she had let him and Mourad go along.

"Cousin," Ghazi said. "Call her cell."

Aziz thought that might provoke Mourad. It implied a special worry. But Mourad looked glad Ghazi had suggested it. He had been wanting to call.

"Maybe they went to meet Linda's new husband," Aziz said.

"We should have gone with her," Mourad said.

"She has a firm mind," Ghazi said.

Mourad was dialing. Listening.

"The cell-phone user you have called has either turned off the phone or is out of the signal area."

"It's off, or she's way outside Boston," Mourad said.

"I can't keep up with all we're supposed to read," April said. She was having trouble concentrating. She didn't know when she'd eaten last. They should open the door, get some air.

"Nothing on Kamal Gamal," Blake said.

"What does that mean?"

"Algerian intelligence has no information on him. He's never come to their attention."

"Okay."

"Nothing on Abdelrafik Ghezil. Or the Khaled brothers. Or Dhakir Yahyouai. Same for Taffounnout Belghazi and Mourad Arkoun."

"Mark. I'm sorry. I am in need of sustenance."

"So let's order something. We're here for another hundred hours. At least."

"Sure. Sure. I'm making a run to the machine for some Fritos in the meantime."

"Get me some licorice."

. . .

It was a Sunday night and it was January, so Dorfman Street in East Boston was empty. They decided to use vans, but beat-up white ones, none of those superfly SUVs. One said MCTAMNEY AND SON PLUMBING. Another said ANDRETTI'S LOCK AND KEY. The ninja look—that was out. They went in dressed like working men. Inside the apartment building, they pulled out white paper vests that said FBI, U.S. MARSHAL, INS, and BOSTON PD in fluorescent orange. They took AK-47s out of toolboxes. There were gas masks in a vestibule under a tarpaulin, delivered by an agent masquerading as a pizza deliveryman an hour earlier.

Battering rams were a thing of the past. They had microscopic drills, silent ones. No sparks.

Lights were off in apartment 8. The suspect was in bed. The stake-out report indicated Kamal Gamal had arrived at twenty hundred hours accompanied by a female in traditional Islamic dress. The female exited at twenty-one hundred hours.

Abdelrafik Ghezil had been followed to a nightclub at 295 Franklin Street called Reach. A SWAT unit in two limousines was positioned for his exit. Three agents inside, outfitted in Italian suits, were incommunicado due to excessive noise.

"Thank you, sir," April said. Thc director had called. "I appreciate that, sir.

"I'll keep that in mind. . . .

"Sir? . . .

"Sir, I was raised in New Hampshire. . . .

"That's correct. Live free or die. . . .

"At this point in time, no, sir. . . .

"I will notify SIOC. . . .

"If the assistant director feels that is important. . . .

"No question. . . .

"I've been briefed. . . .

"I'm crossing my fingers, sir. . . .

"You're very welcome. . . .

"I will sir. . . .

"Yes. Goodbye, sir."

They used black SUVs for this sleepy little Everett neighborhood. Looked like everyone here was snug in bed by nine. They could have touched a chopper down at the intersection and no one would have stirred. Drills were not authorized here. They had cased the door weeks ago. It was only going to take a heave-ho to gain entry.

It was past midnight. The cups were bundled together, sorted by language. They planned to get up early and drive around to the subway stations circled on their map. They had found one station that Ghazi thought might be close to a halal butcher shop. Good chance of a Muslim community around there. And Mourad was going to talk to the airport manager about the possibility of the parking garage.

But they weren't really thinking about the next day. Everything was about Heather. They didn't know the name of the restaurant. They didn't know where Linda lived. Mourad and Ghazi wanted to go out and do something, drive somewhere, call someone. There was no one to call and nothing to do but wait.

"Sounds like the director likes you," Mark said to April when she hung up the phone.

"I don't know what the assistant director said to him about tonight, but it sure wasn't the truth," she said.

"You look good, the assistant director looks good, the director looks good, the bureau looks good."

"They're all sitting around SIOC, waiting to hear how the arrests go."

"Strategic Information and Operations Center, where the UBL room is."

"Why is it *Usama* Bin Laden for the bureau, and *Osama* for the press?"

"Vowels."

"Vowels?"

"In the Arabic alphabet, most vowels are diacritical marks. They don't always correspond to our vowels. There're disagreements about how to put them into English."

"Right." Diacritical? Jesus. She looked at her watch. Almost one. They should be hearing something soon.

Command was established in unmarked GMC Suburbans in the satellite parking for Logan at the end of Brooks Street. The situation was not optimal. Lights were on as of 1 a.m. They awaited word on whether to go in while the three targets were awake or defer until lights out.

April slammed down the phone. "We are so fucked."

"What?" asked Mark.

"Kamal—gone."

"Gone? Where?"

"They go in and find some woman in there."

"Wait, wait."

"I'm telling you. He's gone."

Lahouari, Ali, and Hamid were sleeping in the living room on a mattress and a chair and a couch. Their five roommates were distributed in the kitchen, the hallway, the bathroom tub, and a bedroom that was really a closet. If you wanted to take a leak in the middle of the night, you went out the window of their ground-floor apartment and pissed in the bushes.

A naked Lahouari had tiptoed over his brothers and darted through the January air to his favorite spot behind a hedge. He was almost done when he heard what sounded like burglars. Before he could think, two men pushed him to the ground, smashing his face into ice-hard dirt and the smell of warm urine.

"Rafik made them," Mark said. He had just hung up the phone.

"How could he? That's not possible. Limo, Italian suits—"

"It's two a.m. The club just closed down. They searched. Unless he's underneath the floorboards, he's not there."

They wanted permission to turn on the engines and get some heat in the Suburbans. They'd been sitting there thumb-twiddling for five hours. It was freezing. The SAC said no. Everyone agreed she was a bitch.

"They're never going to go to bed," April said.

"I don't get it," Mark said. "My God, it's three in the morning."

"You don't get it? I do."

"What."

"They're worried about Heather. She never came home. Those lights will stay on past sunrise."

Mark looked at April. "That's what you heard."

"Heard?"

"Listening."

"Oh, in the van."

"Yeah. You heard it in Heather's voice. How they care about each other."

Aziz, Mourad, and Ghazi had gone back to inking cups to keep their minds off the obvious. It was four-thirty. Something bad had happened to Heather. They'd already had the conversation about calling the police. That's what Americans on television did. When someone went missing, they called the cops. Officer always said there was nothing they could do. We need a body, they always told the frantic family.

In the home country, no family would call the police. Police were the ones who ferried the missing to guest treatment under orders. Ghazi would call the army if he thought *irhabiya* were involved.

"But what could a bureaucrat answering a phone really do?" asked Mourad.

"What would you do?"

"I would call your father," Mourad offered.

"Him?" Ghazi sneered. "My father's a coward. Useless when you fear."

Mourad remembered. Yes, when Aziz was feared dead, all Ghazi's father had was a lie.

Maybe it wasn't so bad that Aziz and Ghazi being illegal meant police were not an option. They would have had to explain why Heather was carrying so much cash. They would have, Ghazi knew but didn't say, had to explain him giving her that kind of cash.

So when the knock came, Mourad said, "She must have lost her keys." He had such a smile. He hugged Aziz and said, "She couldn't drive home. That's why. That's why."

"Her cell ran out of batteries," Ghazi said. "No car lighter to recharge it."

Only Aziz was not surprised to see armed men when he opened the door. They were enraged, eyes rimmed wine red, rifles ready. They had waited so long, but they had found him. While his brother and Ghazi had been talking about Heather, Aziz had stopped listening. What did her parents do when she did not come home? Who did they call? Did they walk into their orchards, past the lemon trees, into the juniper? From a distance did they realize the foundling—wrapped in broken dress—was Soumeya? Up close, as she came clear as herself, no one could have sensed her shroud was made for love of another.

. . .

They put all of them in solitary. It was for their protection. From the other inmates, who watched television, which liked the story. Terrorist cell in Boston linked to Al Qaeda. Explosives found in Everett U-Stor-It. East Boston harbored hardened militants. FBI foils plot to kill thousands. Plan targeted Boston subway.

Ghazi was on suicide watch. So was Lahouari. Kamal was in Jakarta. Dhakir boarded a plane in Montreal for Amsterdam the day before the Boston arrests, his final destination unknown. Rafik never made it to Italy. His flight went through Frankfurt, and he decided to stay. They released Mourad on bond, and he and Heather ran to Mexico. Eventually, the Khaled brothers were deported after pleading guilty to membership in a terrorist organization. Algeria wouldn't take them. Only Sudan, in the entire world, would have them. Ghazi's case went to trial a year after the arrests. A jury didn't believe his story about why his fingerprints were at the U-Stor-It. He was a con man and a thief. The tapes proved he wanted to get to terror camps in Afghanistan. He got thirty-seven years.

Aziz had a good lawyer, a woman who took a liking to him. She did enough of her own investigating to have the terrorism conviction overturned. The immigration judge, though, was overworked and skeptical. He'd heard too many hard-luck stories to believe even half of this one. He just didn't like that Aziz's prints were found at the U-Stor-It. He ordered Aziz deported after a daylong hearing. On appeal, Aziz lost.

Ghazi got one letter from him. He wrote back a few times, but there was no reply. One day, he read in an old newspaper at the prison library that tourists from Europe had been kidnapped in the Sahara. The government said terrorists kidnapped them. They asked for money; the Swiss wanted to give it. But the exchange never happened. But why? he wondered. Didn't they want the money? There was always something missing, too much that made no sense, in anything he read. Into that blurriness, Aziz had gone.

Acknowledgments

This book would not have been possible without the generosity and faith of Algerians. Portions of the novel are based on government records Algerians provided to me; for the risks they undertook, I am particularly grateful. I am indebted to Ali Djebli for his patient schooling in Arabic; even so, all errors herein are solely mine. For her understanding of the Algerian predicament and her loyal companionship, I would like especially to thank Kim Sullivan. Leon Wieseltier read and commented on early drafts; I was inspired by his encouragement. My debt to Katherine Boo, trusted reader, is great. I am obliged to loving readers: L. A. Gladus Adams, T. Taylor Adams, Meredith Breitbarth and Ned Rifkin.